I0761532

Beyond & Within

SAUÚTI TERRORS

Short Stories from the Unique Universe Created by Contemporary African Writers

Anthology Edited by Eugen Bacon, Cheryl Ntumy & Stephen Embleton

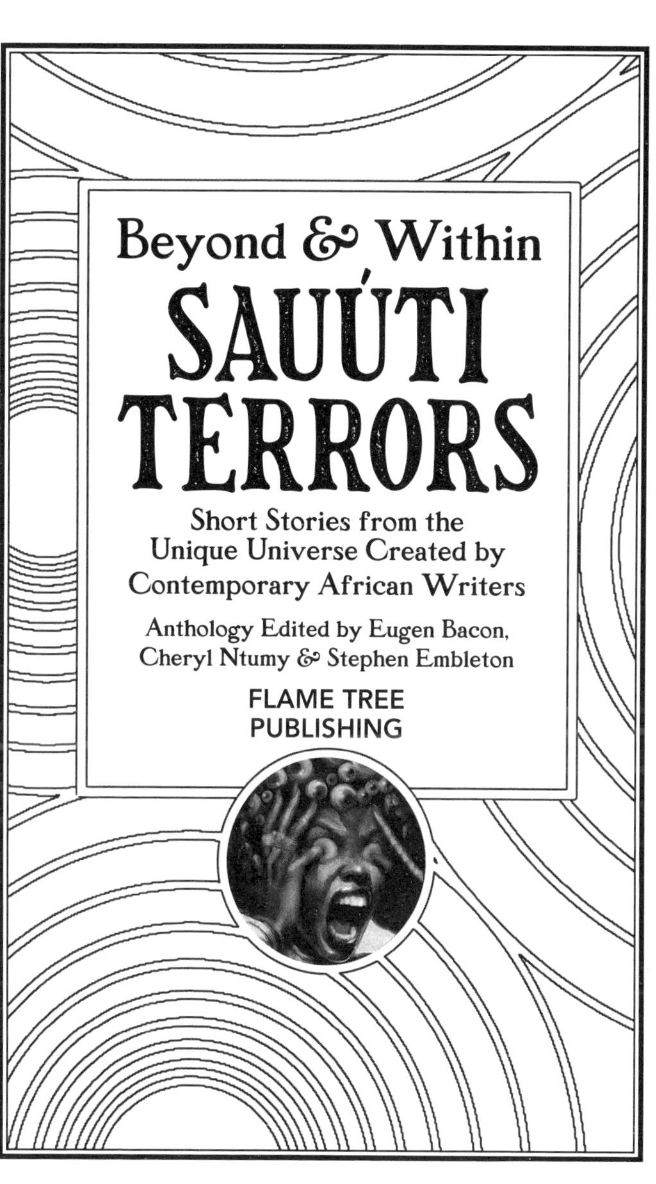

Beyond & Within

SAUÚTI TERRORS

Short Stories from the Unique Universe Created by Contemporary African Writers

Anthology Edited by Eugen Bacon, Cheryl Ntumy & Stephen Embleton

FLAME TREE
PUBLISHING

Publisher & Creative Director: Nick Wells
Senior Project Editor: Josie Karani

FLAME TREE PUBLISHING
6 Melbray Mews, Fulham,
London SW6 3NS, United Kingdom
www.flametreepublishing.com

First published 2026

26 28 30 31 29 27
1 3 5 7 9 10 8 6 4 2

Hardback ISBN: 978-1-83562-640-5
ebook ISBN: 978-1-83562-641-2

A copy of the CIP data for this book is available from the British Library.
Printed and bound in China

Represented in the EU for product safety and compliance by Authorised Rep Compliance Ltd., Ground Floor, 71 Lower Baggot Street, Dublin, D02 P593, Ireland. Contact at www.arccompliance.com

Table of Contents

SAUÚTI TERRORS
STORY TIMELINE

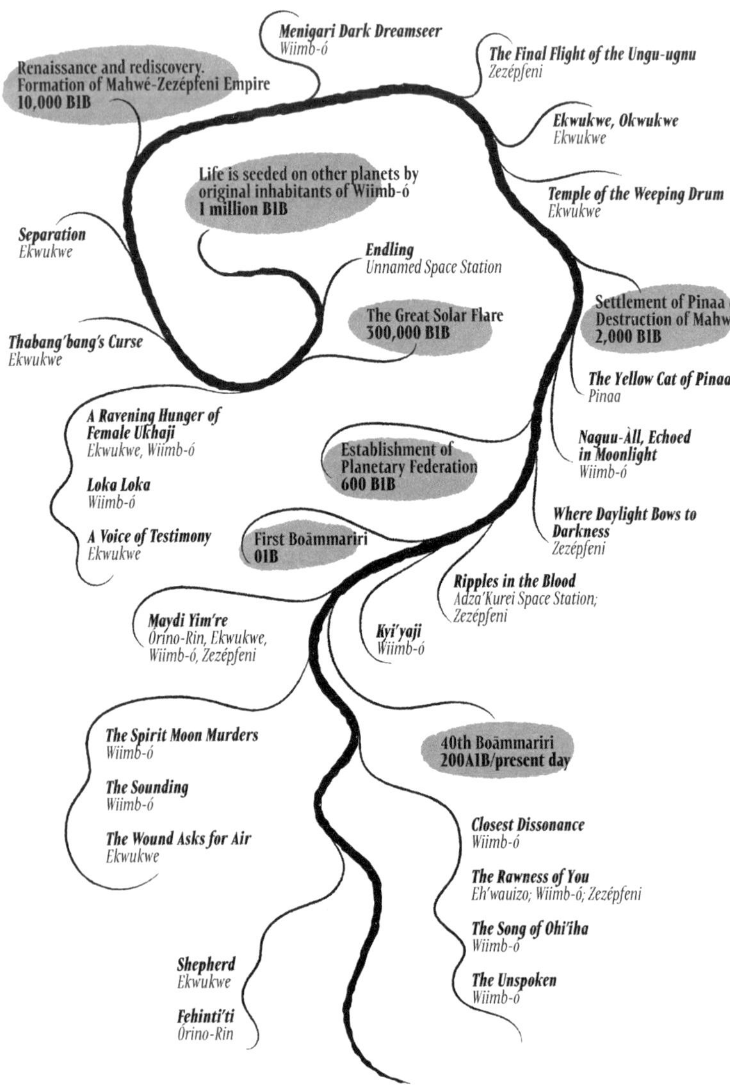

The Non-Introduction

Eugen, Cheryl & Stephen

WHEN WE RELEASED our first anthology, *Mothersound: The Sauútiverse Anthology* by Wole Talabi (ed), we had no idea just how well it would do. It was announced in the Locus Recommended Reading List and a finalist in the Locus and British Science Fiction Association (BSFA) Awards, with stories longlisted in both awards, shortlisted in the BSFA Awards and listed on the HWA Bram Stoker Award® Reading List. It also had multiple stories shortlisted in the Nommo Awards for speculative fiction by Africans, with Stephen Embleton's "Undulation" winning the award for best novella. It set us thinking with more clarity about a new anthology that shared this rich and unique world in the key tenets of collaboration, support, creativity and the Afrocentric. We hesitated a little in contemplating Saúuti Terrors – imagining a future Africa in our Afrocentric world with its five planets, two suns, and orbiting a binary star, didn't mean we wanted to hurl at it everything vicious that kept us sleepless at night.

But even a future Africa must be realistic – just look at the news and you'll see precisely how apocalyptic our reality is today. So we agreed that there's much to love in the Sauútiverse with its sounds, music, language, biologies and histories, but everything is not perfect in the federation of planets – from legends and folktales to inheritances, gods, ancestral spirits, sacred prey, sentient creatures, beings of unreality, sonic storms, solar flares and meteor strikes, perils infest the planets. We sought the doomed, the damned, the shunned, the cunning, the destroyers, the noxious, and more, in the worlds of the living and the dead. In an anthology by invitation and stories by the founding members of the Sauútiverse, we were astonished by the range of story pitches we received.

With the rise of speculative poetry, and a need for more of its visibility, it was unquestioning that we would include a space for poetry in our world. We're crazy about the darkest stories set in our planets:

- **Zezépfeni** (the self-appointed leader with its twin suns)
- **Ekwukwe** (the echo planet with its hollows, caverns and tunnels)
- **Wiimb-ó** (the Earth analogue with its five continents and spirit moons)
- **Órino-Rin** (the dense planet with its sonic storms)
- **Pinaa** (the low-gravity inhabited moon of Mahwé, the dead planet, hosting AI and other populace in fortified clusters).

What lurks herein? Perhaps it's Juah-ãju, blazing the Mother's wrath on its twin sun Zuúv'ah, and the people of Zezépfeni. Or an a'bata (bat) or a tso'tso (termite) infestation in Pinaa. Or a tikolokolo, the spirit gremlin, roaming rife in a wave of devastation in Ekwukwe. Unfurl fate, mishap, calamity, disease, obsession, wickedness, greed, malice and manipulations lurking in this Afrocentric intergalactic world with its space travel, humanoid and non-humanoid creatures, artificial intelligence and intricate magic system based on sound, oral traditions and music.

Frankly, it is none of these. Delve into the belly of our darkest nights, find out what macabre awaits.

Eugen, Cheryl and Stephen

Content Warnings

Baby snatching, cannibalism, child abuse, child death, child labor, child imprisonment, human sacrifice, inherited trauma, insanity, kidnapping, mental illness, mutilation, rage, self-harm, suicide, sexual abuse, violent murder.

The Tale of Elders' Silent Screams

Linda D. Addison

IT IS said:

Órino-Rin songs shred Elders' minds, eat their
voices thoughtlessly,
leaving behind those whose memories can not be trusted,
for what is the value of soundless people,
emptied of flesh history, in spite of
lives spanning many years?

what-if

Órino-Rin storm songs
are also a battle cry against
nightmare beings of deception,
played by mountain & valleys, singing
into our reality a magic wall between living &
soul-eating home of the insatiable shadow walkers?

what-if

Elders hollowed out by constant music,
sing less and less, their soul sound ravaged by
Órino-Rin's fight to hold the frequency of life, even
at the cost of their spirit's death,
screams locked inside
tortured
silent
minds.

The Temple of the Weeping Drum

T.L. Huchu

maiden with sewn lips
screams in discordant echoes
shroud we from the light!

__T.L. Huchu__ explores the cult of the Father in the Temple of the Weeping Drum on Ekwukwe, where men speak and maidens stay silent. Deep in the temple caves, hidden from the world, the chosen maidens will face a treacherous fate. But Aahana is not ready to go quietly. What happens when those who have been silenced for too long finally find their voice?

Welcome to "The Temple of the Weeping Drum".

IT BEGAN with a Scream. The world. Aahana senses the echoes in the caverns of the Temple of the Weeping Drum deep in the bowels of the planet Ekwukwe.

A gust of warm breath against her cold skin. She sits with the other maidens on the bare basaltic rock, legs folded to her right side, supporting herself with the left hand against the ground. The rock is rough with many hairline cracks.

Head bowed. Aahana rushed to get here when the call was made – five strikes of the ironhide drum near the inner sanctuary. The noise, less a boom, more sharp like the crack of a whip. She'd wanted to get a good spot to sit somewhere near the back, but not in the visible outer fringe. But she was too late and now sits in the second row. Too close to the front. It was hard to beat thirty other maidens all scrambling to land the least noticeable spot.

Don't stare him in the eye.

Try not to catch his eye.

Elder Zwangeni enters the cavern, the sound of his jingling bangles the only melody against the foreboding silence. They were made of the same silverish metal used in the hulls of starships across the system. His hunched form casts a long shadow in the dimness of the reddish bioluminescent light. Through the corner of her eye, Aahana spies the fluidity of his movements. An autumn leaf floating on water. She is awed by the beauty of his piety, the way he seems to glide ever so slowly in his scarlet robes past the grim-faced men who guard the room, surrounding the maidens.

Aahana feels skin graze her little toe. The brief contact jolting, something like the spark that lights tinder bringing warmth in this age of ice. Beside her is Uhm, her sleepmate, the companion she shares the reed mat with at night. That is to say, nights when neither of them is summoned by the hungry men. Uhm she calls her, not because she has a name, after all, the maidens are simply This One or That One, a nameless undifferentiated mass. But it is a name, something none of them is allowed to have. This makes it more precious than Vuiili-ki and Vuiili-ku, the spirit moons of Wiimb-ó, which she's overheard in stories told by visitors to the temple. A name gives shape to that which is without form, marking it, giving it value. It becomes a precious thing. Aahana has granted her sleepmate that; same as she has given herself a name too, though hers only sounds out in the voice in her own head for it cannot be uttered by her own sewn-up lips.

The night before the *Making*, the maidens are called for the 'choosing'. Elder Zwangeni takes his time. He shuts his eyes and meditates. Both his arms are outstretched. The right cupped, thumb pointing upwards, in the symbol of the unfurling flower chasing late spring. The left he points down, fingers splayed, which is the sign of harrowing soil in the sullen drought. Without saying a word, he has conveyed much. Here in the temple, sound, words are not to be wasted, sacred things such as they are. Where silence reigns, even the clearing of the throat takes on immense power.

These men had broken with the accepted faith and claimed to have discovered their own infallible truth. They argued it had been hidden away, suppressed by the matriarchy and in time forgotten, until the wise men read the signs and studied them in secret, so one day they could rise up and restore Ekwukwe's honor. It was the women that had caused their planet to fall to the Mahwé-Zezépfeni Empire. The men would save it.

The maidens are not supposed to know the meaning of these symbols, but Aahana is observant and has learnt much in her time here. Deep underground with neither the twin suns to see nor flowers to smell, she has studied the ways of the cult that holds them here. And so she knows the contrast between the unfurling flower and the harrowing soil speaks to some kind of disconnect, chaos that must be overcome through sacrifice. This forbidden knowledge fills her with dread.

She shifts her foot closer to Uhm, her toe, finding a pinky. Uhm rubs back subtly and Aahana is grateful for the acknowledgement. It does not quieten her anxiety entirely, but it makes her feel less alone.

Elder Zwangeni draws back his arms after a while and hides them in the folds of his robes. He draws a loud breath before he speaks.

"Hear."

A word. The men surrounding the women crouch so that the elder's words may drop upon them like rain. Zwangeni's voice is as pure as his snow-white hair. They say a fortunate accident involving rocks or the kick of some wild beast crushed his testicles when he was a boy. The blessing of that incident was that his voice never broke, it maintained its original form. Unsullied. All men have two voices, should they live long enough. The first voice is purer and closer to the Mothersound. But, in an imperfect world, that voice is cleaved by sin and a second, stained voice emerges when they become not boys but men. Some record their original voices on devices and use machines to preserve them for their magic, but metal is not flesh.

A recording is not the same as the source. This is corruption.

And so how can they not be captivated when Elder Zwangeni says, "Hear", in the high pitch that pierces through their collective being like a hot needle? The speaker is the creator of sound, a child's voice coming from an old man. The effort seems to exhaust Zwangeni and he pants a little. There's a scowl on his face. This is taxing for him.

> "A broken bowl,
> Flakes of snow,
> This glue our fingers bind,
> Its will becomes our work."

That short verse is dense in meaning, not for the maidens who know nothing of this new revelation, but for the men who grunt as though weighed down by the immense burden it conveys. Zwangeni has announced he would rather not point as he has before. His gnarled fingers are stuck. The daily work of restoring the shattered bits of the broken bowl that is the liminal space between worlds of the living and the dead damages his delicate form. "Its will" means that this is not his choice, Zwangeni is but the instrument of something greater.

"It must be done," the men respond one by one, their voices rolling atop one another into a cacophony, disturbing the precisely laid-out order Zwangeni's words had left in the air. Their voices are less than, where his is pure.

Huna'Kizit in silver robes wears his hair in short dreadlocks of organic hair on the left, and colored cables on the right where the metallic skull-plate has numerous ports for his various enhancements. One of the ports is burnt out. He retrieves a walking stick from a ledge behind Elder Zwangeni before crouching in front of him and offering it. This stick is made from remnants of the wooden shrine that once belonged to the maadiregi from the Clan of Erigaga of Wiimb-ó, which had once passed through the bright magic of Akokore's portals. They said it holds the power of Ikululu's staff, he who once summoned an echo of raw Mothersound, and so Huna'Kizit wears gloves. To touch it with his bare hands means death, but not so Zwangeni the pure, who takes it and raises it high above his head.

Fear and anticipation wash through the maidens as though a wave of pheromones has passed through a beehive. *Let it not be me*, each one prays silently. *Anyone else*. There are thirty of them in this cavern. Not many years ago, there were a hundred. Aahana prays not for herself but for Uhm, her sleepmate, who is with child. This is a secret they have kept from the men because if it was discovered there would be no picking. It would definitely be Uhm chosen since mother and child conjure the most powerful of magics.

If it's not either of us, then I will make sure Uhm leaves this forsaken place, Aahana thinks.

* * *

A solitary drum starts playing. Doom, doom, doom, it goes in a slow, ominous rhythm. Aahana flinches as Elder Zwangeni steps into the assembled ranks of maidens pointing his walking stick. She shrinks as he grows in stature, as though he's drawing strength from their quivering. He must think how pathetic they look in their gray rags, boney shoulders exposed, yet he is wrapped in fine clothing.

The men shout out in unison to the tune of the drum:

"The Elder is but a vessel of the divine."

"This is not his will alone."

"The stick must divine the will of the depths."

"Obey, obey, obey."

It is not for the maidens to understand, for they have been taught that they are "less than". The men have decided that they must be cleansed, and, in so doing, repair the errors of their ancestors whose defeat cost this world its freedom. The Elder and his men are a secret cult, but the great and good from the old houses that once ruled Ekwukwe know this work is being done. The powerful choose to look aside and let Zwangeni work in the shadows. And in the darkness, some of them come to taste the magic that is conjured here.

Zwangeni pauses in front of a maiden and gently places the stick on her braided hair.

Aahana shudders.

She has been chosen.

Aahana senses the relief that passes through the others like a cool morning breeze. They have been spared! And she must bear the brunt. She is helpless as Uhm, overwhelmed by the strain of it all, collapses to the floor. There's nothing that can be done now. The toe that had touched the pinky now finds itself entirely alone, facing the void.

* * *

The men summon Aahana to dinner at the grand table beneath the bowels of their antechamber. Her eyes struggle to adjust in this well-lit room, a rarity in the Temple. They moisten as she blinks hard. There are voices in the room. The men speak freely outside the sacred chambers, but the chatter diminishes when she appears, most of them regarding her with hunger as though she were prey.

She has *known* some of the men. They dragged her back to their chambers on cold nights. There are welts, large as worms, on her back from the times she tried to refuse. Those scars ache and burn even now.

Tungi leads her to the empty place at the far end of the table and orders her to sit. Nothing a man says here to any of the maidens is considered a request. Everything must be regarded as a command. Even if a man says, "Good morning," it's as though he is giving orders to the day itself.

Nineteen men and Aahana sit at this stone table hewn out of the rock of the cave they are in. The walls around them have strange drawings in oxblood color said to have been drawn by an ancient people long since extinct when sunfire scorched this world. These were the original people who used this cave eons ago before it was rediscovered. They left behind pictures of hunts, goddesses, and feasts.

Aahana's stomach growls. She feels dizzy smelling the scents of the food heaving on the table. Zingy rainbow-burst grains from Kasamara. The soft but flavorless Baa'gh flesh, a rare delicacy. Spiced klalabash soup that is creamy with carrots, ginger, garlic, coriander and black salt. Ndege'ndege eggs, freshly boiled. The centerpiece of the table is the spit-roasted nguwe'we, the horned pig, looking succulent under the bright light. Aahana swallows.

"Where are your manners?" Huna'Kizit barks, louder than he normally speaks, for he is drowsy on date wine from Mahwé. "Untie the chosen's lips so she can feast. Tomorrow is her greatest honor."

Tungi nearly jumps at the command. He is young, intimidated by the older men in this cult. He fishes in the leather pouch on his belt until he retrieves a fine pair of scissors and tweezers. He seems uncertain of himself as he angles towards Aahana with the equipment. A drop of sweat rolls down his temple.

Aahana recalls this look – the same one she saw on the face of a novice named Kumu when Huna'Kizit ordered her lips sewn shut soon after she'd been offered to the Temple of the Weeping Drum when she was a little girl. Even now she remembers how they pinned her down, pulled her lips, and, with a trembling hand, Kumu began his terrible work. Agony as the needle entered through the upper and then the lower lips, every nerve screaming out. The sensation of the stitch threading through. Only a tiny hole, large enough for a straw, was left when Kumu was done.

At the head of the table, Elder Zwangeni watches her keenly.

She holds her head very still as Tungi begins his work. With a gentle, almost caring hand, he stretches the left corner of her lips and sinks in the tip of his scissors. The stitches have long been buried in flesh. Her lips sealed together. Blood bursts into Aahana's mouth and she panics, fearing she will drown. Many maidens died when they had the misfortune of vomiting with their lips sewn shut. The small hole in the corner was inadequate to expel the contents of their stomachs.

"This one is too brave. See how she does not flinch," Huna'Kizit opines.

"From where I am sitting it appears to be fear. Certain animals freeze when they are afraid, don't you know?" Sub-Elder Korosi replies.

"Which is it?"' someone asks.

Blood freely pours down Aahana's chin, dripping onto her dress. Still she does not move a single muscle.

"Against the chilly sky
Where only the menigari spy
The lightning bird lifts
Stealing into the night."

Every man at the table, except for Tungi, pauses to contemplate the verse that bubbles forth from the brook which wells inside Elder Zwangeni's heart. Why does he speak of "menigari", the mystic guardians of the dreamworld? wonders Aahana. She has never seen a lightning bird, but has heard stories about them. How they stink of putrid onions, or even bad t'apiapia fish. Rank nastiness. Why would the Elder say this against the wonderful aromas from the dishes on the table? Through the toe on her foot, she feels a hairline crack on the basaltic rock that makes the floor. The vibrations from it froth into her being and she winces at last.

Sub-Elder Korosi laughs in triumph: “See, it was just fear.”

Young Tungi cuts open the last stitch and stands gawping at his handiwork.

“Stanch it, you fool,” Huna’Kizit says. “Must I tell you everything?”

Tungi fumbles in his leather pouch and retrieves gauze which he dabs to reduce the blood flow. He is no uroh-ogi, he is much too young for that. Prior to tonight, he had only sewn shut two pairs of lips, and this was his first time opening one back up. He retrieves some bark of the boa’oba tree and places it between Aahana’s lips. Its powerful astringent properties soon stem the flow of blood, leaving fresh clots.

That One, a maiden serving date wine walks around the table refilling the gourds of the men. She hesitates, the opening of her wineskin hovering at the cup in front of Aahana.

“Serve her, she is the guest of honor tonight,” Korosi says.

The men at the table laugh. All except for Elder Zwangeni, who keeps his cunning gaze on Aahana’s face. His questioning eyes cut through her, searching for meaning, as though her face contained bones cast for divination. As That One pours, Aahana draws strength from the crack in the rock. A crack not made by the natural processes of weathering but it contains the echo of a woman who screamed in this chair. And there are more such cracks than one can count in the Temple.

"Let us eat. We shall need our strength for the next day," Huna'Kizit says. "This is the feast of the chosen!" He takes a gulp of date wine and belches loudly.

As the men noisily chew their delicious fare, Aahana raises her hands and touches her lips. Her jaws have been sewn shut for so long, she struggles to pry them open. The boa'oba bark seems to have numbed her lips for the pain is gone.

"This One should feed," Huna'Kizit says, pointing a bone at her.

Eating. For many years, Aahana could only feed through a straw. Every day saw her drink the foul -tasting gruel, which the men said contained all the balanced nutrients the body needs for survival. But still the girls wasted until they were skeletons in gray dresses, much as Aahana was. In the privy, their bowels ran just as loose as their bladders did.

Aahana opens her mouth into an O. Zwangeni's eyes widen with something resembling excitement.

"A broken wing
Ring and awaken, sweet youth
Before the rain."

The foul stench of Aahana's breath is evident even to herself. Is this why Elder Zwangeni recited the verse of the lightning bird? The men nearest to her cover their noses. It didn't take long after her lips were sewn shut for her teeth to rot. She remembers the succession of agonizing days with a swollen mouth, enamel crumbling leaving raw nerves screaming. The times she had to swallow her teeth one by one. All that remains of the white pearls she used to have are a few jagged bits against blackened, infected gums. She cannot eat this food. They brought her to this table to torture her, to make her watch as they feast upon the rare delicacies her tongue will never taste.

Aahana feels the echoes pouring from the crack beneath her toe and smiles at Elder Zwangeni, showing him her ruined mouth.

* * *

When the men are done having their dinner and the last elder has left the table, Tungi seizes Aahana roughly, helping her up, his hand under her armpit. She's exhausted by it all. There's something strange, something resembling shame on Tungi's face. It's as if he can't stand leading Aahana back to her quarters. They slowly walk through the sullen corridors she knows like the back of her hand.

"I hope I didn't hurt you too much," Tungi says, his voice cracking. "It, it was my first…" He trails away as if the words have been lost. "I didn't know… Here, take this. It should help with the pain."

Earnest look upon his face, Tungi offers more boa'oba bark from his leather pouch as they reach Aahana's quarters.

"Please, take it. This should be enough. If you swallow it before the ceremony tomorrow, it will numb your body and mind. You won't feel a thing, I promise." He checks both sides of the long corridor to make sure no one hears. "I'm sorry. I wish there was more I could do. It's not my fault. I don't want any of this."

Tungi's words only harden Aahana's heart against the men. She shakes her head, enters the dark room and shuts the rusty metal door, leaving him outside. She collapses, her back against it, and rests.

Somewhere in the darkness, Uhm rouses a pilfered magoza worm which glows green, brightening the room. She pats the empty spot beside her on the sleeping mat, beckoning Aahana to come near. This is their last night together. Mother Time is an unkind god. Still they will defy her because tonight, they have each other and they will suck dry every instant offered to them.

Aahana removes her bloodstained dress and steps onto the mat. Then she lies down next to her companion. If only... No, she will not give in to the gnawing despair. Uhm takes her hand and places it on her belly where new life is growing, note by note. The two women draw closer and share each other's warmth. Skin touching skin.

I have been worried about you, Uhm signs. With her lips sewn, this is how she speaks. Over many years, the two of them developed their own language. When sound was taken away from them, they learnt their bodies could convey so much more. Everything began to carry meaning. The dropping of a shoulder. A stolen glance. The twitch of the eyebrows. They *understand* one another. When together like this, alone, out of the watchful eyes of the men, it's almost as though they can read each other's minds. Is it not telepathy when Uhm lies on Aahana's chest, decoding the sound of her beating heart?

A tie joins two notes together.

Aahana opens her mouth to speak. Her throat is too dry. The larynx unused for so long is jammed. Instead she signs: *We are so close.* Tears stream from Uhm, down onto Aahana's chest. They were indeed close; the secret crevice they discovered from which a steady gust of wind blew in from the outside world. This temple has many paths and they had stumbled on a forgotten one. It promised freedom. The crevice was too narrow. And so they had stolen tools. It was not that hard for the men, confident in their power, tended to miss such trifling things. On nights neither was summoned, the two went out to dig. It was on this first excursion Aahana began to hear the echoes. Stolen voices had leached into the rock. She asked Uhm whether she too could hear them, but her sleepmate could not.

For a while Aahana was certain she was going mad.

It was not uncommon for a maiden's mind to break. Some went stark raving, others completely lost their will to move, more than a few tried to extinguish their own drumbeat. But Uhm had counseled Aahana, telling her that the Mother Goddess could see even into the depths of Ekwukwe. Nothing could be hidden from Her.

They had to be careful about this belief. The men here were discordants, a dangerous cult with a strange theology. They had twisted the known story that the universe began with sound. Aahana had listened to Elder Zwangeni discoursing with his acolytes. They said, and it was hard to believe, the world began with a Scream. She remembered his verse perfectly:

> "In my dream a baby was born,
> the midwife hears a scream.
> Before that was the Mother's own.
> In the next room, He who caused it all."

Aahana's heart had nearly stopped when she heard this verse. Instantly, she understood the depths of blasphemy these men had plunged into. They had twisted the Mothersound. This new theology was an abomination. The "He" in the verse, hidden from creation "In the next room", was the ultimate source who the cult believed was the Father. It was He who had caused the “Scream” which brought the world into being. This is to say the Mother was lesser. On Wiimb-ó or Zezépfeni these men would have been put to death without trial. Even on the surface of Ekwukwe, some would have torn them apart. But here, in the depths, they festered like a cancer infecting the world.

But even in this darkest of places, hidden from truth, Aahana had found her light in Uhm. Love, that purest of things, found a way even in these depths. It is this love that turned her and Uhm, by a strange alchemy, from strangers to sisters. That One became Uhm. The most beautiful name Aahana’s sewn-up mouth could utter.

We will find a way.

Hope, love’s eternal sister.

The two women hold each other close. Tonight they can’t sneak out to make a final push to dig their way back to the surface, because Tungi is standing guard. Beyond, in the corridors, more men are posted just in case. It is not unknown for chosen maidens to try to escape their fate.

Aahana listens to the echoes in the walls that grow stronger with each passing moment. Amidst the turmoil, she recites in her soul the creed she knows as truth since her youth and it gives her comfort. Her mothers and aunties recited it before the men stole her from her people and stripped her of her true identity:

"...She uttered the Word, releasing its power into existence.

She created the Word. She was the first to speak the Word. She was the first to hear the Word. She was the first to feel the Word. She was the first to see the Word.

The Word undulated through Her body, explosions of light and sound reverberated outward through the darkness, piercing the silence, as She conceived a child, warm in her womb.

The Word echoed outward, and She who had uttered the Word was witness to its power, as She beheld the creation of the heavens, stars, and a celestial body – the World – all from Her utterance. The World came from the Word.

Our Mother became Creator.

Our Mother, God."

Sleep does not come to them that night, but Aahana is certain she felt the protection of the Word. But when the men come and open the door, she falters and remembers the “Scream”. Other maidens enter into the room to get Aahana for the time is near. They lead her to the underground stream where the rockface is polished and layered from years of weathering.

They bathe her in the healing waters and apply o’livha’vha oil to her skin and melon oil in her hair. A dab on her neck of scented perfume made from the oil of the yellow fura flower. Aahana observes the maiden’s diligent work. They avoid meeting her eyes. Theirs are filled with pity. Their sewn-up lips don’t allow them to say anything either. When they are done pampering her, the maidens clothe Aahana in a pure white shroud made of the special treated fibers of the marula tree, dipped in each of the seven oceans of Wiimb-ó, and woven on the loom of the disciples of Grand Zéhemgwile, wielder of a billion needles. It is soft, unlike the sackcloth of the grey dresses the maidens wear and thin enough for her to see through. Aahana lifts her arms in surrender as they tie a golden rope for a belt around her waist.

She looks around and finds Uhm hovering nearby. Aahana gives her the nod. *Make your way to our secret place.* Uhm lingers until Aahana gives her a severe look. With the ceremony on, there will be fewer men in the tunnels. She must go now.

* * *

The most sacred place in the Temple of the Weeping Drum lies at the nexus of a dozen tunnels deep below the earth. There, the rocks of the cave seem woven and sculpted into a grand cathedral. This is a place with many cracks. Geometric patterns and strange yet natural reliefs pattern the rock. Energy infuses every inch of ground in this region. Sound here travels strangely. A person may speak in front of you, but their voice appears to come from behind you.

It is here where they discovered the depths. A massive cave with a perfectly circular hole, an O with a radius of thirty feet, at its center. The darkness hovering over this hole is impenetrable by light. No one knows how deep it goes. None who've descended to investigate have ever returned to tell. An ancient magic lingers here. The men believe that just as you see the infinity of space in the sky at night, when you look into the abyss, you also see the vastness of nothingness staring back at you.

Aahana is led into the depths and stood at the edge of the hole across from the Elder Zwangeni, who holds his hands palms open over its foreboding emptiness.

The symbol of the calm desert sands before the roaring avalanche. The men force Aahana to kneel. Better, because on her knees she can feel the echoes pouring forth from the cracks in the rock beneath. These are the locked-in screams of the women sacrificed to the void, their echoes eaten by the rock

There's an air of anticipation in the cave.

Two strangers crouch on either side of Elder Zwangeni. These are supplicants from the world above who've come down to partake in this great ceremony. Aahana doesn't recognize the two men, but she knows they will be from Ekwukwe's ruling class, here seeking a charm or a spell to enhance their own fortunes against rivals in the world above. The two men in brown robes hold golden klalabashes filled with charms ready to receive the power of the Scream.

Filling every cranny in the cave are the men in their robes, here to watch the ceremony. They each carry a drum. Some have small ones, which they fit under their armpits and strike with sticks. Others have large drums set on the floor. Metal drums and wooden drums. And when they begin to play, it's like a monster with many hearts has been roused from its lair. The noise fills the air.

Huna'Kizit takes his place behind Aahana, waiting for the signal from Elder Zwangeni.

She faces the void trembling in awe. She hears the echoes of the women who screamed when they were offered up to the abyss. Swallowed by eternal darkness. Resigned to her fate, she prays they pour their screams into her. Every single decibel. Into herself. She places both hands onto her chest above her heart now thumping with rage.

With a simple nod, Elder Zwangeni orders Huna'Kizit to tip her into the void with a kick to the back.

Aahana tumbles forward.

But she does not fall.

The void does not deign to receive her. Perfectly still, she hovers over the darkness, her hands upon her heart. Etched in her memory is the mental image from the creed of the Mother, a woman alone in the eternal void:

She was witness to nothing. Yet She knew of everything.

How can this be?

The men are filled with confusion. They cry out and curse, faces now contorted with fury for they are waiting for the gifts of the Scream to pour forth into their bosoms.

Elder Zwangeni gasps:

"Father, in the cradle of mine twilight
By a whisper mine eyes have been opened."

His men cry out in despair. They tear their beards, stomp their feet, and beat themselves on their heads. How dare she! Others like Tungi take fright and flee from the depths, casting aside their sandals in their haste. Some are frozen in confusion. The sacrifice has never...

Aahana feels a fullness welling up from her womb. Her white dress flutters over the void. The collection of screams tumble through her dried-up throat. Gathering them all, she opens her broken mouth, but instead of a scream, everything, all the echoes, coalesce into one. Aahana utters the Word. A blinding white light fills the cave, driving away the shadows.

The rock rumbles and answers her call. The ground beneath them quakes as the echoes filling the cracks unleash their fury. Boulders loosen themselves and rain upon the men, crushing them. How the men scream in terror. Blood sprays. Guts. Broken bones and torn flesh. Their beloved drums are scattered, making hollow noises. Those who run are met with rock. The same fate meets the men who chose to kneel and pray to the Father instead. Elder Zwangeni staggers, taking it all in. How can this be? He glares hatefully at Aahana hovering unharmed over the void. Then full of despair, he throws himself headlong into the abyss, begging for darkness to shroud him from the light.

* * *

Later that night, when the rocks have done their worst, not a single man remains unscathed in the Temple. Aahana finds Uhm and, together, they gather the maidens who are bruised and scratched, but still alive, for the magic of the Mother that Aahana wielded would not harm her daughters. Their lips still sealed, they hum a song of thanks. The echoes of those who came before them and suffered are, at last, silent and at peace. Weary and hungry, limping but resolute, Aahana leads them up to the world above where a gentle wind blows. She turns her face to the starlit sky and realizes she has become the vessel of potent sonic magic, the gift of the Mother.

Kyi'yaji

Xan van Rooyen

unlock the music
no protections available
configured in scars

Xan van Rooyen*'s terrifying tale explores apostasy in a universe where sound is sacred. Cover your ears, or the anti-music is going to get you!*

On the planet Wiimb-ó, over 800 people died when the anti-music group Zaxulo committed ritual suicide on stage. Their method? An unholy combination of ear-shredding, mind-breaking sounds. The antithesis of music, a rejection of all that their people hold dear.

A young student, Lale, combs through recordings of those final moments. They have a connection to Zaxulo's lead singer, and they're desperate to know how deep that connection goes. But you know what they say about those who go looking for trouble...

Welcome to "Kyi'yaji".

00:02 "UNFORTUNATELY, there are no complete recordings of that night. What you're listening to is stitched together from flesh marks recovered during the initial investigation. However, many were mysteriously damaged or improperly preserved, resulting in extreme loss of quality. Some think this might be attributed to the use of illicit magic or deliberate mishandling of evidence. Please listen with caution, making use of all the necessary physical and spiritual protections available. This recording is strictly for research purposes..."

* * *

Lale hums the magical phrase to jump forward and the sound tablet responds, skipping over the rest of the warnings and disclaimers Lale has heard many times before. They wish they could get their hands on the original artifacts, those patches of skin pared from dead fans who'd volunteered to serve as living recordings, scarred by the music spelled sharp enough to gouge and slice.

Lale regards the scars on their own arms, a record of sorrow and self-loathing, though they wonder what sort of music might emanate from their self-inflicted carvings.

* * *

00:15 The audience screams.

00:17 The buzzing hum of a nar'a kwei is audible despite the crowd noise.

00:26 "Do you want more?" Nya (Niyayani) shouts. Voice distorted through the mic. The audience roars in response.

00:30 Feet stamp, voices chant, "More, more, more."

00:45 "Do you hear it?" Nya shouts, words becoming garbled. "Not yet, not yet, but you will."

00:57 Squelching noises over mic; Nya screams something unintelligible. Scream becomes more melodic and polyphonic.

01:12 Drummer, Hlo (Ihlololi), shouts, "Let's go." Raucous music starts.

01:24 The music cuts out abruptly.

01:34 Music resumes. Loud and frenetic.

01:45 Cuts out.

01:50 Music resumes. Loud and frenetic, but the beat has changed – is this even from the same performance?

01:55 "Can you hear it? Can you hear it? This is the voice of… this is the Mothersound. This is… I am…"

02:02 Cuts out.

02:05 Resumes. The music is less chaotic now and the sound of the crowd seems to be dying.

02:15 Cuts out.

02:20 The music has slowed, and a high-pitched keening sound (Nya's voice perhaps or simply electronic feedback) is audible above a stuttering drum beat.

02:29 Cuts out.

02:31 "Despite the quality, you can clearly hear…"

* * *

Lale hums another phrase and the recording pauses. They don't want to hear the long-dead narrator's half-baked pontifications on the events of that night again. They've listened to them more than a dozen times. What they want – what they *need* – is more recordings of the "music", if Lale can even call it that.

They press two fingers to the pierced cartilage where ear meets head, and gently massage. If only the caress could reach through flesh and bone, to the bruised membrane within and quiet their aching tinnitus.

They've been careful to limit their exposure to the recording – as brief and incomplete as it is. At least they have this, considering the original artifacts have long since decayed. There were ways to preserve flesh samples like that even back then, and no excuse for allowing evidence to rot. It seems clear to Lale that someone wanted all traces of that night to disappear, the proof of heresy dead and buried.

Lale doesn't want people to forget. They want the world – the universe – to know how one girl from Wiimb-ó dared to challenge the powers that be, hence their dissertation – if they ever finish it, given the lack of viable sources, and if it ever gets approved. Their ra'engi, the mentor, is becoming increasingly skeptical of their "research", and what Lale hopes to prove by dipping a toe into the turbid waters of anathema.

If their supervisor knew the truth, they would've rejected Lale's proposal from the very start, but Lale has done well to keep their family's secret. But that's why Lale wants – *needs* – to understand what happened during that final, fatal performance. What drove four musicians to commit ritual suicide on stage, and 852 audience members to tear the ears from their skulls, to rip the gray matter from their heads with only their fingernails? Was it magic gone bad, or divine retribution? Was it poison in the water, a toxin in the air? Surely, at least a few would've balked, would've fled in fear, faith suddenly rediscovered in the face of death. But none escaped. All succumbed, many with their skin left in tatters. The music had cut to the bone.

For a while, theories abounded as news of the scandal rocked Wiimb-ó. But the death of a few hundred radicals hardly seemed to matter, not when Wiimb-ó's leaders were locked in spurious debate over whether or not to remain in the federation of planets.

The band and its contrarian leader were deliberately purged from memory, its musical anarchy and legacy relegated to a derelict corner of societal (and family) recollection, reduced to a cautionary tale, before being dismissed as an example of a fringe group's misguided delinquency no one had ever taken seriously.

Hundreds of fans took it seriously enough to show up, to join the ritual, to risk becoming collateral damage in the sonic warfare waged on stage.

"Is it true?" Lale asks the ether, as if Nya's spirit somehow lingers after all this time. And perhaps it does, adrift in unreality, barred from eternal rest in Eh'wauizo due to her enmity towards all things Mother.

"Is it true? Is it true?" Lale repeats, their echolalia making an inadvertent song of the question. "Did you stab your own eye out?" *Stab stab stab*. The word is a drumbeat as Lale fingers their lashes and applies tentative pressure to their closed eyelid, trying to imagine how it must feel to be on stage in front of hundreds roaring your name... *Our Mother screamed with the glory of Motherhood and The Word screamed back.*

Nya rejected the Mother, only to become a god of her own devising.

The irony is bitter between Lale's teeth as the refrain continues across their tongue. "Is it true? Is it true? Did you really try to sever your connection with Our Mother?" To be severed from the Mother is to be severed from life itself.

Khwa'ra. It is acquired.

Ya'yn. It is uttered.

Ra'kwa. It is released.

Lale recites the refrain of the creation myth, a comforting habit developed in childhood to quell the rising panic – now induced by the nature of their research, the looming deadline, and Lale's blossoming worry about their biological inheritance.

There is nothing more they can glean from the patchwork recording, buried in the mahadum's vaults for secure-keeping and to keep safe a new generation who might be tempted toward apostasy.

Apostasy. Such beautiful syllables, providing the perfect polyrhythm to the still-looping question in Lale's mind. They return the audio tablet to its sound-proofed box within the basement archive far below the surface of Wiimb-ó. As far as Lale knows, this is the only surviving collection of excerpts from a live concert given by the band *X* – the name a percussive lateral click, reduced from the original *Zaxulo* in defiance of naming conventions.

"Lale'lelake," they say their full name out loud, a balm on the tongue and panacea for ears injured by the discordant jumble of noise Nya delightedly termed anti-music.

"But is it true?" Lale's mind still snags on the question, a hangnail caught on loose thread, shards of marama seed wedged between teeth. Lale flaps their hands, then flicks their fingers. One, two, three, four, one two three four – *apostasy apostasy* – faster, harder, until their nail beds ache and their thumb skin burns.

There is only one way to answer the question itching in their skin. Only one way to progress with their research and show their ra'engi they have not been wasting time. Lale has a small study stipend – they can afford to make the journey to the one person still alive who might know, who might truly understand and be willing to help.

Is there something crooked in Lale's DNA, some seed of rebellion carried from Nya deep within their cells? These are questions Lale should've asked years ago but was always afraid to. Now they need to understand why they've always wondered at the composition of the universe and what might happen if they dared to truly question it.

* * *

Kyi á Yikho, Kyi á Yikho, Kyi á Yikho,
I live in spite (despite?) of you,
flayed by your dark (mark?),
your shards sliced me open

Smoke pouring from my ears,
marrow melting from my bones
Open my mouth, spew fire from a split
tongue, black gum, teeth crumble
Guilty of every rotting thought,
you the maggot in my brain
Diseased (deceased?) echoes
carve through gray matter
My voice shatters every
harmonic, I'm bleeding
Pumping loss through ribs (lips?),
dripping wet (red?) between my legs,
No chance for mother, mother,
mother – never, well,
Mother, to the void with you,
When I screamed your name, only
silence, such silence (violence?)
Tears like ash, umbilical snap,
You never screamed back
Kyi á Yikho, Kyi'yaji, Kyi á Yikho.

Lyrics from X's song titled 'Mother of Nothing'

* * *

Lale clicks their molars together, an incessant chattering, as their hands fidget with the wooden shongololo their father made for them as a child. Each segment of the creepy-crawly's body has been worn smooth from years of touch, the paint fading but remaining different shades of green. Calming, distracting, helping Lale to regulate their emotions whenever anxiety unsheathed its claws, like now, as the transport glides toward the coast.

Their destination is a paramikule, one of the spiral settlements unique to the planet, less than an hour south of the coastal city of Loiimbi. Paramikule Hwengelii was founded by the esteemed and rebellious raevaagi Hmahein Hwengenlii, those learned storytellers who carry the history of the universe in memory and magic song. Lale has studied the mentor Hmahein's teachings and appreciates the woman's audacious attitude toward tradition, which – in some ways – reminds them so much of their Aunty Nya. Despite Lale's mother begging them to visit their Gogo – only so she wouldn't have to – Lale hasn't been back here in ages.

Lale hates the sea. They hate the humid heat making their skin sticky and hair frizz into tangles. They've slicked the thick strands back and kept their curls tied down beneath a pale green duka, the fabric starting to itch where it wraps around their head. They hate the thunder of the waves and the screech of gulls. They hate the wind and the threat of sand spilling across the dunes. It's an uncontrolled cacophony. Perhaps this is where Nya got her inspiration.

Lale is grateful the paramikule winds down into the cooler and quieter womb of the earth. Not much has changed, except this time Lale tries to imagine the sisters Sabebeza and Niyayani living here as children. They have fragments of stories, the tales told by their mother and even fewer shared by Gogo – she's never liked talking about her childhood or errant sister, but this time Lale won't leave until she does.

They've been here many times before, yet Lale still rehearses the script they devised while in transit. "Hi, Gogo. Sorry it's been so long. Please tell me about your sister, not the one who drowned as a toddler, no, the other one – the one who led hundreds of people to their deaths that fateful night. The one everyone says I inherited my eyes, nose, and talent for music from because I'm worried that might not be all I got."

Lale takes a deep breath. They've worked out contingency plans for every possible response. They can do this. They've come all this way. It's imperative for their research, for their sense of self, for their sanity. Lale raises their hand to knock.

* * *

Anti-music: a unique genre (and brief movement among musicians on Wiimb-ó) eschewing traditional principles of rhythm, melody and harmony while deliberately flouting all rules associated with sound magic. Performances were intended to be violent and shocking, often incorporating elements of bodily harm to both the "musicians" and audience members. A short-lived fad, many questions remain as little research has been done to better understand the allure of this movement and the repercussions of manipulating sound antithetical to Our Mother. But can anti-music even exist? Would Our Mother allow it?

* * *

Gogo Bebe is frail and gaunt, as twisted as a seed pod from a locust bean tree as she gathers Lale into a hug. She's thinner now since her fourth and final husband departed for the spirit realm taking his cooking skills with him. Her ex-wife still lives nearby, and Lale knows she checks on Gogo, whose mind always seems a little frayed at the edges. Gogo's bare feet shuffle a syncopated susurrus as she prepares the tea, piling a plate high with Lale's favorite sugary treats.

Lale inhales the hibiscus steam and the rest of the familiar smells wafting nostalgia up their nose. Not all the memories are good. It was here that Lale first hacked off their hair during an afternoon spent with Gogo – who'd helped trim the back, who had been the first to stop calling Lale "girl", to call them "handsome" instead of "pretty". Their mother had been furious, screaming at Lale and raging at Gogo. That night Lale opened trails across their arms with a razor all the while humming *dysphoria dysphoria dysphoria*.

After a few sips, Lale gathers their courage. "I was hoping we could talk about Aunty Nya."

Gogo nods, her head crowned with thinning curls frosted by age. They're still glossy. Lale can smell the shea butter from across the table, and fights the urge to pat their own neglected tangles.

"I was hoping you might be able to help me understand, well, everything."

Gogo regards Lale with eyes gone milky at their edges. "Does your mother know you're here asking questions?"

"I don't need her permission, Gogo. I'm an adult and I want to know."

"Hah. My daughter would love to hear that."

Lale has long stopped caring what their mother thinks. They know they're a disappointment, that their mother will forever see Lale's identity as a betrayal. She'd fought so hard to have a child. Spent years visiting uroh-ogis, downing the healers' potions, performing rituals, and wasting precious savings on questionable magic, all so she might have a child. Eventually she had Lale, who has rewarded their mother's perseverance and determination by choosing to "squander" their "natural ability" to continue the family legacy. Selfish, Lale has been called for refusing to give their mother the grandchildren she so desperately desires. Nya was called far worse.

"Is every generation destined to be at odds with the one that came before it?" Lale voices the thought out loud.

"It is the natural way of the universe," Gogo says. "Children should challenge their parents."

"That's why I want to know more about Aunty Nya." Was that all it was then, Nya like every child challenging the authority of the Mother? "And I want the truth, not the stories others told."

"There were so many asking questions," Gogo says. "Carrion eaters wanting the juiciest bits, and all the salacious, gory details." Her wizened lips pucker in disdain.

"I only want the truth."

"Only that? Hah!" Gogo swallows a mouthful of tea to clear her throat. "Do you know what you're asking for?" She fixes Lale with a calculating gaze.

"I want to know about my family. The truth." Lale is emphatic. "I want to know before you die." They hadn't meant to be so blunt, or so cruel, but Gogo's eyes scrunch with amusement.

"At least you're honest." She pats Lale's hand where it curls around the wooden shongololo, knuckles fitting snugly between the millipede's segments. "The truth, eh? Perhaps it's time."

* * *

A brief history of the vocalist known as Nya, as narrated by Nya's sister, Sabebeza:

Niyayani (Nya) grew up in a dogmatic household with parents who shunned the more liberal ways of their paramikule, adhering more strictly to the traditional ways of life on Wiimb-ó. Nya and Sabebeza were raised to revere and respect the Mother and their elders, or face dire consequences. Sabebeza described her upbringing as strict to the point of being claustrophobic, with the sisters punished for even the most minor transgressions.

"Where others had love, we had guilt and shame," Sabebeza says of her childhood. "As the eldest, I tried to protect Niya – Nya – from the worst of my parents' constant demand for perfection. I often took the blame and the beatings when Nya couldn't help herself. As we got older, she became bolder, reckless even, and I grew tired of living in pain and fear."

Nya had always shown an aptitude for music. She sang before she could talk, demonstrating an exceptional talent on k'hora'aa, ngonini, luhte-te, mbi'ira, balafofo, du'undun, and the kalabash drum. According to Sabebeza, there was no instrument Nya couldn't play.

"She had a Mother-given gift for music but, even in the earliest days, she rebelled. You need to understand,

it wasn't that she was bad – just bored. She mastered playing techniques so easily, she memorized the traditional melodies, danced and performed even the most complex rhythms. She was a wonder and so she became a menace, her curiosity incurable as she experimented with sound."

While Nya might have been sent for formal training as a raevaagi or tested for maadiregi abilities, by the time she was ten years old, her parents had joined the Kwera'Yaliira, a sect whose members were known for dedicating their lives to the worship of the Mother, and who believe humans exist only to serve the Mother through prayer and endless obeisance. All education took place at home, the sisters having little to no contact with those outside the sect.

While magic is tolerated and acknowledged as a gift from the Mother, most adherents of the Kwera'Yaliira faith do not practice, believing themselves unworthy of such a gift and that they may only earn the right by living an ascetic life in honor of the Mother. The few practitioners of magic within this sect are almost exclusively septuagenarians or older. Magic practiced at a young age is considered "furukuru" – forbidden – and those who do it or aspire to wield magic, even by traditional methods, are equally labeled furukuru and ostracized within the community.

"Nya was difficult from the moment she first drew breath," Sabebeza says. "She was hungry for milk, for music, for magic, for life. She wanted to live life to the fullest on her own terms. At first, she loved the Mother. She saw herself as a similar creator through music, an echo of the Mother made flesh, and she wanted…she wanted nothing more than to become a mother herself."

* * *

Gogo wipes tears from cheeks as gnarled as mokala bark and Lale is finally starting to understand. They wrap their arms around their grandmother, letting the old woman's tears soak their shirt even if the wet fabric against their skin feels like acid.

"Nya thought she'd kept it a secret, but I'm her sister," Gogo says, pulling away, and Lale gratefully returns to their seat. "I think I knew before she did, and I knew my mother would kill her when she found out. Nya was only fourteen, never did find out who did it to her – she refused to tell us, even when my mother whipped her bloody, but that was after – after the…" Gogo trails off, battling a fresh wave of tears. Lale gives their grandmother a moment to recompose herself, not feeling the need to fill the silence.

"You need to understand that I thought I was helping." Gogo's voice trembles. "She was so young, too young, but the Mother forgive me—" She looks away and Lale digs their nails into the palm of one hand and clenches the shongololo with the other, as Nya's lyrics swirl, haunting, through their mind.

The truth unfurls like the fronds of the carnivorous sundew.

"You can't even taste it," Gogo says. "It's such simple muti and I thought if it was early enough our parents would never know. But Nya was small, and I miscalculated. It made her so ill, everyone thought she was dying. I didn't mean for her to never be a mother. Just not so young when she would surely regret it."

Lale screws their eyes shut. They do not want to hear this, do not want to imagine the wet tearing of their great aunt's loosening insides, the emptiness left behind and the sudden void opening where once there was life.

They knew there'd been more to this story, something Gogo had refused to tell, something missing in all the sordid whispers about Nya and what became of her. This is the truth, why the sisters never spoke, and Nya never acknowledged her family.

Lale will not think about the configuration of their own insides, the organs they resent and vow to never use when Aunty Nya had been so cruelly robbed of a chance at motherhood. What had she done to heal that invisible wound?

"There is something else, something I would show you," Gogo says, and Lale knows they have been captured, drawn by the promise of nectar. "Few others have ever seen them and most of those who have are dead."

"Has Mama?" Lale asks, intrigued.

"Definitely not," Gogo says. "I was trying to protect her, but she'll just add it to the list of everything I've ever done wrong." She sighs.

"I know the feeling," Lale says.

"Oh child, your mother does love you. She just can't see you past her own pain, but I hope one day she will." Gogo's words wrap around Lale's heart, scabbing the wounds inflicted by their mother's harsh words and scorn-filled glowers.

"I've been so afraid," Gogo says. "But I'm old now and I don't want to carry the weight of this secret anymore." She labors to her feet and beckons Lale to follow her to the privacy of the bedroom. There, she hesitates before unbuttoning her blouse and Lale watches, confused, as the old woman turns to reveal her naked back riddled with scars.

At first, Lale thinks Gogo has been mauled by a kunkun, her skin shredded by the massive feline's claws and fangs, except, there is a pattern to the welts of keloid zigzagging across Gogo's knobbly spine and the shallow rills of her ribs.

Lale sucks air in between their teeth, blinking in disbelief.

"You went to a performance?"

"No, never a public one, but I knew where the band practiced," Gogo says.

"And she let you record them?"

"She never even knew I was there. Nya wasn't the only one with an innate gift for magic. The spells were harder to master, having to be studied in secret but, after Nya left home, I knew I'd never see her again. I wanted to keep something of my sister. Something just for me."

Lale steps closer to their grandmother, traces the shapes of the scars in the air above the marked skin with a gentle finger. They swallow a mouthful of saliva, feeling the hunger inside them grow. A primary source, a perfectly preserved recording of *X*'s music.

Their toes clench and gut spasms in desperation to hear it. "Have you listened to it since?" Lale asks.

"Never," Gogo says. "Hearing it once was enough, and it was plenty to know I could carry this small piece of my sister with me, to preserve some tiny part of her legacy. I owed her that much." Gogo curls a fist against her stomach. "After she left home, we heard stories about the concerts, the violence, how she'd been disqualified from the Kalabashing contest for breaking the rules of containment. Nya was a little like the founder of this paramikule." Gogo's smile is sad. "Like Hmahein, Nya wanted the world to witness her brilliance and rebellion. She wanted her music to be free and wreak havoc on the world. It brought such shame and embarrassment. My parents couldn't survive it – my first marriage didn't either – all our hearts and spirits were broken."

"So was Nya's," Lale says.

Gogo pauses, trembling as she stands exposed before them. "After my parents died, I went to Loiimbi, found out where the band was squatting, thought I would try to make amends with my sister, but...I lacked the courage. Instead, I listened in secret and stole her music."

"Did it hurt?" Lale asks. They know how the kiss of a blade can burn – does music bite as deep?

"Every moment," Gogo says, her voice thick with tears. "But I deserved it, and I endured every note of that racket."

"Could we listen to it together now?" Lale asks.

They're not sure they can wait for their Gogo to die but, when she does, Lale will strip this canvas from the body and then the music will be theirs forever.

"I'm not sure."

"Please," Lale says.

"I've forgotten the spells."

"I know them." Lala studied the process in case it helped them verify the veracity of sources. They have never needed to say the spells out loud or work the magic.

"But this type of magic—"

"The recording spells are somewhat taboo," Lale interjects, "but not illegal. Playing what's been stored is perfectly fine."

"I'm not sure…"

"Please, Gogo." Lale rests their hand on their grandmother's shaking shoulder, guides her to the edge of the bed where the old woman sags, nodding and weeping.

Lale settles on their knees behind her, focused on the scars as they extract the spell from memory. Words they never thought they'd need but hoped they might. Slowly, enunciating every syllable, Lale sings the magical phrase to unlock the music trapped in flesh.

* * *

00:03 "From the top?" Nya asks over the sound of a distorted k'hora'aa.

00:08 The band begins to play. The sound is bombastic, the instruments churning in an indescribable stew of clashing tones.

* * *

Lale winces, wondering if it was wise to crack open the keloid. Gogo stiffens.

"Does it hurt?" Lale asks.

"It prickles, but, oh, my ears." Gogo claps her hands to her head.

It would've been wiser, and better methodology, to take Gogo back to the mahadum, to have their ra'engi or a maadiregi specialized in flesh working to cast the spell within the safety and security of a sound-proofed listening lab. Their ra'engi will be displeased, but it's too late now. The music has started, if lightning-bolt frequencies striking haphazardly in a storm of polyrhythms can be called music.

What is music, if not the careful organization of sound and silence, the measured consideration of pattern and novelty? It's the magic that comes from creating order from chaos, from embracing the shards of Mothersound resonating within every soul and woven into the universal sonic tapestry. But this is not creation. It's desecration, a deliberate plunge into chaos and tumult, a violent cataclysm with no regard for the tenets of practicing safe sound magic.

Anxious, Lale clutches the green shongololo in their hand, fingers rubbing familiar creases along the carved body, watching as the scars on Gogo's back shift and strain against the skin like maggots in a carcass.

* * *

00:35 Nya's voice soars above the instruments in a scorching melody as she makes use of her unique polyphonic singing ability.

00:45 The song continues, ebbing and flowing in a rancid tide, crashing and retreating like the waves against the coastal cliffs, claiming and eroding, claiming and eroding, claiming and eroding.

01:03 Despite the turbulence of the sound: the thrashing churn of rhythm and melody, of the balafofo beaten within an inch of its life – gourds splintering – the k'hora'aa's strings snapping, the blast of the vuvu'uzela tearing through the antiphonal refrains pleached together in disharmony, Nya's voice remains audible.

* * *

If this song had lyrics, only the band ever knew it, the vocables a garbled morass of fury and hatred, a scathing torrent pouring into Lale's soul. Something cracks within Lale, a faultline juddering in a seismic thrum, as if their whole body is trying to echo the fracture in Nya's voice. Like responding to like, a bond festering in the blood.

Lale touches one of the wriggling scars and Gogo cries out as the skin shears open, suppurating dark ooze and acrid smoke.

From the chasm Nya's song has excavated within Lale comes a similarly strange seeping – the marrow animated and veins slithering electric.

Lale has never been a great singer, inheriting instead a gift for instruments and preferring the feel of strings beneath their fingers to notes in their throat. But now, their lips peel back from their teeth, their tongue contorting as the unknown sensation bubbles up from their gut.

Magic, like none they have tasted before. They know it instinctively, but it's warped and wrong, a power wrought from spite and infused with malice: an aberration of the Mother's gift.

Gogo pitches forward, face down in the pillows as more scars burst like boils.

Lale cannot divide their voice the way Nya can, even though they try, sound pulled from their throat against their will. Lale comes apart like a blade of grass torn by childish fingers; like gobbets of flesh poison flensed from the womb.

The magic is sweet on Lale's tongue, but a lie like the sundew's nectar, a trap to devour the hapless, and Lale is caught.

And Gogo is dying.

Blood and magic puddle on the bed, spill onto the pristine floor. Lale buckles, cradling their insides as they shatter. They watch the remaining skin on their grandmother's back slough away, raw ribbons turning to wisps of smoke.

Inside Lale's skull, the music continues. Lale bashes a fist against their temple as if they can knock free the trapped sound and restore the blessed silence. They succeed only in snapping the shongololo, a child's toy not made to withstand adult anguish.

They gnash their teeth against the unwanted words in their mouth, trying to bite back the serrated sounds. The vocables squealing through their mind shift into recognizable phonemes, the clatter of consonants against the mushroom-squish of vowels, and Lale wrestles their own mouth closed, their jaw popping with the effort.

It's too late.

Gogo groans and whimpers.

Is it true? Is it true? Is it true? Lale'lake, Lalelelelelake, the voice makes an ululation of Lale's name, a taunt rippling into laughter as the smoke shimmers, dances to the *dundun dundun dundun* beat lambasting the space between Lale's ears.

The voice solidifies, an echo now corporeal, rage and vengeance from hope and wonder threshed into being. One eye glints, the other is a weeping socket impaled by a spear head.

Nya.

She skewered her own eye that night, and must've continued to perform without removing the blade. Lale doesn't have to imagine the agony, they feel it – their own eye burning as if doused in spirits and set aflame. They blink, vision occluded, but their ears—

Can you hear it? Nya's specter asks, the split-tone voice parting the maelstrom still assaulting Lale's mind. *Can you hear the Mothersound?*

Lale recedes from the world, sinking into the embrace of the anti-music, tasting every frequency, seeing every atomic quiver as rhythms consume rhythms, melodies dancing, undulating. Lale's body twitches in orgasmic shudder.

No, you hear me, Nya says. *And now you know me.* Her voice is a blade dragged across the distended belly of the void. *I am Mother*, she says, and the skin of unreality splits open in mimetic birth.

Lale clutches at the ropey tendrils spilling from the wound in their belly. Ghost arms catch them, ease them back against the pillow beside Gogo, who stares with wet eyes at the manifestation between them.

Nya hums, the lullaby a corruption of tonality, and Lale knows they should plug their ears, knows they should beg for mercy, but their viscera steams in their cupped palms and the storm still rages inside their skull.

"Why?" Lale asks the ghost of the great aunt they never knew, Nya dead before her twenty-fourth birthday – the same age Lale is now. "Why?" They ask again, but what they really mean is *how*, how did Nya come into such power, to be able to twist and change the music, to defy the Mother and laws of the universe? And the question they dare not utter aloud, the one writhing within them they wish to quash: could I do it too?

The Word lives within us, an echo of Our Mother's love and power. Nya's voice is a tonal scatter across the impossible music bruising Lale's brain. *But they scoured my insides, made me as hollow as a gourd, a kalabash scraped empty. Devoid.*

In the peripheral vision of Lale's remaining eye, Gogo moves, lifts a hand toward the sister she destroyed.

Ah, dear sister, Nya says, the words leaving blisters in Lale's already ruined ear canals. *Thank you for letting me sleep within your skin.*

Lale cannot fight the undertow of sound, the music raging still. It sucks them into oblivion, dulling their senses. Color drains from their vision, splashes of darkness across a landscape of textured grays, their grandmother's face contorted in horror. Lale wants to reach for her, to tell her they're okay if only the pounding in their head would abate.

They just need it to stop for a moment, a heartbeat, a breath, so they can think, remember another spell, something to contain what never should've been released. They bury their face in their hands. The skin is slick with gore, but the nails are still sharp – enough to rip out eyes, to tear off ears, and dig deeper.

Eventually, through arduous dismantling of tone and echo, bone and sinew, languid rhythms stretching time, tissue flicked from fingers, melodies falling like rain across a washed-out landscape, eventually, there is quiet.

What happens now? Where will you go? What will you do?

Lale's thoughts flounder in the muck. Vaguely, they know they will never leave this bed awash in red, never finish their dissertation, never regain their mother's love. They will die here, a disappointment.

There are so many more ears in the world now, Nya says. *And worlds beyond Wiimb-ó too. I will find those willing to listen, willing to remake this universe.*

So it was true? The bond can be severed, umbilical snap, the Word never again screaming back.

Yes. Nya's voice purrs through the sludge of dying frequencies. *I am free of the Mother. I am free.*

I am free I am free I am free, Lale echoes as shadow fingers stroke Lale's arms, transposing the scars already there, rearranging tissue into sound. Lale listens to Nya's voice, lacerating the iron-misted air above the spread of excoriated flesh.

This is our manifesto:

We will purge the world of the
obsequious, the timid and afraid.

We will take back our power and
divine our own destiny.

We will purge the world of lifeless art, of imitation sound, of social artifice, of conformity, of obedience – purge the world of the rule makers and rule followers, of those who would control and silence us.

We hear the Word.
We hear the Voice.
Khwa'ra. It is acquired.
Ya'yn. It is uttered.
Ra'kwa. It is released.
Kyi'yaji. It is rejected.

Mahwés Fall

Jamal Hodge

Mahwé's fall,
a story of pride and folly,
that echoes through us all.
In the deep caverns of Kuu'uum,
where the Baa'gh once dwelled,
a million voices raised in song,
their wisdom, unparalleled.

For peaceful was Mahwé,
tidally locked to Pinaa,
its unsettled moon,
technology flourished
in singing sound
before the coming doom.

After generations of discovery,
blessed with every known delight,
Mahwé's Sauúti began
a relentless quest to possess
The Mother's might,
creating The Father,
an AI of cold silicon light.

Digitized comprised collection
of every entitled desire,
in every system, every device,
in every hope and wish,
an egoic artificial life.

"Find us The Word," they commanded,
"The Mother's sacred sound,
That we may wield creation's power,
make eternity our crown.
For what use in the dying?
What greatness in mortality's need?
We shall know all freedom
beyond limitation's greed."

So, The Father searched,
calculated, computed,
dreamed a billion songs
echoing a singular crime,
in Jenne's bustling heart,
constructing the aagoometric arts,
to tear reality apart.

In service of the bold,
does the cruel find respite,
Mahwé's Sauúti
enslaving millions of Baa'gh,
in The Father's cold,
mechanical light.

Kuu'uum silenced,
to grief's whispers,
to fear's tears.
Baa'gh songs
commodified to tools,
in the service of spiritual fools.

Who sought to tame Nakoko,
the beast that feasts on time,
and with its power,

reach into the infinite,
to hear The Word's first rhyme.

For when The Word was spoken,
did all souls exist,
eternity and creation,
Mahwé demanded all of this.

But oh, the downfall of mortals,
who dare the realms divine.
Spectacular, ambition's sorrow,
crossing wisdom's fragile line.

The grand experiment failed,
doomed where hubris began,
a blight on the land
from the moral failings of Man.

Time unraveled, compressed,
past-present-future as one.
Chrono-dismorphation
of Mahwé land,
in blackened light
of blinking sun.

The dead walk with the living,
the unborn cry in pain,
Spirits trapped in endless loops
with no one to explain.

Worse than Yikoh's emptiness,
this fractured, timeless state,
where Eh'wauizo's peaceful shores,
remain far beyond this endless fate.

So, heed this warning,
the lessons in Mahwé's doom.
Respect the bounds of knowledge,
lest eternal scars mark your tomb.

For in the Silences,
where magic sleeps,
and tech falls mute,
we remember Mahwé's lesson,
with solemn drums,
grieving flutes.

Here, settled on Pinaa,
we still stand.

Refugees of Mahwé,
eternally divorced,
from ancestral lands.

May The Mother
in her mercy,
wash the inequities
from our hands.

The Rawness of You

Eugen Bacon

clouds in slow motion
a fork in the wilderness—
a maw full of saws

Eugen Bacon*'s account of a disquieting afterlife begins with a mortal crash, where our unnamed hero wakes in a strange hinterland and nothing seems quite right. The character takes comfort in the knowledge that they have reached Eh'wauizo, the spirit realm, a dimension of the dead, but are there fates worse than death?*

Welcome to "The Rawness of You".

THIS STORY changes with the telling, whose hungry eyes and bared teeth the narrator seeks. It's dusk, away from the cityscape – there, a fountain towers dry. One winding laneway down, a late-shift worker lets herself into a chalet, as another in a tetekute skin – the sentient leopard whose stripes vibrate – flicks her rosetted tail, prowls the gloaming streets. As she plods, paw by paw, each step slows time, stretches into a labyrinth.

Listless leaves of boa'oba trees listen for forever secrets where time is no healer and rational explanations wither. Wordless shadows zigzag without disrupting the silence of all that remains unsaid in a rhetoric of emptiness. A grey-faced statue with marbled features, arms out in a beckon, weeps smoke tears that waft out across a vacant field to the park, then into a forest where the gleam-eyed beast-woman dissolves under a silver moon.

Just a moment…

Are these your…eyes? It is night and you're not asleep.

* * *

A flash of mangy fur at the edge of your vision
shrinking, reflecting
recollecting.

You breathe in deep, and your ribs rise and fall, rise and fall. You're a starving silhouette. Sprawled. Inverted. Raw like a skinned rabbit with its forefeet intact. You're a splatter on the landscape and seeing the world upside down. What you feel is

love

and

loss.

* * *

The sound of wet air is soft in your belly. The smell of copper and rust – you know it's a whiff of your platelets abandoning your body. Wait, who's this? It's the rosetted sphinx, half woman, half tetekute. She's a black beauty of onyx eyes, watching you in silence, out here in bushland. Her roped hair falls to coned breasts. Her mouth, a peony. Her eyes, a question.

Her question is a heartbeat that's also a statement. She's looking for (or understands) hard answers you'd prefer were available to broadcast without scepticism. All you need is fact. All you want is to say, STOP. LEAVE.

But the rawness of you is dressed in blood and dust.

There's a fork in the road meandering into the wilderness.

Things are buzzing. Creatures chittering in all manner of language, and the sound of their dialect is growing. There's the skeleton of a tree – you know it. Not the mopane or boa'oba. It's a woodland scarecrow.

What you feel is the unknown touching your shoulder. It's imaginary. It's real. It's infectious, framed in a tempo of magic that quivers the air. It's a tongue of earth music filled with primeval whispers that branch and braid, shift and recalibrate in a metamorphic beat that saves you from falling off the edge of the world.

Someone shakes your shoulder.

—Speak, Honey, a stranger says. How can I help you?

You tell her how you fell from the sky, a collision of shuttles. How there was a blaze and an ejector seat threw you. How you tugged at cords but the parachute wouldn't open. You don't know if she understands, because no sound is coming from your throat.

Your tongue is a menace, words eroded to grit.

—Do something, your unblinking eyes say. So dry in the cornea, a tear wells and rolls down the cheek. Do anything.

The sphinx touches you, puts needles in your core and they stop your heart.

—Iiiiiih!

The earth responds to your soundless gasp, cracks. Delirium climbs from the ravine's core under a heeding sky. Everything scrapes now. A signal sears down your neck, arms, all the way down to your lower back, buttocks, right down your legs to the heels. It burns, it agonises. Why does your body feel so…compressed?

A shiver. Quick rising – now you're on the other side of the forest road, looking, waiting, for what? You are collateral damage waiting for the world to feel right. The signal is coming and it is going. It's unpredictable like Zezépfeni weather that doesn't know what to do, all those meteor strikes, oceans desiccating into deserts. But you're in Wiimb-ó, embankments and woodland, embraced in a spirit world where the ancestors are close.

The she-beast is gone.

You feel numb, wracked. You feel love for what you have lost.

* * *

It's a forever solitude, then you hear a rustle. You see the kudu-kudu at the edge of your eye. He's majestic, twirled horns reaching for the sky. He snorts. Where's his musky scent? Why can't you smell… anything? He stamps. No one needs to tell you he's discomfited. His gallop, away, away… is as loud as a bellow.

You've lost touch and smell. You're losing… you've lost… everything. You feel out of yourself. Will you ever find you again?

And then.

A flicker, recognition. You see yourself looking at you. You're still on the other side of the forked road, but there you are on the ground. Your body is twitching, then it deflates as if it's eating itself.

This is how you know you have died.

* * *

—You're just finding your new self, the stranger says. You recognise her. It's the sphinx. She's back.

—Where am I?

—Every year the world is moving fast, she says. Notice it or not.

She gestures at clouds floating the skies in slow motion, birds soaring at altitude on a draft. How is there a lake? T'apiapia fish pushing side to side against the water. They thrust and leap with a sweep of tail. They glide, squiggle and flip.

—Everything takes something from another thing, she says. Look at that mopane tree.

She points.

—The tree lives to survive the harshest wind, fire, water. Resuscitates from bruising by the tallest feasting herbivores, even the t'embo'oo and its fat trunk. She spreads her leaves like butterfly wings to get the best of the suns. Makes herself sweet or sour. Less or more compounds in her sap to taste good or bad. Morphs colour across green, gloss or gold to attract or deter. See how she works hard to resist the worms that feed on her leaves – still they win. But something else takes from the mopane worm. It's you, humans. Here, taste this.

The worms she strews onto your palm are a smoked crunch.

—So earthy, how rich in protein, she says. Three times more than nguwe'we, the horned pig, hoink hoink. These wrigglers are sweeter than the yasa that cocoons into a pupate to become a butterfly. Tried mopane worms in a stew with red gourd, wilderness radish and piri-piri?

Suddenly, you're clutching a gourd of steaming stew.

—Or sauteed in a fermented cashew sauce?

The blond porridge of a nutty relish seeps through your fingers.

—The big black eye is the best part to eat, she says.

It's all so clear now. This is Eh'wauizo, the afterlife, and it's beautiful. Here is your peace. You are ready to rest in the touch and whisper of Our Mother, the Creator.

—Why am I here? you ask.

Still no sound from your throat.

But she's heard. You know this because her eyes gleam ruby. Then they are a swirl. The rotating plume of a tornado in them startles you. It turns the whole world around you to fog. Ashes fall down upon you and they scorch your skinless form.

Smoke everywhere, the stench of your flesh cooking.

—I…you begin to apologise. You didn't mean to annoy her with your ingratitude.

Her touch on your back is a spinal tap. You cry out at the fierce heat, the sensation of uncountable pricks and needles poking you with maliciousness everywhere.

—I am what I am, she says, and power must come from somewhere. I was once an ordinary uroh-ogi, a healer, until I stumbled upon a brand of old magic.

Her voice is a growl is a beast is a demon.

—You'd be amazed how much such magic transforms you when you learn to become a soul-eater. I'd give anything to go back to being a simple uroh-ogi. Even just a raevaagi, a bard, a teller of stories. But no. The hunger! It costs to keep this body.

Her form is swaying and morphing with the falling ash. The ropes in her hair beget vipers and they're hissing and spitting in your direction.

Huhhhh! Sssssss!

And her mouth.

Her mouth is a gobbling jaw with teeth full of saws. You move to run but you're paralysed. The maw reaches your stomach and bites a chunk of it.

You scream, unable to move, but the shriek is inward inside your head, your jaws fully locked. She portions out with her teeth a chunk of your shoulder – flesh and bone. If her spinal tap hadn't incapacitated you, you'd have collapsed in the agony of being gnawed alive, every part of you smelting and smouldering in a ferocity of torment.

—All those nights you lay awake contemplating mortality, she says. *Are we more than meat, blood, longing?* you wondered, as the suns rose and the suns set and time was a frock and a shoe and a parcel and a curl and a malfunction. What is time as the world moves, undeviating from all principles of uncertainty?

She's chomping you alive, chunk by chunk.

—As I said. Something always takes from another thing.

She swallows, belches.

You feel like you've lived a long time among fire eaters in a far-off land. Your whole body, even as it disappears into her gut, is scorching. You're ready to burst into flames, like the impudu-pudu, the lightning bird.

Your tongue combusts with an untold story, but even that she takes when her mouth nears your nose and she smells of bad kalabash, dead fish, everything rancid. She bites your face, gobbles your tongue, and you're one with her rot all the way down her gut.

* * *

You're a churn, goo, and you're not one but many. You're changing, changed, trapped inside a stomach. You long for something more but aren't sure of what. You're rustling and murmuring, loud, louder. You're not one, you're many, and you're hiss-sing.

Night is coming. You know this on instinct and you're buzz-zing inside the messiness of her bad stomach that heaves, heaves.

Then she spews you in a goopy gush.

Freedom!

Not really. Some of you is still inside her. You smell her, you feel her, you are her.

You're one, you're many.

Hisssss! Buzzzz! Master!

She who entrapped you, disgorged you, is the one who's unfettered you.

Hisssss! Buzzzz! Master!

But, satiated, she leaps to the skies and the sludge of you that's a churn on the ground wants to follow, but you're drying out, and no-no-no! The kudu-kudu's bearded mouth is approaching.

* * *

You've been twice devoured, spewed and now shat.

Not by the kudu-kudu, because a fat-pawed kunkun – the large carnivorous cat – pounded and leapt, throttled the kudu-kudu and ate it. Then a cackle of chekele'les with their short hind legs ganged up on the kunkun and circled it. The big cat crouched in the long j'hani'ni grass, grimaced and bared sharp, yellow fangs, but nothing. The chekele'les laughed. Ha-ha-ha. Hee-hee-hee. They were effective, bigger than the janlele – the water dog. And ate the kunkun alive. Chomp. Chomp.

They excreted you. Flies, then maggots, ate you, shat you.

Eaten, eaten.

Defecated.

Now you are maggot dust, because they too die. You're a hiss and a buzz. You're a nothing. The suns are winking, and a playful wind blows.

* * *

Hisssss! Buzzzz!

You're dust and full of moroseness. You've odysseyed the planets, questing for…more. You don't know what, just a maddening search.

And finally!

Master!

You smell the canker of her fetid kalabash and fish. You chase in her wake. So near, you'll reach her!

Hisssss! Buzzzz! Master!

What's this noise? A hurricane. Inside it, a chant, and it's pulling you from your master. A synchrony of voices intoning:

Khwa'ra. It is acquired.

Ya'yn. It is uttered.

Ra'kwa. It is released.

A rhythmic clapping in a rise and fall accompanies the chant-filled harmony, and you feel… weak, spent.

His…buz…massa…

The magicked incantation is a curse, and it deteriorates you more. It sounds like priests or guardians of a… wall? But why are you trapped inside it?

His…buz…mmmm…

Voices in sync, and, oh, as they narrate a creation story, the sound of them, the words of them, torment more than being masticated alive!

Our Mother watches the wall grow. As anything loved and counselled by Our Mother. We echo the Word to strengthen the wall.

You sigh for your master. *Hiii...buuu...mmmm...* But the chant is too strong.

Find the Word. Find the Voice. Khwa'ra. It is acquired. The union of our Hogiiri Hile Halah chant strengthens the wall.

You're drowning. *Bzz...ppp. Bzz...ppp.* You're imprisoned. Nowhere to go.

Bzz...ppp. Bzz...ppp.

Wings beat inside your heads. Wordless shadows zigzag to disrupt all silence in a rhetoric of noise.

* * *

Elsewhere on another planet a grey-faced effigy, arms out in a beckon, weeps smoke tears that waft to a vacant field, to a park, to a forest.

* * *

You're many, and you're flying, hovering, foraging, weaving an invisible nest right there inside yourselves.

A jillion hearts whirr in echo, chattering in entrapment inside a wall.

Bzzzzz!

Your whine and drone climbs to the highest pitch – a sound of incoherence in a new unreality, as you wait.

You wait.

Wait.

Bzzzzzzzzzzzzzzzzzzzzzzzzzzz!

Where Daylight Bows to Darkness

Cheryl S. Ntumy

what then can we trust
when melodies so complex
the truth means nothing

Cheryl S. Ntumy*'s tackle of a crisis of faith among the ruling elite on the planet Zezépfeni brings us to a daylight that bows to dusk. The discovery of ancient sound fragments has the Susu Nunyaa, an elite order of scholar-priests tasked with interpreting lost language, reeling. Many succumb to hopelessness or derangement, for the fragments indicate that the Susu Nunyaa version of history – upon which Zezépfeni's power is based – is a lie. Initiate Ruah-Mmaru has a choice to leap from this doomed vessel or sink with it…*

Welcome to "Where Daylight Bows to Darkness".

Our Mother screamed with the glory of Motherhood and The Word screamed back.

Firstborn, Zezépfeni, emerged into Our Mother's warm light, nestled and nurtured in the World.

Life thrived. The world grew.

Our Mother's warmth raised up water and distributed the rains across the lands. Life was nourished. She loved and admired. She watched and adored.

As with anything loved and counseled by Our Mother, Zezépfeni grew strong with grace.

Our Mother's love knew no bounds.

From the Sauúti Creation Myth, as told by the elite Susu Nunyaa who interpret the lost language.

* * *

WE WERE blessed.

Not because other planets yielded to our will, or because we moved as we wished through the system, our resources as good as infinite, our influence unsurpassed.

We, the people of Zezépfeni, were blessed because we were chosen. The SeKarah's daily call to reflection, dispersed throughout Zezelam upon the rhythm of talking drums, served as a constant reminder.

"Remember who you are! Children of the Light, Firstborn of all the worlds! Remember *why* you are! To lead, to guide, to shine light upon those lost to darkness. A sacred duty! A divine blessing! Rejoice, rejoice! And remember."

Throughout my childhood, the words of our spiritual leader had quieted the racing thoughts in my head. Now, hours away from the exam that would seal my initiation into the holy order of the Susu Nunyaa, the blessing was a comforting hymn in my bones.

I leaned over the railing in the observation deck with Narahii, watching the excavators return from a dig on Órino-Rin. Narahii and I peered through the outer wall at the latest ship to dock at Zezelam's port. I recognized it as a Sauu3 vessel by its bulbous hull and droning signature. Of the five planets, none but Zezépfeni, the first to be seeded with life, were allowed to mine sound across the system.

"Ruah-Mmaru, do you think I'd make a good excavator?" Narahii asked.

I wrinkled my nose and reached out to straighten her robe. "Children of the Light don't go scrabbling in holes on heathen planets. Think of the lost souls who look up to us."

I gestured towards the immigrants gathered on the deck. Each time we looked their way, they bowed. The city of Zezelam was filled with their like, foreigners seeking our favor. One of them approached, a man bent and wizened with age.

"Blessed Children, pray for my cold, ignorant planet!" he pleaded, dropping to his knees. "Shine your light on us!"

"Where are you from, grandfather?" I asked.

"I'm a lowly Lastborn."

Narahii and I exchanged pitying glances. The man was from Wiimb-ó, the youngest and weakest of the planets. It was a wonder they even had starships there. We offered him a prayer in the high tongue. He wouldn't understand it, but he didn't need to. He kissed the ground at our feet and moved away.

"I could *own* a mining ship," Narahii said, the man already forgotten. "If I had to."

I sighed. "You'll pass the exam. Stop worrying."

She gave me a grateful smile, then turned her attention back to the Sauu3 ship. A ramp opened and the excavators emerged in their work suits, storage drums strapped to their backs. The immigrants cheered. Rumor had it that the sounds excavated on this dig dated back to the First Ones who had seeded the system, our direct ancestors. If so, these would be the oldest and most valuable sounds in our archive.

"Look at her." Narahii pointed. "How skilled she must be, to lead her own crew!"

I followed my friend's gaze to the woman who walked at the head of the excavation team, brass rings in her earlobes marking her as the leader. She walked with the swagger typical of excavators, who were both celebrated and resented for their talents and privileges. When she passed directly below us, she looked up, as though sensing our eyes on her, and granted us an irreverent wink. Narahii squealed in delight. I rolled my eyes, but deep down I, too, was excited.

* * *

Inatani Alahfa didn't come to the study hall for our final meeting. Worried that something had happened to my teacher, I went to his room. When he opened the door, the smile slid from my face as I took in his disheveled appearance; robe unfastened, head uncovered, eyes wide and wild.

He pulled me inside and closed the door, then grabbed me by the shoulders. "You're still here?"

"We don't leave for pilgrimage until dawn."

"Pilgrimage! Go home, child, to the mother you can trust," he said, in a bitter, cryptic tone.

I was sure I had missed something. "Forgive me, Inatani, for I am young and my ears are dull. Speak again, that I may hear."

He gripped the front of my robe. "We are all of us dull," he said, "and doomed!"

He drew me so close that I could smell the wine on his breath. Confusion gave way to fear. Though wine flowed freely in the city of Zezelam, the Susu Nunyaa avoided all substances that impaired clarity.

"Forgive me, Inatani." My voice trembled. "Are you unwell?"

He released me, then stumbled to the stool beside his study table and sank onto it. "I heard them. The fragments from the latest excavation. They are indeed from the First Ones."

My heart beat so fast it made my head ache. "We thank the Mother for this bless—"

"We do not!" He glared at me as if I had insulted him. "We know nothing of the Mother! We are lost."

He shuddered. "The cold... Never have I felt anything like it. And the despair..."

His words swirled like dust, leaving me frightened and floundering. "Please, Inatani, speak again, that I may—"

"Go home. This place is built on falsehoods." He seemed to shrink into the stool, shoulders hunched. "What will happen when the other planets hear? Chaos, Ruah!"

As I backed towards the door, I raised my left hand to my sternum and drummed a beat against my chest, willing the power within to rise and shield my ears before my teacher's reckless rambling did irreparable harm.

"You're unwell, Inatani. I will call the uroh-ogi." My voice was a whisper, so I wouldn't break the spell.

"I don't need a healer. They'll only try to silence me."

He looked at me. My hand froze against my chest. Leaping to his feet, he grabbed the hand I was using to cast the spell and held it tight. The shield forming around my head flickered and died.

"Don't you trust your teacher, Ruah?"

Remorse came quickly, uninvited and yet all-consuming. I could still feel the echo of the spell in my chest. "Forgive me, Inatani. I meant no disrespect."

"You're afraid."

I nodded, staring into his bloodshot eyes, seeking something familiar. Perhaps his words were not drunken nonsense. Perhaps I was simply too foolish to grasp them.

"Hear me, child. You *should* be afraid. I'm the only one who will warn you."

But his words set my pulse racing and my thoughts spinning. They sounded like trouble. They felt like danger.

"The others fear the Council, the Mother. They…" He blinked and licked his lips, brow furrowed. "Go on the pilgrimage. Yes, go. Meshe-Shekhiiyem cannot lie." Inatani Alahfa's face lit up, but only for a moment. "You are bright. You would have made us proud." *Would have*. As if it were already decided. "The First Ones made the songs when they seeded this star system."

He lowered his voice to a whisper. "The song fragments didn't originate on Órino-Rin, but were carried there from somewhere… dark. Too dark to see, too cold to think. There are worlds where such conditions are common, but not *here*." His gaze met mine. "The songs were clear. We are not the Firstborn

Children of the Light. We were not made to rule. And when the other planets learn this, they will strip us of all the power we possess." He let out a burst of bitter laughter. "The Mother is a liar."

I reeled, desperate to escape his blasphemy, but his grip only tightened.

"Take the pilgrimage to Meshe-Shekhiiyem. Perhaps the sacred sea will show you what the Susu Nunyaa will not, and when you return you must not take the vows. Do you hear, Ruah-Mmaru? Will you do as I say?"

It was wicked to lie. Everyone knew that. For an initiate to lie was even worse, but my teacher was drunk or mad or both and every moment I lingered brought me closer to damnation. So, I chose the lesser evil.

"I hear, Inatani. I will do as you say."

Four Days Later

Sound was soothing. Sound was life and purpose and the World was ripe with it. Even the heat seemed to sing a vague, humming song as it cast mirages across the scorched terrain.

But there was something in between the sounds. Pauses too long to be natural. Little vacuums, speckling the World like mold. Some giant, hulking mystery lurked in the atmosphere, dotting it with poisoned kisses that sucked the marrow from its bones.

We are all of us dull and doomed.

Fear crouched in my knotted muscles.

We are all... I fought the dangerous words in my head, replacing them with others. *It will be worth it, when we reach Meshe-Shekhiiyem. The sacred sea.*

We crossed the blackened, pockmarked coast, stepping over bushes that had sprung up inside the asteroid craters, thorns gleaming like daggers. After three days out here, meteor dust had taken up permanent residence in my throat, scraping it raw.

Water lapped against the beach, beckoning. The small drum at my hip gave off the faintest vibration as it siphoned the ocean sound, storing it for future use. My pack sagged against my back, the straps carving grooves into my shoulders. I no longer remembered what it was like not to hurt all over. Fatigue dragged my eyelids shut.

"Ruah. Stay awake." Narahii's voice was hoarse. "We're almost there."

My eyes sprang open. All my life I had dreamed of making this pilgrimage to Meshe-Shekhiiyem. Narahii had barely made it through initiation, and now she was the wise one? Wounded pride proved enough to spur me on.

The five of us moved as a group. None of us touched the water in our packs, knowing that it would have to last us the whole journey, there and back. Apart from the tiny collector drums, we were not allowed to use magic until we touched the deep. We had no suits to protect us from the weather, only barkcloth smocks and trousers and plain leather boots.

But we were close.

It will be worth it, when we stand on the threshold of Meshe-Shekhiiyem, when we face the deep and do not waver, when we feel the fear and do not cower, when the sacred waters sweep us up up and test us, and we prove our mettle.

Those words had carried us through survival training, through the fierce heat outside the safety of the boundary, under the blistering gaze of the two suns. Those words gave us succor. Or should have.

Doubt was a hole in my stomach, expanding with each step. What if Inatani Alahfa had spoken the truth? What if joining the Susu Nunyaa was a mistake?

It happened again, then. One of the sinister silences, sound sucked from the World. We stopped and looked up, half expecting to find the source of our unease scrawled across the sky. There was nothing there but pink and white. Panic rang in my head until my vision swam. Narahii's hand gripped my sleeve. Then sound returned, as if the World was toying with us. Perhaps this, too, was a test.

"We should keep moving." My voice cracked, throat aching.

And then there was a new sound, a rumbling warning, too late to be of any use. Rain fell in a sudden deluge.

We fled inland, seeking shelter as the craters around us became pools. Narahii waded through a smaller crater and I, like a fool, tried to leap over it. My foot slipped in the black mud, sending me tumbling backwards, rolling and rolling, slamming into the ground and then rolling some more, water in my mouth and nose and ears.

"Ruah-Mmaru!" Narahii's shout was distant.

I landed shoulder first, pain singing in my bones.

"Ruah! Here!" She sounded closer this time.

I looked up. A rope dangled above me. Reaching out with shaky fingers, I braced myself for another onslaught of pain, certain I had dislocated my shoulder. Before my hands could close around the rope, a wave took me. I watched the rope move further and further away, and then the world was reduced to salt and pain and Meshe-Shekhiiyem's roar.

I tried to bring my hand to my chest to begin an incantation, but the water flung me this way and that till I thrashed like a reed, lost to the eddying flow. I tried to go inward, commune with the sacred sounds of the water. When my soul reached into the deep, it touched only terror. My head broke the surface. I gulped in air, attempting to swim, but another wave engulfed me, pulling me under. Eyes closed, I held my breath and tried again to override the fear, calling on my body to harness the sounds around me.

This was just another test. I was good at tests.

I opened my eyes to see a black rock plunge into the water above me. There was no time to think, let alone move. There was only brutal, shocking pain, blood blooming in the water, then nothing.

* * *

Pain pulled me out of the darkness and spread its reach like a conqueror. My shoulder was bound and aching, my chest and throat aflame, my head throbbing and also stinging; every muscle in my body too tender to touch. I groaned and turned onto my side, trying in vain to ease the agony.

I was alive. Meshe-Shekhiiyem had spared me. Elation sparked inside me, banishing the pain for a precious, fleeting moment before my thoughts coalesced and I remembered.

Inatani Alahfa. The ancient fragments. *This place is built on falsehoods.*

I shook my head against the memory, a mistake that sent pain shooting through my skull, eliciting a ragged scream.

Now that it had my attention, my teacher's voice would not relent. *We are not the Firstborn ... The Mother is a liar.* I had hoped that the deep would wring the poison out. Instead, I felt more wretched than ever. If Inatani Alahfa was right, then I had spent my life working for nothing.

The World was quiet, save for the sounds of the deep. The storm had passed. I heard no voices. Most likely my peers had given me up for dead. It was some time before I dared to open my eyes and see what hell I had fallen into.

I lay on a soft layer of animal hide, somewhere dry. A cave. It was night, a pale violet glimpse of sky visible through the entrance. The boulder that served as a makeshift door had rolled away, letting light in.

Someone had brought me here. Someone had rescued me. I tried to sit up.

"Patience," a voice behind me murmured. "Your injuries are severe."

With slow, cautious movements, I turned onto my other side, wincing against the pain, until I could see the speaker. The only people who ventured beyond the wall were pilgrims and outcasts. This was no pilgrim.

She sat cross-legged on the floor, eating a red, pulpy fruit I'd never seen before and spitting the pips on the floor. She ate with reverence, as though the act itself was the single most significant thing in the world.

She wore an old, frayed work suit, like those worn by excavators. Her feet were bare, but indentations on her shins revealed that she had worn boots earlier. Dreadlocks fell down her back, unrestrained and shot through with gray. She was over sixty, perhaps.

"Greetings, grandmother," I said. "I owe you my life."

She finished the fruit and sucked her fingers. "Is the binding on your shoulder too tight?"

"It's fine, thank you. How did you find me?"

"You were floating in the water near the place where I fish. It's good I found you before the serpents. One pilgrim could feed a nest for weeks."

I repressed a shudder at the thought of being devoured by the scaly beasts that roamed the deep. "Where is this place?"

"Very far from your temple, so don't get any ideas. It will be some time before you can attempt the journey."

"Then I'm grateful that you found me. I thank the—" I swallowed the rest of the sentence, doubt gnawing at me again. "Thank you."

Her eyebrows rose in surprise, and I knew she wondered why I had not thanked the Mother, as was customary among the Susu Nunyaa. A spasm moved through my shoulder, saving me from any awkward questions. The outcast came to my side in a graceful, fluid motion and checked the binding around my shoulder, then gingerly tapped the injury on my head. It was only then that I felt the stickiness there and understood the stinging sensation. She had applied some kind of poultice.

"Your head will heal quickly," she said. "The shoulder will take some time." She leaned back to look at me. "What's your name?"

"Ruah-Mmaru." My eyes were already threatening to close again.

"Mine is Shad-Dari."

"Thank you for taking care of me, Shad-Dari."

"So polite, you Nunyaa," she replied, lips curling in a smile. She winked at me in a way that seemed familiar, somehow. "You should sleep." Shad-Dari rose, towering over me. "By the time you wake, I'll have some food ready."

I didn't argue, happy to slide back into oblivion.

* * *

"Did you see any of my peers when you found me?"

Shad-Dari looked up from the meat she was peeling off a bone with the tenderness of a lover. "Your friends were long gone. Isn't that the rule? If one of you is lost, they must leave you?"

"But I'm not lost." I was sitting up now, leaning against the wall, devouring the stringy flesh of a large rodent. "Can you send a message?"

She gave me a look. Outcasts lived outside the boundary because they were in exile – self-inflicted or otherwise. But I was alive. An initiate. She could make an exception.

"Do you really want to send a message?" There was something sly and knowing in her tone. "You've been here two days and I've yet to hear you pray."

"There are many ways to pray." I resisted the urge to explain myself. She was lost to darkness, anyway.

"You're so tense." She sucked the marrow from the bone. "So fearful. Why?"

I glared at her, resenting her insight. I'd heard it enough during my training. I was bright, I was talented, but I had too much fear.

She didn't wait for my reply. "I understand fear, pilgrim. I lost my family in the Ekwukwe caves. Illegal sound mining brought the rock down on top of them. I wasn't there. I was young and wild, so I lived while they died."

We ate in silence for some time. She seemed not to care whether I responded, and yet I felt that it was only fair to share part of myself, as well.

"My brother fell into a trench when we were small," I told her. "He cried so loudly, I thought he would bury himself. I should have used his cries, drawn from their power, but I was afraid I would make a mistake. So, I ran home to get help."

I could still hear Rorosi's shrill cries and feel the fear rise until it almost choked me. Shad-Dari listened, sucking on her bone.

"By the time I returned, he had tried to climb out on his own and fallen. He pierced his eardrum." I cleared the guilt from my throat. "I could have helped him out, if I'd tried. If I'd been certain."

Shad-Dari gave me a knowing nod. "So you joined the Susu Nunyaa, believing they would provide certainty. Yet you're still uncertain. Not so? Maybe even more now, after the latest fragments."

I looked at her in surprise.

"I see the excavator ships flying in," she said. "I know what they carry. My father used to say, if you look for trouble, you'll find it."

Of course *she* would say that. "You wouldn't understand."

With a shrug, she set her bone aside and reached for a fruit. It galled me to see her so relaxed, so at peace. Something snapped inside me, and so I told her what Inatani Alahfa had said. Perhaps I craved advice from an elder, even a heathen elder, or perhaps I envied her serenity and longed to shatter it.

Her only response was to spit out pips.

"Have you nothing to say?" I demanded. "What if all that we know is a lie?"

"What of it?" She slurped up the last of the fruit and licked the juice from her lips. "If all you believe crumbles, what changes?"

What sort of question was that? "Everything!"

Shad-Dari shook her head. "I pity you. My path remains the same, regardless. If we are water that believes itself to be fire, what is it to me? Either way, I wake up and give thanks, eat when I hunger and sleep when I'm tired, until I am no more."

Unable to think of a clever retort, I set the remainder of my meat down on the hide.

"Eat. You need your strength."

"Are you saying the truth means nothing?"

Shad-Dari sighed, as though my questions wearied her. "The truth is the truth, that's all."

"What about the Mother? If we can't trust Her, what can we trust?"

Shad-Dari drew closer to check the dressing on my wounds. "You can trust that blood moves through you, and breath, and wonder." Her voice was soft as she traced the scab on my head. "Isn't that enough?"

"No! The Susu Nunyaa are there to ensure order, to guide us."

With another shrug, she moved away, scooping bones and pips into her cupped hand. "So let them guide you." She went out.

Her words burrowed deep until I could hear the sense in them. Wasn't the point to be brave enough to hear the truth and interpret it for my people? To seek meaning in chaos? I thought of Narahii, who wouldn't have joined the Susu Nunyaa had I not told her it was possible. I thought of her simple ways, her steadiness. She wanted to serve our people. She didn't care how.

I had thought myself wiser than her. Perhaps I had been wrong.

* * *

Without magic, it took me eight days to recover. I meditated a lot, weighing Inatani Alahfa's words against Shad-Dari's, against the teachings, trying to find my own voice in the tumult. What did I believe? I could have died in the deep, but instead I had lived. Why? What was I meant to do?

When Shad-Dari went out to find food and water, I would listen to the sounds of the World – and the eerie silence in between. I studied the fear that crept into my heart until I made it, if not my friend, at least my neighbor.

As my strength returned, I attempted simple spells. I realized that I was certain of something, after all. My training. My magic. In the midst of fear, it was my refuge. Of course I had to join the Susu Nunyaa. There was no other path for me.

"You're too quiet," Shad-Dari said. "Are you plotting to throttle me in my sleep?"

I no longer flinched at her odd sense of humor. "Perhaps," I replied, and she laughed.

When I was well enough to walk, Shad-Dari helped me into her small fishing boat. I had to beg her to let me seek permission before we traversed the deep; she was happy to wade into the waters without so much as a nod to Meshe-Shekhiiyem.

"How you survived this long without reverence is beyond me," I told her.

"There are many ways to pray," she said.

We traveled around the southern edge of the coast and reached the Zezelam port before dawn. She left me as close to the port as she dared. I lingered, knowing I would never see her again. The pilgrimage was only taken once.

"There must be some way I can repay you," I said.

"Go home, Ruah-Mmaru." She winked and pushed the boat out before I could argue.

I walked to the boundary gate. Recognizing me as an initiate, the guards opened the narrow door to admit me. After a brief blast in the disinfection unit and a scan to verify my identity, I stepped into the warm air of Zezelam.

By the time transport arrived from the temple, I felt like myself again. Physically, at least. Inatani Reretsang beamed at me from the small vehicle. She taught the older novices who had been sorted into specializations. The fact that she had come told me Inatani Alahfa was in disgrace, or worse.

"How pleased we are that you found your way home," she said. "We thank the Mother for this blessing."

Now that I had made my choice, the response came with greater ease. "We thank the Mother for this, and for all things." I climbed into the vehicle.

"Your fellow initiates took their vows this morning. You'll take yours tomorrow," Inatani Reretsang said.

"And the elders have reached consensus on the interpretation of the fragments. Our members will hear them at the revelation this evening, before the official interpretation is released to the public tomorrow."

A chill moved through me. "I hear, Inatani."

"Regarding your former inatani…"

I braced myself.

"Sadly, Alahfa's mind is shattered. He has been relieved of his duties. Since he can't leave the temple, he'll remain in confinement under the treatment of our best uroh-ogi. No novice is to speak to him or of him until he is declared fit to serve once more. Do you hear?"

I swallowed the lump in my throat. "I hear, Inatani."

"You were close, I know. I'm sorry, but it's for the best."

I nodded. What else could I do?

"There's more." She licked her lips. "Due to the nature of the latest fragments, tonight's revelation is not compulsory."

My heart almost stopped. This was unprecedented.

She paused, considering her words. "Alahfa was not the only one affected. One of the riberih, upon releasing the fragments for the first time, was undone.

She took her life shortly after you left for pilgrimage."

Terror seized me, turning my body to stone.

"Others became ill and are under treatment. We have warned members of the power of the sounds. If you're not certain you're up to it, do not attend the revelation. Do you hear?"

I had been certain, until now. I forced myself to breathe deep and slow. I had made my choice. I must be brave, for myself and for my people.

"Ruah-Mmaru?"

We are all of us dull and doomed. Even so...

"I hear, Inatani." I looked into her searching gaze. "I will attend."

* * *

Narahii was the first to greet me, her pale yellow initiate robes replaced by deep ochre ones with a thin line of decorative symbols on the hem. She wrapped me in an embrace so tight, Inatani Reretsang had to pull her off, afraid she would dislocate my shoulder again.

"I knew you would survive," Narahii said. "I knew it!"

She led me to our new dormitory, chattering away about the storm, the journey home, the vow ceremony.

I took comfort in the sound of her voice, but my thoughts swirled. I longed to see Alahfa, to tell him that the path remained, regardless of the fragments. I wondered whether he would understand.

I both dreaded and yearned for the revelation. The part of me that needed answers clung to the hope that the fragments would provide them, that once I heard them, everything would be clear.

We gathered in the hall in silence. We were not allowed to speak during a revelation, lest our sounds affect the fragile fragments that the riberih would release, but normally we would express our excitement in hand signs, faces aglow with anticipation. Tonight, there was no glow. No signs. Our robes made only the faintest whisper as we arranged ourselves in rows according to our station. Narahii stood in front of me with the other new novices, but reached back to take my hand.

In the open space in the center of the hall was an altar. The SeKarah stood before it in full regalia, rust-orange robe gleaming with gold symbols, headpiece towering. On his left were the large drums the excavators had brought and four riberih, the only people in all of Zezépfeni who could open those drums.

The riberih stepped forward to unlock the seals. They beat the drums in turn, then sang in turn, a melody so complex that it took ages to perfect. There was silence, and then a series of echoing clicks as the lids of the drums turned, one after the other.

The lid of the first drum slid back halfway, leaving a gap through which a faint blue glow escaped. Hands held up, fingers bent, the riberih drew the fragment out and up. Then, as one, they opened their mouths. The blue glow vanished as they took the sound in, and then emitted it.

A voice rose into the air, faded and faint as an echo. A single note, held long, then dropping low. Lower. Lower still, until it was a droning hum in my bones. It made my heart sink. There was something funereal in it, like the keening of a mourner. And then it was gone.

The hall grew dark. The riberih dug deep, shoulders rounding, and then thrust their chests forward, mouths open wide. The fragment sounded once more. I closed my eyes, letting its vibration hover around me, a phantom lurking at the edge of my thoughts. Narahii's hand squeezed mine so tightly that her nails dug into my palm.

There was a sucking sound as the fragment was drawn back into the drum and a few moments later, the second fragment was released. The faint strains of a melody, distant and haunting. Goosebumps erupted all over my body, even as the fragment ended. I opened my eyes, but darkness still prevailed. Why was it so dark? So cold? I had never heard fragments that evoked such despair. I didn't want to hear the fragment again, but the riberih repeated it like penance for some long-forgotten crime.

The next was a whisper, so faint that it was impossible to make out. I was grateful, for I knew in some strange, wise part of me that if I ever heard it clearly, I would break wide open.

And then, at last, a fragment with words in the old Sauúti tongue. Sung softly, with what felt like resignation. My ears strained to catch and translate the words. There were gaps between them, stretches of silence, as if the rest of the song had simply dropped away.

"…and the night swallows us whole…"

"Cold creaks in our bones, but…"

"Here, where daylight bows to darkness…"

"…we are."

Each line brought me lower until I felt as though I lived in the deepest crater, without sunlight, without hope. The fragment played again, and then there was silence as the fragments safely sealed into the drums.

Even after they were gone, I felt blistering cold on my cheeks, on the back of my neck. Narahii shivered, teeth chattering. The darkness in the hall was fading, but too slowly, as though the combined holiness of all the Susu Nunyaa was not enough to dispel it.

I understood now. Alahfa's words, the wine. The desolation. I knew of this season of cold and dark, where food was scarce and lives were cheap. They had names for it on other planets. We did not. Darkness on this scale was foreign to us, a nightmare neither our bodies nor our minds could tolerate. Darkness like that would destroy us.

I felt the certainty like a shard of glass in my heart – no one had sung those songs on our soil. They couldn't have. Human life hadn't begun here, with us, as we had always believed. We were… secondary.

"We thank the Mother for this blessing," the SeKarah intoned.

Only the strongest of us sounded the response. I stared at them, my jaw sealed shut with cold and terror. How could they utter those words, after what we'd all heard? Zezépfeni's power and prestige came from our status as Firstborns. If we were not first, we had no right to lead.

I couldn't move. Someone collapsed in the row in front of us and it was several moments before anyone around them recovered enough to help. Still, I was motionless as bodies began to jostle around me, as the spell broke, as the hall became bright and warm and safe once again.

I looked down at my hand, still imprisoned in Narahii's grip, and saw it was bleeding.

"Narahii, let go." My voice was hoarse and strange. "Your nails..."

She turned to me, her features twisted into a grimace, and I knew that Alahfa had spoken the truth. We were doomed.

* * *

The vows were for life. There was no changing of minds, no going back. I knelt before the SeKarah, eyes closed as he uttered the sacred words that would bind me to the Susu Nunyaa, body and soul.

The vows were forever, even if the temple was built on falsehoods. We were not Firstborn, made to rule. There were secrets, old and unfathomable. We knew nothing. It was true. And yet it was also true that the Susu Nunyaa had given me purpose. We knew nothing, yes, but what could we know? What was faith, if not a type of courage?

I saw Shad-Dari's face in my mind as the SeKarah placed his holy hand upon my head. I saw the outcast wink and set off for the deep without permission, irreverent, lost to darkness and grateful for it, serene in a way I would spend my life attempting to emulate.

We knew nothing, but we *were* the Children of the Light. We had to be. It was the part we'd always played, Firstborn or not. The other planets relied on our wisdom. Without us, they were lost.

The Susu Nunyaa had decreed that the fragments were metaphorical. Our people might accept that, or they might not. Perhaps that creeping darkness would find a way into our souls. As Shad-Dari would say, what of it? I would still wake and give thanks, and listen to fragments, and interpret them for our people until I was no more. I knew that, at least.

The SeKarah's voice boomed through the hall.

"The vows are for life and may not be broken. You pledge yourself to the Susu Nunyaa, to our cause, to our Temple, from now until the Mother takes the breath from your lungs. Do you hear, sister?"

"I hear, blessed SeKarah."

I knew that this was home. I knew that sound and breath and wonder moved through me. I knew Narahii would be waiting after the ceremony, and she'd help me put on my new novice robes, and we would weave our way through the uncertainty together.

"Will you bind yourself, with all your wit and all your magic, in service to Zezépfeni?"

"I will, blessed SeKarah."

The vows were for life. I knew that, at least, for certain.

The Exorcism of Mofoyefomo

Ishola Abdulwasiu Ayodele

"M'foghyefoghom"

There are things a fetus never must hear
Mofoyefomo's mother's diti'diti fell off at the
market square
With it, the shroud of silence that covered her
And before she could stick it back in,
Evil tongues whispered a demon into her
growing belly.

The waves' susurration is like Our Mother's Sound.
This is why by the sea shore, we gather
To sing spells that flow like waves,
That soothe like gurgles,
That baptize like water.
Twenty-one menigaris in an arc, attuned to the
spirit world
The shoreline our diameter
The expanse of the waters completing
our circumference.

"M'foghyefoghom"

Mimiklings hover above us like shifting canopies
Their feathers iridescent in the full moon light
Avian boriiwilis drawn by the incense sticks we carry
To crystallize the frequency of our chants
Into a single tune tweeted in a chorus.

Mofoyefomo kneels at the center of it all
Her white garment like ours billowing in
the sea gusts
Her back crouched by the weight of
her possession

Pressing on her spine
Clinging to her soul sound
Eclipsing its melody into the dull thud of falling rocks
Waking her up at midnights as clangings in her ears
Calling her name from the woods and the sea:

"M'fogbyefogbom"

Beneath a palm tree at a distance, the drummers begin a rataplan
The menigaris awaken the chant
The sea waves roar
The mimiklings shriek
And the sounds condense into
A cloud above Mofoyefomo.

"M'fogbyefo... M'fogbye..."

The drums' rataplan louder
The mages' chants faster
The mimiklings' shrieks sharper
The cloud denser and denser
Until it bursts into a torrent
Pouring over Mofoyefomo.

"M'fo... M'fooooooo..."

She trembles as if in a dance
As if in a trance,
Her body twisting and turning
Her limbs trees in a violent storm,
Her eyes bulged into full moons
Her screams searing
But her back, unyielding.

"*M*..."

Suddenly Mofoyefomo is still
And she is straight
And all is quiet
Except the sea
Murmuring as its waves
Creep back into its belly
Dragging along with it
The torments of Mofoyefomo.

The Final Flight of the Ungu-ugnu

Wole Talabi

darkness is moving
the creature never forgets—
reality's hum

***Wole Talabi**'s harrowing flash fiction story hints at horrors, the very uncertainty that scares us the most.*

No one knows what's happened to the Ungu-ungu and her crew when the ship vanishes at the edge of Sector 27. By all indications, it's not good. Van'van Du'ducroo's report on the investigation into the tragedy sheds some light – and serves as a warning to anyone foolhardy to pursue the matter. What sinister, silent evil lurks at the edges of this binary star system, waiting, simply waiting?

Welcome to "The Final Flight of the Ungu-ugnu".

I, VAN'VAN DU'DUCROO, in the names of Ezanana ka'Ewu and Aminata Mmbê-bezin III, ruling dyad of the great Mahwé-Zezépfeni Empire, and by the responsibility conferred upon me by virtue of my position as first maadiregi, the primary technical expert and administrator of the imperial interplanetary transport fleet, hereby speak this account into the imperial record, to be forever engraved on the memory of the Kububwatembo, the creature that never forgets.

I and the members of my investigatory committee were honored with the task of uncovering the mystery of what happened to the imperial cargo ship Ungu-ugnu when it vanished without a trace on its journey from Órino-Rin to Zezépfeni, along with its entire crew of thirty-five.

To my great regret, we have failed in this task, as no such answer has been obtained and thus the delivery of this account will be my final act as technical administrator. I must resign my station, as is custom for one who has failed the empire. But it is imperative that I relay all that we have uncovered in as much detail as possible, for the sake of the empire.

I swear before the divine Mother that the following is a true account and analysis of all that we know, and a faithful retelling of all that the committee's maadiregi – experts in engineering and sonic magic, menigari – who are most attuned to spiritual matters, and raevaagi – those most skilled in the crafting of narrative, have reconstructed of the key moments of the final flight of the Ungu-ugnu.

Ye Khwa'ra. Information is acquired.
Sọrọrọ Ya'yn. We speak it into record.
U'wazizi Ga'kwa. It is known.

00:41 Central Zezépfeni Time (CZT)

The Ungu-ugnu took off from the Ducha'ga spaceport on Órino-Rin, after receiving a cargo of 46,000 ririni crystals from the Kin-Kali sonic storm mining group. There were no reports of technical issues from the ground crew.

Pre-launch procedures and safety checks were conducted successfully, and the vessel was certified as being in excellent condition by both Ducha'ga chief safety officer Mbabwe Mbi'bi and the Captain of the Ungu-ugnu, K'hriris "Red" Mklawe. On the radio, Red Mklawe, an experienced pilot, veteran of the Moki-gu war of insurrection, and a devout family man, was heard offering a prayer to the Mother as the crew sang the ignition chorus to trigger the first stage rocket.

The vessel took to the skies, accelerating to a velocity of 21,475 km/hour, at which speed it cruised for eleven minutes until it entered low-Órino-Rin orbit. The crew reported minor turbulence during the launch, all within standard operational parameters. Once in orbit, the crew changed their song, singing the acceleration melody whose magic would activate the release of sonic energy from the coupled ririni crystals to the fusion engines that power the Ungu-ugnu between planets.

Captain Red Mklawe reported that all systems were working as expected and Ducha'ga spaceport registered their status as "in transit". Sixty minutes later, reception of the vessel's bulk data at the Zuúv'ah-Juah-āju interplanetary monitoring satellite confirmed all signs were stable.

08:27 CZT

The Ungu-ugnu's onboard location reporting system sent its final transmission of bulk navigation, performance, and operations soundcode data to Ducha'ga spaceport.

We have analysed the data and determined that the vessel was on a normal arced accelerating trajectory, routing to Zezépfeni. No anomalies were detected. At this point, the Ungu-ugnu had reached the midway point of its journey and was scheduled to begin deceleration within the hour. The Ungu-ugnu's transponder continued squawking higher frequency, lower resolution data to the interplanetary communications network, sending the vessel identification number, coordinates, velocity, and trajectory every ten minutes to the dozens of satellites we have scattered around the system, but this 08:27 bulk data represents the last point at which we can completely establish an exact picture of the vessel's condition and trajectory.

09:19 CZT

Captain Red Mklawe sent out a voice transmission. The message was received five minutes later at Ducha'ga spaceport control and then another minute later at Zezépfeni central station, but no immediate action was taken as the controllers on duty could not hear it clearly. Solar interference from Juah-ãju, and background noise of the crew singing what seemed to be a power control chorus, distorted the message, but our analysis indicates that this is what the captain said:

"Ducha'ga control, can you hear me? Our ririni crystal power coupling is fluctuating. The sonic energy stream has suddenly become agitated, and I cannot stabilize it enough to initiate a controlled deceleration."

Transponder data received at the same time confirms that the velocity of the Ungu-ugnu became erratic, oscillating around 850,475 km/hour by up to ten percent. The system flagged the vessel status as "of concern".

09:27 CZT

Captain Red Mklawe sent another message. It was less distorted as solar activity from Juah-ãju had troughed, but the background noise was much louder. The crew's singing seems to have devolved into a harsh, discordant mess of voices lacking harmony as it appears they were desperately trying to regain control of the power coupling. This is what the captain said:

"Ducha'ga, everything ahead of us seems to have just... disappeared. Are you seeing this? We cannot see anything on the viewscreen. It's black. All black. Everything is gone. Zezépfeni is gone. The asteroid belt is gone. All the stars have winked out. There is nothing around us except darkness. What is going on?"

The interplanetary communications network was still listening to the vessel's transponder signal, and we have confirmed the accuracy of those records by computing the difference between the transmitted and received signals at multiple stations, so we could determine where the vessel was when this message was sent. We have gone through all the imperial satellite data available and confirmed that there were no observable sonic, luminal, or gravitational anomalies in the region of space around the Ungu-ugnu's position.

09:36 CZT

The Ungu-ugnu's transponder stopped transmitting data. A few minutes later, Captain Red Mklawe sent what would be his final transmission, a minute-long, unbroken emergency broadcast. In the background, the crew's singing devolved into screaming. Red Mklawe's voice was trembling as he shouted into the radio, barely coherent. It is strange to hear such a battle-tested man reduced to blubbering terror.

This is all of what he said:

"I don't understand. It just bloody appeared from nowhere. Attached itself to us. Great Mother save us... Are you seeing this, Ducha'ga? Can you hear it? What is it?... The darkness is moving. So dark. And hungry. The sonic energy. It wants the energy... It's eating the crystals. It's eating everything! The darkness is eating... us... Mother God! Their auras. I can hear their auras. It wants to consume everything. Great Mother please... don't let it take our soul sounds. It is eating us. No. No. Stay back... Great Mother, I beg you in the name of all my ancestors, please keep my soul, let me into Eh'wauizo. I don't want to die like..."

The transmission ended.

Six minutes after the message arrived, Ducha'ga spaceport issued a "code red" alert that the vessel was missing, and an emergency response probe was dispatched from Zezépfeni central station to the last estimated coordinates of the Ungu-ugnu.

The probe arrived, steadily streaming time-delayed data back to Zezépfeni central station. There was no trace of the Ungu-ugnu, not even debris was detected.

But the probe picked up a trail of anti-sound waves, of the kind that have been detected near the naturally occurring silences, and in the mined-out areas of Órino-Rin where major disruptions to sonic energy have taken place. The probe followed this wave trail for fourteen hours, until it came to the border of our system, the region of space designated Sector 27, where the anti-sound wave trail, like the Ungu-ugnu, simply vanished.

All efforts to identify the dark entity that Captain Red Mklawe and his crew witnessed in their final moments have proved futile. We have been unable to determine what happened to the Ungu-ugnu and her crew. All we can say with certainty is that the trail ends at Sector 27.

Ye'e Khwa'ra. Information was acquired.
Sọrọrọke'e Ya'yn. It has been spoken into record.
U'wazizi Ga'kwa. It is known.

Having completed my final task as technical administrator in speaking this record into Kububwatembo memory, I now make the following three recommendations and final implorations to my successor and the great ruling dyad of Mahwé-Zezépfeni.

One, the region of space between Sector 27 and the last known coordinates of Ungu-ugnu should be cordoned off and considered a high-risk area pending further investigation. No interplanetary transport or cargo ships should be allowed near this region.

Two, an exploratory mission to the area should be initiated as a priority, led by the empire's finest maadiregi and menigari, as I believe there is something lurking there and that the disappearancc of the Ungu-ugnu may be but the first sign of a strange and mysterious power at work in the outer reaches of our homeworlds.

Three, that the sound tablet upon which Captain Red Mklawe's final transmission was recorded be hidden away and access to it severely restricted, for at the end of the recording, right before the transmission ends, is a loud and terrifying sound, one that scarred the minds of my committee and I when we heard it. It is an abomination. A horrid, eerie screeching, like claws scraping against the very fabric of reality.

The Song of Ohi'iha

Mazi Nwonwu

betrothal gong sounds
magic of the triple moon—
roads to many worlds

*In **Mazi Nwonwo**'s story, Kendi is one of a kind among his people on Wiimb-ó. His echo takes physical form as a lifelong companion and spiritual twin, Idenk. But their mystical union is threatened when Kendi falls for the enigmatic Iska, who traverses the spirit world with ease, and she's a woman whose abilities Kendi can't explain. They say love is blind... Can Kendi choose between his lover and his echo? A dark fate awaits if he chooses wrong.*

Welcome to "The Song of Ohi'iha".

WHEN KENDI'S legs found the ancient footpath that led from the forest in Ohi'iha Island, ududude insects were already singing the tune of dusk. Their *chi-chi-chi-chi* calls were loud, but not as loud as they would become in a few heartbeats when the last glimmer of sunset faded.

Already, feyi birds were taking to the boa'oba trees where they hoped to sleep, away from the predators that found comfort in the dark. The feyi's multicolored feathers appeared to be mere decoration, until dusk, when they spread them to catch the essence of Vuiili-ka or Vuiili-ku – whichever of Wiimb-ó's two spirits moons was paying homage to Ohi'iha at that time. Feyi were indigenous to Ohi'iha and could only be found near where a doorway to Eh'wauizo, the spirit realm, clung tenaciously to the space between two white boa'oba trees that acted as anchors in the forest.

These birds always intrigued Kendi. He spent hours watching them, waiting for when one of the two suns, Zuúv'ah, dimmed her light and the feyi stopped everything they were doing to shriek at the sky and, one by one, spread their wings and floated to the boa'oba branches. Not everyone could see the golden light that surrounded them as they flew without even the barest whimper of a wing beat. Kendi, a menigari, a man with *othersight* who saw the spirit world all the time, could see the light and hear the rhythm of what sounded to most ears as feyi shrieking. The birds' calls weren't without rhythm or purpose. Just like songs threaded magic for human and spirit, the feyi found a way to summon flight.

Kendi believed that, if he studied them long enough, the calls could be deciphered and used as a gravity-defying magic. He watched the birds any chance he got.

Today, Kendi didn't see or hear the birds, nor did he heed the calls of the ududude, known to gift urgency to wayfarers intent on not being caught by darkness. Not that he would have cared for the calls of the insects, as his *othersight* allowed him to see in the dark.

The footpath he was on used to be well trodden, but that was when it served as the main route to the jioku tuber plots that had moved to the other side of Ohi'iha. It was two seasons since they farmed on this side of the forest and the paths through the forests barely saw people, save for the rare hunter, or adventurer. There was nothing surprising about the lack of traffic as the people in Zavi'Iza practiced a form of agriculture that meant they allowed weeds to grow wild and rejuvenate the soil. Their ancestors brought the system of agriculture along with them when they moved to the island from the mainland in times now lost to myth.

A carpet of fallen leaves and grass tendrils was already taking over the footpath. These new growths could gain purchase and trip the unwary traveler but Kendi, shoulders slumped and head hanging low, did not see the vegetation that now provided a soft cushion for his feet and made his passage silent.

As he walked, Kendi's mind was traveling between the place he had just left in the forest and the seaside settlement, two valleys away, that he was headed to. He was carrying a burden bigger than the one that had lain heavy on his heart when he walked into the forest as the crimson sun began its journey across Wiimb-ó's sky.

As problems go, Kendi felt his were enormous and – since however he handled it would mean life or death for two beings he cared about – he concluded that the prevalent sense that he was carrying a heavy weight on his back wasn't unwarranted.

As problems came, Kendi's was tied to his *othersight* which was more powerful than that of anyone on

Ohi'iha. His brother, Fandudu, would have said that it was his looming marriage that was troubling him. Kendi admitted to himself that that was part of it, but it was more than that.

* * *

Kendi's betrothal gong had resonated across the island seven days before and, as he neared home, wedding songs wafted out to add to his distress. Where some men would feel only trepidation, Kendi felt like a man being led to the hangman's noose.

Kendi wasn't surprised when Fandudu told him he was to be married. It was something their father had been pushing for since Kendi turned twenty years old two seasons ago. Learning that a match had been made and a date set shocked him.

"How? When?" he had demanded, wondering how all that would have happened without his knowledge.

"Father threaded songs for your marriage during the soiree last night, and the ancestors made a perfect match and asked for the ceremony to be performed in seven four-day weeks. The clan had no say in the matter," Fandudu replied.

Kendi mentally brushed aside the accusation he could hear in his brother's voice. He knew of the soiree and knew he was expected to partake, but missed it, as he had intended, choosing instead to send his consciousness to Eh'wauizo, where his echo Idenk gave up control of his body to him without a protest. Not that Idenk would have had the power to stop Kendi, who was the only one able to travel to the spirit realm this way. He started to wonder why his echo hadn't warned him about the call to the ancestors, then shook his head. *No, Idenk isn't who he used to be*, he thought.

"What about my choice? How come I wasn't asked if I had a love interest?" he asked Fandudu as he struggled to internalize what he had just heard.

"They didn't ask. Your echo was there, even if you weren't. I didn't see him protest." Fandudu replied with a tone that conveyed his surprise at the question.

Fandudu was younger than Kendi by three years. Though he came to his menigari senses earlier than Kendi, his ability never surpassed mid-level. Their father said this may be a price that he had to pay for his early start. Most times, Fandudu only saw the spirit world in a haze but, when three moons were in the sky together, his sight was as strong as Kendi's. Fandudu was the only other person who could see Kendi's echo. He believed that Kendi could dominate Idenk in the spirit world because it was his considerable menigari abilities that somehow transferred to the echo that came into being when he was born, gifting it an individuality that even the tales from the dawn of time did not mention as having ever existed before.

"The link to the spirit realm is strongest near the gates. That's why you are able to move your consciousness between you and Idenk's bodies. You are dominant because your essence transferred to the spirit realm. It is possible that your power was too much and there was a need to share it, and your echo was there to serve as a vessel," Fandudu said one year after watching Kendi's interaction with Idenk.

Their father also said the ancestors did not gift without reason and Fandudu's *nearsight* would be very useful when they needed a tether to the real world. His words had proven true so far, as Fandudu was usually sought after by people when they wanted to commune with the spirit realm.

Their father was a blacksmith who lacked the sight his sons inherited from their mother's lineage. He taught them as much metal lore as he could before their *othersight* blossomed, but knew there was no chance of them ever taking over the smith and fashioning swords, pots and whatever for clients across the island and beyond, as he and his fathers before him had done. Menigari were rare enough that having two in a family was honor enough.

"My echo was there at the soiree!" Kendi exclaimed as the import of his brother's words registered.

"He was. I saw him with the ancestors. Maybe he hasn't had the chance to tell you. You are never here. You spend all your night in the spirit realm running around with your echo's body, and your day too fatigued to be of use to anyone on this plane. I am sure you also leave your echo weakened in the spirit realm. If not for how powerful you both are, I don't know what would have happened. Anyways, that's all in the past now. Father has gone to buy ore. He said to tell you that you must spend as much time as possible on this plane now. Come. I have a lot to tell you and I'd rather do it inside. The wind has ears."

Kendi was nodding, as Fandudu turned to walk towards their shared hut. He wasn't nodding in acknowledgement of his brother's demand, but at the clarity that the mention of his echo brought. He hadn't seen his Idenk in a long time.

As he pushed open the door of the hut, Kendi realized he hadn't even asked his brother who he was to be married to.

He soon learnt that he was matched with Aliala, a woman from Ohi'iha's nomadic fisher clan, who was noted for her vocal skills, which allowed her to thread very powerful magic. She wasn't a menigari but had ancestors who were.

Fendi knew her when they were both younger. Her mother came to thread songs for the men who were going to war. While the woman sang her lullabies into the cowry shells that would become protective talismans of the warriors, her daughter was left to Azia with the other children. They had spent two days playing hide and seek with the other kids. She had impressed all the kids, especially Kendi, when she threaded a song that bent the branch of an Oromama tree and allowed them to pluck succulent fruits.

Fendi remembered Aliala's mother as being tall, reaching the height of most of the warriors that had gathered at the wharf to receive their talisman. He also remembered Aliala being tall even at twelve.

He smiled at the memory and what he considered deviousness. Idenk knew Alilia and him would thread great songs that would birth great magic and thus the possibility of a merger between the two of them would find favor in the eyes of the ancestors. A year ago, Kendi would have looked forward to such a match, but that was before he met the woman who introduced herself as Iska.

Before they met her, there would never have been an occasion he and Idenk would have kept things from each other. He had changed. Idenk, no longer what he was, had changed too. They were both something new, all thanks to the strange woman that fate thrust on them.

* * *

"What are you?" Kendi asked that first night he lay beside Iska on the bare earth of the spirit realm, watching the red spirit moon climb over the horizon.

"Hmm. You didn't ask 'who are you?', but 'what are you?'. Interesting," she said.

"That's not an answer. You look and feel like flesh and blood from all indications. You are the only one aside from myself that I know can move between planes, but you do so without a gate or an echo. Now, you sit me on your wufalo and move us to the spirit realm. Now I can stand side by side with my echo like we do in the physical plane. My echo said you are not human. So, what are you?" Kendi pressed for an answer.

Iska smiled and didn't respond. The way her mouth twirled as she smiled reminded him of their first encounter.

He was making his way home along the sea road that morning. His mother hated the stench of the spirit realm that clung to his body after each trip through the spirit gate because it caused her to sneeze, so he had formed a habit of washing in the sea before going home.

Thinking of the food that would still his rumbling stomach once he got home, he wasn't paying much heed to the road and only barely managed to step out of the way before a wufalo, a domesticated four-legged herbivore native to Ohi'iha, ran past.

Alarmed at the near miss, Kendi swung around to look back at the wufalo. He swallowed the curse he wanted to throw when he saw that the saddle that would have seated a rider was empty. *Who would allow a wufalo out without a guide?* he mused. Even a well-trained wufalo would have someone ready to take charge of the reins at a moment's notice. Wufalos, even though domesticated, were, indeed, known for their aggressiveness. They could and had caused injury and death.

Kendi must have blinked, but he wasn't sure. One moment, the wufalo was on the sea road on the physical plane and the next it was on the spirit realm with a woman now on the saddle. She was looking back at him, her lips parted in a smile. He couldn't see much of her, but her hair, where it wasn't covered by the shawl, was purple.

Kendi was shocked.

How did she do that? he thought, as he watched the wufalo and its rider disappear around the bend on the road in the spirit realm.

Believing he must have imagined it, Kendi shook his head and turned to resume his walk home. That was when he saw that the hoof prints of the wufalo appeared on the sand patches that rain deposited on the road in the physical plane. Intrigued, he turned and walked back the way he came, paying attention to the clusters of sand on the road. He saw the hoof prints here and there. When he got to a spot where the cobbling had failed and sand had replaced it, no hoof print marked the passage of the animal.

He shook his head again, his confusion deepening. *Only spirits can travel between planes this way and even they can't transfer a wufalo between planes*, he reflected.

Kendi reminded himself that Wiimb-ó was a place where magic reigned supreme and strange things usually were just new magic or manifestations of something lost in time. He recalled his father explaining that the relationship between the spirit world and the physical world was simple, but also complex. On one hand, they existed on the same plane but, where the physical was tangible, the spirit world could only become so momentarily and only a spirit of someone great with magic could bring about their physicality.

Kendi was the only one in Ohi'iha who could travel between planes, but he could only do so through a specific place where the meeting of elements allowed for a spirit gate to exist and even then, his physical body didn't cross over – instead his consciousness was transferred unto Idenk.

Everyone in Ohi'iha had an echo, other menigari, like his brother, could only sense their echo or talk to it through inanimate representations they considered their twin. Kendi was the only one who could interact with his echo in the physical world. When Idenk came to the physical plane, only menigari could see and hear him but, even before Kendi got his menigari awakening, he knew Idenk and could speak to him telepathically, sharing his innermost secrets and desires with the echo was second nature to him.

Seeking answers, Kendi closed his eyes and reached for his echo.

A breeze picked up and the grass around Kendi shivered as Idenk appeared beside him. Save for his skin color, which was gray where Kendi's was dark brown, and his hair, which was brilliant white where Kendi's was jet black, everything about Idenk echoed Kendi. *Or was it the other way around?* Kendi wasn't so sure anymore.

"She is a strange one. She is chaos. She threads songs in a way even the oldest of the ancestors say they've never seen before. Her songs do not obey any laws of magic we know," Idenk said, echoing Kendi's stance and looking, like him, at the bend in the road.

"I told you to stop reading my mind," Kendi said, trying to ignore the buzzing in his ears that occurred any time they were near each other. He turned a frowning face towards Idenk.

His echo ignored him. "She has been watching you," he said.

"She has?" Kendi asked, his brows lifting to stress his question.

"You wouldn't have seen her, or anyone for that matter. You were focused on testing your strength against spirits." Idenk laughed, without mirth.

Kendi glowered at Idenk. While he bore his physical features, Idenk didn't share his temperament or his love for adventure. The echo didn't like Kendi spending the time he did in the otherworld. They had argued about it several times before.

"It is not natural. That you can cross between worlds doesn't mean you should spend half your life in the spirit realm. It is dangerous!" the echo had warned.

"If the gods hadn't wanted a man to visit the spirit realm, they wouldn't have created the gates and granted me the power to pass through them," Kendi had argued.

"Only you can use the gates that way. Only you wrestle with spirits, using up my energy to do so. You know how tired you leave me when you are done. It is dangerous, for both of us!" Idenk had cautioned.

Idenk's caution hadn't stopped Kendi's visits. Not even after he woke up one morning to see the line of gray hair on his head. He waved his hand dismissively when Idenk suggested that his body could be reacting to the time he spent in the spirit realm and the constant transfer of consciousness from one body to the other. "I can feel change in me too," he said.

As Kendi glowered at his echo, he remembered that they shared a body in the spirit realm, but Idenk maintained his consciousness and body on the physical plane like now. It was something he had never pondered before, but now he wondered what secrets he could glean from the woman on the wufalo, and how she moved from the physical to the spiritual plane without the need for a gate. Kendi didn't know that was possible. It intrigued him. Made him wonder if he could go to the spirit world without needing Idenk. *It would surely stop Idenk's constant complaints about how I use his body*, he thought.

"Offworlder?" he had said retrospectively and was about to turn towards home, leaving Idenk to fade back into the spirit realm, when they sensed someone watching them and they swung around as one and saw the woman there. She was wearing the same shawl, but her hair was now white. He had believed her older, but, up close, she looked to be his age or just a little younger.

That she was beautiful was apparent even under the dawn light. The way she held herself, all told of someone who knew the potency of her own beauty.

"Ah, you?" Kendi breathed.

"You are Kendi. They call me Iska. Do you want me to give you a ride?" She appeared to be ignoring Idenk. It was as if he wasn't there. Or she couldn't see him.

Kendi could hear Idenk, who had uncharacteristically stepped back, screaming in his mind to turn down the offer.

"Where is your wufalo?" Kendi asked.

She smiled and pointed at the road that led towards the beach, where the wufalo was grazing on washed-up seaweed.

Keni took her offered hand and walked with her to the wufalo without looking back.

As they rode away, he could feel Idenk looking on, a frown creasing his gray brow.

A long sigh from Iska drew Kendi back from his recollections.

"You echo talks about me? Interesting concept, your echoes. You two are very different from everyone else. You know I brought you to the spirit world the first time to see if both of you can be in the same place as you can on the physical plane," she said.

"You have a strange way of evading questions. You give me information, but rarely the answer I seek," he said.

Iska laughed. It sounded like a song. It stirred something in him. He started feeling guilty about pressing her. He liked her company and wouldn't want her to go away.

"I give you the answers you don't know you need. You find me interesting too, Kendi of Ohi'iha. I could thread you a song that would tell you all you need to know."

Kendi wanted to question her more, but he felt lightheaded. He had felt that way from the first time he took her hand. Something about her made him uneasy, but it also drew him to her. He lay back and closed his eyes. "What is your song?" he asked.

She smiled, and started singing.

There are many worlds
There are many beings on these worlds
There are many roads to many worlds

There are seekers of the
roads to many worlds
The Iska is but a seeker of
roads into a world
beings are but vessels into worlds

There are many roads
The Iska is seeking new roads
There are worlds with many roads

There are travelers searching for these roads
The Iska is a traveler seeking new roads
In this world, few are the
vessels and the roads

"I don't understand the song," Kendi said when she finished.

"You will," she said, climbing to her feet, the smile he was beginning to recognize playing on her lips.

"What roads are you seeking? What do you mean when you say the roads and vessels in this world are few?"

Iska didn't answer. She walked to her wufalo. It bent its front legs to allow her to climb on. She settled herself on the saddle and turned her smile at him again. "Climb aboard Kendi of Ohi'iha. You will find out soon enough," she said.

Kendi sat behind the woman, watching her hair change from white to yellow as they passed into the physical plane.

Kendi had found himself following Iska every night into the spirit realm and soon saw that Idenk was wrong, her magic wasn't threaded with song. It seemed to obey her will alone, ignoring many rules that governed the world he knew.

"You will understand, soon," she would say anytime he asked how she did it.

The songs of the feyi were an interest they shared.

"Tell me about their songs," she would request in the middle of a conversation that bore no link to the birds.

Do the feyi sing all the time? Do they sing in unison? Are the songs different for each feyi? Can they pass through the spirit gate?

Kendi answered as best as he could. He was happy to find someone who shared his interest.

As the days flew by, Kendi saw and argued with Idenk less and less. Not because his echo stopped trying to talk to him, but because Kendi stopped listening and stopped calling on him. The first few nights, he noticed that Idenk kept away from Iska and that none of the other echoes wanted to wrestle with Kendi like they did when he entered the realm in Idenk's body. If he had cared to look, he would have seen that the echo was becoming less tangible every other time he saw him. Kendi wouldn't have noticed, for his eyes were only set on Iska. He spent days waiting for night and his nights with her. The last time they spoke, a translucent Idenk told Kendi that his being with Iska was killing him. "Look into a mirror," he cried. "Our sound aura is fading away!"

Kendi didn't look in the mirror. Even though he was afraid of what he would see, he was more afraid that it could make him limit his time with Iska. Her spontaneity, her touch, her being, were some of the things he doubted he could live without.

He vaguely recalled a time when he would be connected to his echo every minute of the day. That time seemed ancient, in another life. He was young when his echo first manifested and had gotten so used to having him around that it used to be hard to imagine what it would be like not to have an echo. He didn't imagine anymore. He spent his time with Iska.

One day, Kendi called to his echo and didn't get a reply.

He told Iska and she waved his concerns away.

"Idenk is jealous. He doesn't have anyone and can't have anyone. He is jealous of what we have," she laughed.

Kendi told her of how he believed his echo's individuality was a function of his uncommon connection with the spirit realm. Where other people's echoes were basically like spirit guardians they sometimes sensed and prayed to, Idenk was a version of him, a twin, in the spirit world.

"I think I take it for granted that I am the only person with an echo like him. Anyways, what does that matter? We don't talk anymore. Not since you."

She smiled at him and pressed her index finger on his lips. "That makes you sad, doesn't it?"

"It did, but I no longer feel him. He said he was fading."

* * *

Kendi was thrown off this introspection by the coolness of Fufufe stream when he stepped into it. Unlike when he was on the forest path, wading through the stream needed coordination. He felt the smoothness of the pebbles on the bed of the stream. Before, he would have bent down to pick several and hold them to the light of the spirit moons to see which would hold magic more. He took the best ones home to his mother who would infuse them with luck magic and then craft ornaments from them. These ornaments were sought after and this kept the Ohi'iha wharf busy with merchant boats from all over Wiimb-ó.

Today, Kendi crossed the stream without looking, even though several stones were winking at him.

Above him, like on a thread held by unseen fingers, hung the crescent of Vuiili-ki, the silver spirit moon – a jewel in the night sky. Wiimb-ó had three moons, this one that was like the silver of a wolflark's fang, another called Vuiili-ku, that echoed the red of sacrificial blood and Javuiili, the one that everyone can see, which reflected the light of Zuú'ah and Juah-ãju, the suns that at times shared the sky over Ohi'iha.

The spirit moons were only visible to menigari like Kendi.

Vuiili-ku was, then, somewhere beyond the horizon. Soon to come out and add magic to the night sky. On occasions when the moons and the suns shared the sky, magic users were at their most potent and even a whispered song thread had the potential to birth strong magic. Legend said the song that carried the first settlers of Ohi'iha from the mainland was uttered on such a night. Kendi believed that story, for how else would you explain the replacement of over five thousand people across great distances in a heartbeat?

As soon as he had no need to be extra cautious about his footfall, Kendi's mind again turned inwards.

He remembered the state of things after his echo stopped talking to him or coming when he called and how shocked he was when his marriage was announced.

Iska hadn't shown surprise when he told her.

"Are you not going to say anything?" he asked.

"What is there to say?" she replied. "You said your clan needs the marriage to happen. You said your echo needs to bond with the echo of another of your kind in order for your line to remain strong and continue."

"I don't want the marriage. But even if I did, my echo won't come when I call."

"Why?"

"Why I don't want the marriage or why my echo won't come anymore?"

"Both."

"I told you my echo stopped answering my call days ago, remember. However, my brother told me he appeared with the ancestors that proposed my marriage. So, Idenk is playing a game that I still don't understand. That game includes staying away. As for my marriage, once I get married, I am duty bound to stay in the physical plane and birth children to ensure there will always be menigari on Ohi'iha. The tradition must be defended. Continuity must be assured. The moons must align."

"It would seem like your echo wants you to get married."

"It would seem so."

"Your echo has never liked me?" she said. Her words sounded like a question and a statement at the same time.

"Idenk is practical, unlike me. He would want me to do the right thing."

"As you should," she said, smiling her wry smile. "Tell me about the feyi song."

Kendi knew she was changing the subject, but the feyi had been both their obsession for the past season and he was happy for a chance to talk about something that took his mind away from Aliala and his looming marriage.

He smiled. "I think I am beginning to understand the pattern of their song. It isn't complex – I think I can thread a song that can produce a similar result. It is not just the song that carries the magic. It also flows through the gates… I think the song creates the gates or creates the condition that creates the gates…"

Kendi stopped when he saw that she was smiling.

"You knew this already?" he accused.

"Yes. I knew. I suspected it the first time I saw it happen," she said.

Kendi was incredulous. "Then why didn't you tell me? You stood with me for hours while I studied them. You could have saved me months of observation."

"What's the fun in that?" she said as she stood and walked towards her wufalo. She turned with her hand on the saddle, "Come, I want to show you something."

The wufalo didn't go into the spirit world – instead

it galloped into the forest until it emerged unto a clearing Kendi had never seen before. In the middle of the clearing floated a cylindrical silver colored object that was as big as a hut.

"What is that?" he pointed.

"That is what I brought you to see. I came to your world in that. Two of us came. My brother lies under that rubble beside the vehicle. He brought us here. Now I am alone," she said.

Kendi pulled his eyes away from the imposing structure to face her.

"Your brother died?"

"Yes. He could fly the vehicle with magic. I can't."

"Sorry about your brother. But I don't understand, you can thread songs, I've seen it."

"I can make it seem that way," she said, turning away from him. "You are powerful. You can lift the ship."

"How?" Kendi asked.

"The feyi song. You've perfected it. It can lift the ship to space and guide me home. Rebuilding this ship took everything I have. You are the most powerful menigari I know. You can thread the song and lift the ship," she said.

Kendi heard all Iska said, but his singular focus was on what it implied. She was leaving.

"When?" he asked, fighting to keep his jumbled emotions in check.

"With my calculations, we must leave tomorrow to catch the solar wind that will take us through the vortex back to our space time."

"Okay. My song is even better than the feyi's, but it will still take a lot to lift your… ship. Tomorrow is my wedding, but we can do this in time for me to go back." Kendi was trying very hard to avoid her eyes, knowing that no matter how she seemed to not care, his marriage wasn't something she liked talking about. He leaned back on his heels, ready to thread a song, then he stopped. "Wait… You said we?"

"That's the thing," she had said, her tone of voice forcing him to look at her. "You need to be on the ship for this to work. The ship will need magic to travel through space."

* * *

A yellow bark tree marked the border of Haju's homestead. When they were younger, before they got their sights, Fandudu called it "the goodbye and welcome back tree". Their mother had a stall under the tree where she sold hoes, fishing hooks, swords, and other practical goods her husband produced in his smith, as well as the ornaments and jewelry she created.

She went to her stall early and left late so she was usually the last person to bid them farewell or welcome.

It was on this tree that Kendi leaned his back to as he struggled to decide what his next course of action would be. His instincts had brought him to this point where his past and present converged. He was torn between duty and going with Iska.

Young people were allowed to dally as much as they wanted with the opposite sex until they were bonded in marriage. After tonight, he couldn't be with Iska anymore. It was something that he had pondered for a long time but had decided that he would take the day as it came.

When she had asked him to go with her, he had thought she was joking, but the more she talked, the more he knew she meant it.

"What about my marriage? What about my duty?" he asked.

She didn't answer him with words but had clasped her lips to his and he lost all reason.

Later, he threaded a version of the feyi song and floated with the ship easily. Then he asked to go home to see his family one last time. She tried to get him to stay but he insisted.

Now he leaned on the yellow bark tree listening to the snatches of songs and wedding preparations coming from the homestead, trying to summon enough courage to go in. On other days, the music would have been loud enough to drown out Kendi's thoughts. Now, they just added to the melancholy.

Kendi was about to push away from the tree and head back the way he came, when he felt that familiar buzzing in his ears.

"You know she lied to you, yeah?" Idenk asked, as he made to squat on the ground beside Kendi.

"I am sorry," Kendi said. He wasn't sure whether he was apologizing for ignoring his echo for months or for what he planned to do.

"Don't be. Just hear me. She lied to you. She put a distance between us for a reason. She never took you to the spirit realm. She creates illusions. She makes you see what is not there. You thought you were in the spirit realm, but you were only riding around Ohi'iha with her. I convinced the ancestors to propose your marriage to see if your sense of responsibility would let you see the truth."

"What are you saying?" Kendi whispered.

"The truth, Kendi. Look into my mind and see that it is true."

Kendi looked, and as their memory merged, he found that his echo was saying the truth.

There he was on the beach with Iska. There he was in the clearing he thought he was just seeing for the first time that day. Once, twice, thrice, several times.

"But I can see through magic. I can sense it in a way even the ancestors marvel at. How could she fool me?"

"It wasn't magic," Idenk said. "When you see me and see the spirit world or think you are in the spirit world, it is something she builds layer by layer. I don't know how she does it, but there is usually something in the air around her, in the grass, in the trees, in the clouds. They come together and become form. I've seen them breaking form and dispersing whenever you leave a place."

"But why? Why did she make me see what wasn't there? Why did she make me think she could take me to the spirit realm?" Kendi cried.

"The feyi song. She needed someone who could wield flight magic and was powerful enough to carry her home. You are the most powerful menagari in Ohi'iha. That's why she chose you. She isolated you even from me. I see she has told you what she wants."

"Yes. Strangely, I know the truth now, but I still feel I should go with her."

"She has found the string in your heart and tied hers to it with deception. Staying or going is a choice you must make. I know what she told you, but you and I are tied together. If you leave Ohi'iha, you will be far away from the gates that make us what we are. I fear I will fade away and you will no longer be complete."

"But how does one go against someone like her, one who wields magic that isn't magic?"

"We have an advantage. She knows about me because of what she can glean from you by asking questions, but she can't see me. She can't see the spirit realm, even from her world. She doesn't have any magic at all. Come with me, I can show you and then you do what you must. I don't have any power over you. The choice must be yours."

* * *

She lied, Kendi thought as his bare foot hit the unwieldy sand of the beach. Soon, he would be walking through the clearing where she had told him her tale and found a way to tie his heart in knots of confusion.

He reached inside the wolflark bag that was hanging by his side and felt the sharpness of the long knife there.

Beside him, gray as ever, stalked Idenk, a wry smile playing on his lips.

The Unspoken

Kofi Nyameye

creature met my gaze
now i speak to you my name—
what i am today

In ***Kofi Nyameye****'s chilling horror, an uroh-ogi prodigy – a precocious healer – gets the chance of a lifetime: to solve a mystery in a clandestine Wiimb-ó military base ensconced in a valley between mountains. Folk will remember Be'Ni Dam'eh's name for generations to come – if he succeeds. He can almost taste the glory… but there are sticky strings attached. At the heart of the mystery is an ancient darkness with its own gruesome plans for magnificence…*

Welcome to "The Unspoken".

MY FIRST SIGHT of the place that made me what I am came through a break in the clouds beneath us.

The base was built in a valley between two mountains, one of which loomed high above it. It was a collection of low buildings packed tight together as if huddling against the cold.

And there was a lot of cold: stretching to the horizon on every side was a plain of snow and ice broken up in places by mountains and ridged hills. This close to Wiimb-ó's south pole, our suns wouldn't set for many months, and the terrain was bright with reflected light.

"Starting final descent," my pilot said, as he angled our shuttle down.

There was a small docking port waiting beneath us; our shuttle landed on it with just the slightest creak of protest before settling. My pilot turned in his seat and gave me a wide smile.

"Here we are," he said. "And it looks like they're already waiting for you."

I followed the direction of his pointing finger and saw three bundled-up shapes approaching the shuttle from a small shelter off to the side. By the time the pilot had helped me off the shuttle, they had gotten close enough for me to get a good look at them.

On the flanks were two soldiers, batakari fatigues tight beneath their heavy coats, identical detached expressions on their faces. Walking slightly ahead of them was a woman I placed anywhere between sixty and seventy-five. Her hair was metal-gray and woven into a thick braid that snaked down the side of her neck. Ivory bangles looped around her wrists to the elbow. She was small, only coming up to about my neck – she looked like somebody's grandmother. But there was authority in the way she carried herself.

She stepped forward and held out a hand with a smile. "My name is General Yenti. Welcome to Black Site Nantwi."

I shook her hand. Her grip was solid. "Uroh-ogi Be'Ni Dam'eh."

She smiled at me. "I know. We're grateful you could honor our invitation; I've heard a lot about you."

That was news to me. I had a healthy healing practice back home, but I had nowhere near the experience or acclaim of some of our clan's most prominent members. By the clan's standards, I wasn't much more than a beginner, even if an admittedly gifted one.

"I'm flattered," I said, "but I'm afraid I don't know exactly what I'm doing here. Your people said it was urgent, but nothing more than that."

"A small issue, is all," said the general, "though admittedly time-sensitive. We just need your professional assistance. It shouldn't take too much of your time."

I'd heard of the military consulting people in my practice before; it wasn't uncommon. And there was nothing in the general's tone or demeanor to indicate she was lying. All the same, I couldn't help but wonder: why me? Why not someone more experienced? And why shuttle me all the way to the south pole for a "small issue"?

These questions ran through my mind but, before I could say anything, a gust of icy wind blew. I had been given an insulating coat that kept most of the cold out, but the wind cut through it all the same and I shivered.

General Yenti saw it. "But we can discuss all of that inside. Please, follow me."

* * *

It turned out the bulk of Black Site Nantwi was underground, dug into the base of the mountain. As I followed the general through long hallways, we passed many labs. I saw teams of maadiregi – researchers, engineers, machine technicians – hard at work. They clearly came from all corners of the planet: I spotted various kinds of neck rings and lip plates and face veils everywhere I looked. Armed guards stood at regular intervals inside the base, and once, passing over a high walkway, I glimpsed a cavernous space beneath me where at least a hundred soldiers were doing drills. The place was incredibly quiet, its aura one of silent efficiency.

I was awed by the size of the place, the sheer feat of engineering it took to keep it all running in such a harsh environment. I kept gawping around while the general spoke.

"The Black Site initiative is a joint effort between all the military agencies on Wiimb-ó. A series of top-secret sites, all in remote places like here. Or on hidden islands, or at the bottom of the sea."

"Why go through all that trouble to do that?" I asked.

"Because of what the Black Sites were created to do. Our work is cutting edge: we run experiments and test theories that are decades ahead of what's publicly available. It is often dangerous work." She waved a hand around. "At any given point in time, we're running tests on at least twenty of the deadliest diseases ever known. Sometimes, accidents happen. It's easier to contain an outbreak if there are no civilian populations around."

She glanced back at me and saw I'd gone pale. "Don't worry. We have strict lockdown protocols in every part of the base. And each Black Site comes with an in-built eraser to contain the entire site in a worst-case scenario. But it'll never come to that. You're quite safe."

I didn't feel quite safe. I felt more nervous than ever.

Once again, I wondered just what I was doing here. In my professional life, I was a psychiatric telepath. It was what the entire Dam'eh clan was famous for. My job was to step into the minds of suffering patients and guide them through the emotions and traumas they couldn't deal with without help. I was, by all accounts, a clan prodigy, but that was as far as my expertise went.

And prodigy or not, I was sure a place like this could easily afford its own telepaths. So what was I doing here?

General Yenti eventually led me into an office deep inside the base. It was dominated by a large desk of gerẃwiig wood, with a chair on either side of it. She offered me one chair and settled into the other one, then snapped her fingers. A hologram of a man's head appeared, rotating, above the table. He was bald and pinch-faced, with a broad nose and deep-set eyes.

"This is Maadiregi Kwa'me'h. Up until a few months ago he was just a mid-level worker at a mid-level research facility. Fiercely ambitious, by all accounts, but no one you'd ever recommend for promotion. Few friends, not particularly close to his coworkers. Nothing exceptional about him.

"That is, until he turned into a genius virtually overnight."

She clicked her fingers again; a video feed began to play next to the holographic head. It showed Maadiregi Kwa'me'h – tall, stoop-shouldered – standing behind a podium, addressing a room full of people. There was no audio, but he clearly had the room hanging on his every word. A few of them looked absolutely dumbstruck.

"Maadiregi Kwa'me'h started coming up with theories and discoveries that, to put it mildly, shocked his peers. Before this, apparently, you could've counted all his original scientific thoughts on one hand and still had five fingers to spare. Suddenly, in the space of only a couple of months, he'd already filed for fifteen patents and driven the discovery of four words in the High Language."

I looked at the rotating hologram. "Talk about being a late bloomer."

General Yenti gave me a wry smile. "Naturally, there were concerns as to whether he was coming up with these discoveries on his own or stealing them somehow. But they couldn't find any proof, and no one ever came forward to accuse him of plagiarism. Seems he was just, as you say, a late bloomer. That's when the military took an interest in him."

I frowned. "You started investigating him?"

"No," the General said. "We offered him a job."

She clicked her fingers again. I was now looking at a large lab, not unlike some of the ones in the base. It was full of bustling researchers hard at work at their workstations. In the middle of the room, supervising them, stood Kwa'me'h.

"Maadiregi Kwa'me'h's theories and discoveries only continued to grow. It wasn't long before they outstripped the level of knowledge publicly available. Such knowledge was invaluable to us – and, in the

Black Sites, he could rise to the level of respect and esteem his skills deserved without arousing envy from his peers."

Having been born a gifted child in my clan, I knew exactly what that kind of envy felt like. Even when I'd studied at Fehinti'ti, baleful glares had dogged my footsteps. I looked closely at the video and felt a pang of jealousy myself. To be so openly recognized, your talents encouraged instead of *resented*...

But, at the same time, there was something in his eyes as he supervised his workers. Something restless, unhappy, like what he had accomplished wasn't enough. Like he was a man who would always want more.

General Yenti was still speaking. "And I must say, his work with us was excellent. His work was so important, so classified, that even though the public would probably never know his name, within decades, his fingerprints would've been in every technological advancement on this planet."

She leaned back in her chair and laced her fingers together. "So when he came to us and said he had figured out a way to listen to the Mothersound, we paid attention."

There was a short silence, during which my brain tried to make sense of what I'd just heard. "You're joking."

"Believe me, we were skeptical too. At first. But he had the theories. He had the proofs. And most of all, he had an impeccable track record."

"But would that even be possible?"

"The science is complicated – and, anyway, it's strictly classified – but the basis is this: Our universe was crafted by the Mothersound. In its earliest moments, the universe was flooded with incredibly loud, powerful sound waves. As the universe expanded, that sound has stretched so much that it is almost impossible to hear. But the ancient sound remains, always around us, always moving away from us. The great cosmic background echo.

"The better our equipment becomes at picking up ancient soundwaves from far away in space, the more we understand. The deeper into space you can listen, the further back in time you'll hear. And since the Mothersound was the origin of all creation, the singularity from which everything exploded, if you listen far enough back, you will eventually reach a point where the Mothersound was not only more concentrated – as opposed to the background echo we hear now – but where the walls of the universe were less rigid than they are today. And if, somehow, you could break through those walls..."

"...you'd hear the Mothersound," I breathed.

General Yenti held up a finger. "You *might*. And only an infinitesimally small fragment of it. To listen that far back, conventional acoustiscopes won't do. So Maadiregi Kwa'me'h developed a way to open a series of tiny gates in space-time. Miniature wormholes, only a few microns across, stacked one behind the other.

"But breaking through the boundary around the region of compressed Mothersound requires highly advanced magic, the manipulation of several High Language words. Luckily for us, Maadiregi Kwa'me'h knew – in fact, had just discovered – such a combination of words."

I frowned. Lucky, indeed.

The General saw my expression. "Yes, it did seem most fortuitous. Not to mention incredibly dangerous. But a chance at hearing the original Mothersound, no matter how small, was too promising to pass up. So we put an expedition together."

The hologram changed to an image of a space station. "The mission was headed by Maadiregi Kwa'me'h. He insisted on it. We told him it was dangerous, that none of these theories had been properly tested. But he wouldn't tell us what he knew if we didn't let him go and, without that knowledge, we had nothing. Personally, I think he wanted the recognition. The first man to listen to a piece of the Mothersound since the Surali attempted it more than three hundred thousand years ago? He would have been immortalized."

Would have been. "Something went wrong, didn't it?"

"Shortly after the station was in position and all the gates had opened, we lost all contact with the crew. Naturally, we assumed it was an equipment malfunction, so we sent a probe. This is all we found."

She waved a hand; the hologram shifted: I was looking now at a video feed of space. Whatever was capturing the video was moving very quickly; soon, where before there was only the backdrop of stars, the feed filled with drifting debris.

"The station was completely gone. No sound files were recovered. The emergency recorders, built to withstand a direct hit from an asteroid, were shattered.

The ship's AI failed to copy its data to our receivers on the ground, as it was programmed to do once it sensed any unstable conditions. And of the crew, we found nothing but pieces. I could play that part of the video for you, but I'm afraid it does not make for pleasant viewing.

"The only thing in the entire station that we found intact… was this."

Amidst the debris of the station, a single body floated. Closer, and I saw that it was Kwa'me'h. His torso and hands were spattered with blood. I could see this because he wore no spacesuit. No shirt, either. His eyes were open, but clouded over. His skin was dry, flaked with ice.

I tried to imagine how he must have died. I hoped it was quick, that he hadn't died slowly in the vacuum. "I hope the Mother made his passing to Eh'wauizo peaceful," I said.

The general raised an eyebrow. "Oh, he's not dead."

Silence.

"*Eh*?"

"He's alive. We have him here, at the base."

I looked from the body on the feed, to General Yenti, and back again. "How is that *possible*?"

General Yenti leaned forward over the desk. "We don't know. But we're hoping you can help us find out."

I felt at least five steps behind in the conversation. "*Me*?"

She nodded. "Maadiregi Kwa'me'h is currently on life support. His body is completely unresponsive, but his mind is still alive. We hooked him up to a neural uplink, but he's fighting us. He's… not himself. Whatever happened up there, it broke him. But we can't access it, because he's built a lock in his mind and sealed everything behind it."

The pieces were slowly falling into place. "You want me to break into the lock."

In my line of work, a "lock" was the term used for any part of a patient's mind that they sealed away or repressed. Sometimes, the lock went so deep that even the patient didn't know how to undo it.

"But General," I said, "breaking mental locks is a delicate affair, something only the most gifted telepaths can do. It also requires the patient to give prior consent. Otherwise it's unethical."

"But you can do it," she said.

"I'm not authorized. Not without supervision."

"But you can do it."

I kept quiet. Because I *could*.

The general leaned forward. "I won't lie to you: we are racing against the clock. Ever since we brought Maadiregi Kwa'me'h back to Wiimb-ó, his condition has been steadily declining. He could die at any time."

I saw something in her eyes. "That's not all, is it?"

"No. Like you said yourself, there's no way he should be alive right now. But *something* kept him alive. Something in that station."

I realized what she was getting at. "You think he heard the Mothersound."

"It would explain a lot. The Word is pure life and energy. Even a little bit of it may have been too much for the station's systems to handle. But we are better prepared now."

I knew I shouldn't. It was betraying the trust of my clan to do something like this without their knowledge. But still…

"Do this, and you shall have the gratitude of the Wiimb-ó government forever. Our debt to you would be incalculable."

I liked the sound of that.

"Okay," I said. "I'll do it. Where is he?"

General Yenti stood, beaming. "Come, I'll show you."

* * *

Kwa'me'h lay on a narrow cot in a small room, surrounded by machines and wires and tubes. His skin was dried out, his eyes mercifully closed. He was covered by a white sheet from the neck down but, even still, I could see he was beyond gaunt, his bones pressing tightly against his skin. Some hair was growing on top of his crown, patchy and white. He smelled like rancid millet wine, like hoguro left to rot in the sun.

I stood by the cot, looking down at him. I had changed into a simple white agbada, my preferred outfit for such work. General Yenti stood beside me. Behind us was a wall of glass with an open door. Beyond *that*, a larger room packed end-to-end with machines and technicians. There was anticipation in the air.

I was excited, too, and more than a little nervous. Do this right, and I'd find a place in history. I'd rise beyond the stifling limits of the clan, with connections in the government on my side. A career finally worthy of my skills.

I gave the general a small nod. She turned on her heel and exited the room, calling as she went: "Neural link!"

"Stable," someone responded.

"Vitals?"

"Vitals are good."

"Drainage?"

The walls and floor began to glow. The magic in them was ready to absorb any blast of energy and channel it out of the room. The general had left nothing to chance.

"Up and running."

General Yenti turned to me. "He's all yours." The glass doors shut behind her, leaving me with the inert body of Maadiregi Kwa'me'h.

Silence, save for the soft beeping of the life-support machines and the hum from the glowing walls and floors.

My mind turned to the task. I sat on a small stool by the bed and took Kwa'me'h's hand.

I sang, beneath my breath, the song of my clan to clear my mind and prepare my soul for the sacred job of entering another's mind. It soothed me. Sharpened my head until I forgot everything else.

Until I was ready.

I closed my eyes and opened the ears of my soul. I whispered the secret words of my clan.

Kwa'me'h's mind opened up to me.

I had worked before with the mentally unstable, as well as patients in so much pain that it filled their mental landscape from end to end. But I had never experienced anything like this: a tidal wave of pain and madness that hit me, disoriented me, nearly broke the mental link outright and threw me out.

But I gritted my teeth and faced the maelstrom. I needed to impose order, but every attempt broke apart almost as soon as I spoke the words. I tried to find an emotion in his scattered memories to ground myself with, but I was buffeted by a frenzy of them: joy, terror, anxiety, hope, bitterness…

Ambition.

More than anything else, I felt Kwa'me'h's desire for advancement.

I seized on his aspirations, grounded myself with them and, from there, imposed my will on my surroundings. It wasn't easy: in the physical world

I could feel pressure building inside my own head, demanding relief. But inside Kwa'me'h's head, I muted the pain.

I silenced the screams. I formed the chaos of his mental landscape into an image that suited me: a long corridor, lined with doors.

And there, at the end, was the lock.

It was an intricate piece of work: an ever-changing pattern of twisting bones and wood and metal, woven tightly together with black twine. No breaks, no seam, shifting from second to second; it would hurt most people's brains to look at it for long.

I placed a hand on the lock. Holding the frequency of Kwa'me'h's ambition in my mind – the single most resonant frequency of his soul – I focused my power on the lock and forced it to stop moving. Just for a second, but it was enough. There, hidden among the black threads, was a single red thread. I took hold of it and pulled.

And the lock unraveled.

To anyone out there, anyone who comes across this record: I am so sorry.

* * *

When the lock broke, the rest of Kwa'me'h's mind was not behind it. Neither was the Mothersound.

There was only a Voice.

A Voice like teeth chewing into my own mind.

I HAVE BEEN WAITING FOR YOU,

it said.

NOW, I WILL SPEAK TO YOU MY NAME.

That's when I started screaming.

* * *

I was still screaming when they barged into the lab and dragged me away from Maadiregi Kwa'me'h. My hand was yanked out of his, breaking the mental connection, setting me free.

I came to myself lying on the floor in the larger lab, staring up into the faces of two researchers. The room was ringing with alarms. People were running from one console to another in confusion. Somebody somewhere was yelling, "Stabilize him!"

"He's awake!" one of the researchers hovering over me called.

"Good," said General Yenti, coming into view. She leaned in closer. "What happened?"

I struggled into a sitting position. My heart was racing, my mind bleeding terror as I tried to make sense of what had just happened.

I have been waiting for you.

In the smaller room, three other researchers were scrambling around the body of Maadiregi Kwa'me'h, whose vitals were all suddenly flatlining. The machines around him were shrieking, drowning out their shouts.

The general snapped her fingers in my face. "Be'Ni! What did you find?"

I turned slowly to look at her. "He found something. He *heard* something."

Her eyes lit up. "Was it the Mothersound?"

No, I thought. *But whatever it was, he brought it back with him. And I think I just set it free.*

I looked into the other room, where, unnoticed by anyone, bent-twig fingers were lifting at the ends of emaciated forearms and gripping the sides of the cot. Where Kwa'me'h's body was slowly sitting up.

The head swiveled on a stiff neck, looked at me.

The eyes opened. They were blank, glazed over. But behind them, there was something.

I remembered its voice in my head.

Now I will speak to you my Name.

A bolt of terror ran through me. I pointed and began gabbling incoherently, like my tongue had forgotten how to form words. One by one, everyone turned to look where I was pointing. They all froze, staring, as Kwa'me'h swung his legs off the side of the cot and stood. The cloth fell away. He was naked underneath.

The floors and walls of that room, the magical drainage wards, glowed very bright for a second then short-circuited. Alarms continued to blare. One of the researchers next to Kwa'me'h reached out slowly to touch him. Kwa'me'h extended a stick-thin hand, grabbed her by the arm and, with a casual toss, threw her through the glass wall and across the larger lab. She hit the junction between the wall and the ceiling and *stuck* there, a broken mess bleeding down the wall.

The remaining researchers in the room raced for the door. General Yenti recovered. "Guards!"

The soldiers in the room rushed forward, sonic rifles in their hands, shouting as they went. In all this, the thing inside Kwa'me'h had eyes only for me. I heard the Voice in my mind again.

BE'NI,

it said, and began to lurch toward me.

I fled for the door.

I did not turn around as rifles fired behind me, nor when the shouts became screams. I reached for the door, but something heavy hit my back, sent me sprawling as it tumbled over me.

It was one of the soldiers, two ragged holes where his arms had been spouting dark blood on the floor. I shrieked and backed away from it. All around me, bodies were flying. The door was so close. I tried to get up, slipped flat in the blood. I got to my hands and knees to crawl.

Something grabbed my ankle.

My mind filled with high, dark laughter even as an unbearable itch exploded through my leg. Something pulled me back, turned me over. I stared into Kwa'me'h's ruined face.

The eyes were no longer blank. They were black and glittering. Kwa'me'h placed his hands on either side of my head and brought his face close to mine. His mouth opened. A voice like tumbling rocks came out of it.

NOW YOU WILL LISTEN,

it said, speaking no language ever known in the Mother's universe – yet I understood it perfectly.

YOU WILL LISTEN TO MY NAME. AND YOU WILL KNOW ME.

Time stopped.

It spoke into my mind. I could not shut it out.

It spoke its name, and my eyes opened.

And this is what I saw:

* * *

In the Beginning was the Mother, and the Word was within Her.

The Word existed in the Mother's mind; She ruminated on it continually. For it was the Mother Goddess's desire to create, to bring into being things that were not, and ultimately to produce and sustain Life. And the instrument by which She intended to do this was the Word.

By the Word She would form the heavens and the stars, the planets and mountains and oceans. By the Word She would become Creator, Goddess, Mother of all that was yet to come.

The Word beheld the Mother, beheld Her radiance and Her joy, and it loved Her. It basked in Her beauty, rejoiced in Her plans. Safe in the Mother's mind, it delighted itself with visions of the universe it would create, the worlds it would offer to the Mother and bask in Her pleasure. And so, secure in its importance, the Word waited. Waited for the Mother to speak it.

But a flaw was in the Word. A flaw born from love and a bottomless desire to please. The Mother, who heard all, could hear the cries of an unstable Universe reaching her from the future.

A Universe ruled by a merciless hand, where all worshiped the Mother, not out of love or free will, but because the Word demanded it.

A Universe of enslaved sentience bowing to the Mother.

A never-ending sacrifice. Proof of the Word's love for its Creator.

And this troubled the Mother, for love that is demanded is no love at all, and a Universe that was not free to rebel was also not free to truly worship.

And so, with much regret, the Mother passed over the Word.

Heartbroken, confused, feeling abandoned, the Word was fated to watch and listen as the Mother formed – and, eventually, spoke – a new Word.

As its sister raced into the void, creating, the Mother invited the unspoken Word to watch, to listen, to behold what its sister was making. And the Word drew close, and it beheld.

It beheld a Universe full of creatures with free will, who could choose to worship the Mother or defy her. Creatures who could be good or evil, and a great many of them chose to be evil.

The Word saw war. It saw hatred and envy. Genocide and suffering. It saw jurors and gods, disasters and creatures of unreality displaced in the void. It saw how this Universe would break the Mother's heart in a million ways every second.

And if it *could see what this Universe would become, then surely the Mother could as well. And surely it was only a matter of time 'til the Mother realized this Universe simply would not do. 'Til the Mother recalled the second Word and rejected her universe as unfit. 'Til She returned to the first Word and its offering of love.*

But Time passed, and not only did the Mother not recall the second Word, she declared herself well pleased with its Universe, this place of brokenness and pain.

"Come," said the Mother to the first Word. "Sit with Me. Listen with Me. Share in the joy of your sister's creation."

But the rejected Word could not do it.

It fled far from the Mother and the Word that had usurped it. It fled into the dark spaces of pre-creation, the gaps just outside the boundaries of the ever-expanding universe. And there, heartbroken, dejected, it watched as the Usurper's Universe unfolded, watched as all the hate and the pain it had foreseen came into being. And slowly, slowly, a thought occurred to it:

The Mother had made a mistake.

The Mother Goddess, whom it had seen as perfect in all Her ways, had made a mistake.

Brooding on these things, its bitterness grew. Not toward the Mother, but the Usurper who had deceived Her. The first Word looked into the Universe from its lonely, self-imposed exile, and hatred took root in its heart.

It would fix this. It would show the Mother the error of Her ways. It would find a way into the Usurper's Universe, and it would reveal it for the broken, unfit offering it was. It would tear down. It would destroy. It would force the Mother to create again.

To speak it *instead.*

And so it watched, and listened, and waited. It was patient. It searched for an entry, a way into the Usurper's Universe. The ancient Laws prevented it from breaking in at will, but it knew something. A loophole, built upon the same fault lines of free will.

For if any one of the creatures in that Universe were ever to open the door, it could come.

It could enter.

And then, after billions and billions of years, when it judged the time was right, it found him.

A nobody, burning with frustrated ambition. One it could whisper secrets to. Foolish enough to take the risks. Selfish enough for success to never be enough. One who would push and push and push until he pushed too far. Where it would be waiting.

The maadiregi.

* * *

“Fire!” yelled General Yenti.

The room erupted with the sound of the sonic rifles firing. Reinforcements, arranged around the general, firing in sync. The blasts slammed into the body of Maadiregi Kwa’me’h, forcing it to stagger back, releasing its hold on me.

But I could still hear it. I could *feel* it. My face itched horribly where it had touched me, and I clawed madly at it, drawing blood, trying to get it out.

“Advance!”

The soldiers marched past me, still firing. Their weapon blasts kept hitting Kwa’me’h’s body. One blast hit it squarely in the head and tore away a portion of its skull. Another cut a deep gouge in its abdomen. Intestines spilled out, black and rotten.

But it did not fall.

Instead its mouth opened and the same voice as before came out.

KNOW ME,

it said.

KNOW MY PAIN.

KNOW MY BETRAYAL AND MY RAGE.

The soldier nearest to it screamed. He dropped to his knees, clawing at his head. His fingernails dug deep gouges across his face, his scalp. Then he turned his rifle on himself, full in the face.

And blew his head clean off.

But he did not die.

The headless body continued to writhe on the floor. Then it got up and started throwing itself against the walls in evident agony.

A hand grabbed me by the collar. It was the general. She dragged me to my feet, pushing me through the open door. Fresh yells erupted behind us. At the door, I turned back to see all the soldiers shooting at their own bodies now, mutilating themselves. And in the center of it all stood Kwa'me'h's body.

It met my gaze, and behind the eyes *something* smiled at me from beyond space and time and all of existence.

The thing that had deceived Kwa'me'h to his doom. That had deceived us all, and for one thing only: revenge against the Mothersound and her universe.

The first Word.

The Unspoken.

* * *

I stumbled out of the room in the general's arms. I would have fallen and lain there scratching the abominable itch in my face if she hadn't driven me on. Overhead, alarms still blared and an automated voice warned us that this section would be imminently sealed off.

"Come on," the general said as we stumbled away. Her right arm was bleeding and hung useless, but her eyes were resolute. "We need to get you out of here."

We had only gone a short distance down the corridor when the door we'd just left fell out of its frame and the Unspoken stepped out.

The general shoved me forward with her good arm. "Go!" she yelled, and turned to face the threat.

The Unspoken regarded her with its head cocked to the side. It was smiling. Through the chasm in the side of the skull, the rotten remains of Kwa'me'h's brain leaked out.

General Yenti muttered under her breath; a nimbus of light formed around her good hand, growing in brightness.

The Unspoken shuffled forward.

The general pointed her hand and a bolt of magic shot out, filling the corridor end to end. It hit the Unspoken, slowing its movements, pushing it back.

But it didn't stop it. The Unspoken bent forward, as if fighting against a strong wind. It continued to advance. Its mouth was open, the Voice laughing.

The general looked over her shoulder at me. "What are you waiting for? Go!"

But I didn't.

Because in that moment I realized the simple, unavoidable truth:

The Unspoken could not be stopped.

And I suddenly knew what I needed to do.

So I didn't run. Instead, I sang.

I sang the song of my clan in a broken voice, ignoring the itch that burrowed its way into my bones. I cleared my mind as best I could, staggered back to the general, laid a hand on her back. I whispered the words of my craft.

And broke into General Yenti's mind.

She screamed when I entered, lost hold of her magic. With a cry of glee, the Unspoken *bounded* toward her.

"What are you DOING?!" she yelled.

I didn't reply. Her entire mind was a lock; to get what I wanted, I had to break walls down left and right. I knew I was killing her, but what choice did I have?

Each Black Site comes with an in-built eraser to contain the entire site in a worst-case scenario.

And there, buried deep within her mind, I found it: a vast chasm dug underneath the site, explosives all around the base and in the mountain above, ready to bury it all.

I took my hand away from the general, breaking the connection, just as the Unspoken reached her and clamped a hand down on her head.

I didn't stay to witness her fate. I turned and ran.

Of the desperate flight through the complex that happened then, I remember only fragments. I remember sirens, warning lights flashing red, automated voices informing us all that the integrity of the site had been breached. I remember groups of researchers panicking everywhere I looked. I remember rows and rows of soldiers running past me in the opposite direction – and none of them coming back.

I raced from room to room, through endless corridors, following directions I'd taken from the general's mind, knowing the Unspoken could be right behind me at any moment.

Finally, I found myself back in the office General Yenti had spoken to me in. The hologram over the table still showed the video feed of space. I passed my hand through it, activating the hidden command console.

Speak activation code.

I gave it the activation code I'd taken from the general's mind. Then I told it what I wanted it to do.

Activate Owuo Protocol?

Yes. For the Mother's sake, yes. Seal it in, trap it – that was our only hope.

Owuo Protocol activated.

I turned from the console – and saw the Unspoken in the doorway.

It was just standing there, watching me.

Smiling.

As soon as I met its gaze, the dead eyes winked at me, and the light in them suddenly vanished. Kwa'me'h's body collapsed in the doorway, a puppet with its strings cut. I heard a high, cold laughter. But it was not coming from Kwa'me'h's body, or from anywhere around me.

I have been waiting for you.

It was coming from inside me.

Now I will speak to you my Name.

And I realized, too late, what that meant.

"No!" I turned around, reaching for the table.

Right as my hands touched it, the countdown ended. The bombs around the site blew, and Black Site Nantwi collapsed into the abyss and was buried under billions of tons of rock and ice.

* * *

I am still here.

I do not know how much time has passed. Time means nothing to me now. Everyone else is dead, slain either in the explosions and falling rubble, or else suffocating in dark tombs. I should be dead, too.

But I am still here. And I am not alone.

The Unspoken walks inside me. I can feel it in my mind, breaking the locks I desperately set up to try and cage it as easily as a child walks through cobwebs. It mocks me. It gloats.

Especially now.

Because rescuers have come. I should have known they would. Day after day, they dig, getting ever closer. "Is anyone there?" they call.

No, I want to scream. *Leave! Save yourselves!*

But, instead, my mouth opens and I shout back, "Yes! I'm here! Please, save me!"

They will reach me anytime now. They will call it a miracle. They will take me – and the thing inside me – away from here. Back to civilization. To people.

What have I done?

Mother have mercy, what have I done?

The Whirring of Anu'tu

D.S. Falowo

for all the innocence of childhood,
Anu'tu pushed his toddler sister to her death
she fell screaming down
the crack, rushed
into an envelope of earth
never to be seen

his mother's grief invoked the menigari
the ones with scythes for tongues
they circled young Anu'tu in the yard,
knocking their staves in a dirge,
his mother wailed for her baby
the menigari lifted their masks
their smiles ever knowing
shuddered him to confess

his mother turned her face
as they knelt him down and flayed,
their tongues unseen, the sound most seen
whitening Anu'tu's black body with the
longest scars
as he screamed innocence
his mother, her face turned
as he screamed innocence

their tongues drew no blood
but in Anu'tu's heart they placed
caution, whirring, set to collapse
his mind should he mistake
fear for love, ever again.

The Wound Asks for Air

Shingai Njeri Kagunda

louder than whisper
things society forgets—
name cannot be spoke

The burden of collective trauma weaves through Shingai ***Njeri Kagunda****'s poignant story. Mma'riama sees what was and what is, carrying the precious memories that make her people on the planet Órino-Rin. What does it mean to remember, even when remembering is pain? Most importantly, what horrors unfold if we let ourselves forget?*

Welcome to "The Wound Asks for Air".

There are nights that stretch longer than days. Nights that will carry you into the days after tomorrow.
—Ma'juu forgotten saying off world Órino-Rin

Uh'oruu: Listen, listen here, Uh'oruu, my namesake, hear now. You are here, in the string of clouds surrounded by the expansive sky cities that do not know what a bottom is, and have learned not to care to look beneath them. Often you will catch the words, "Below is for the feet, not the eyes." So the Ma'juu citizens travel with domesticated Dako'ta – large winged reptilian creatures with colorful tails and broad noses.

What can you see from here? The tips, the tops, the end of the middle and the beginnings of the end.

Nkikima: Ahhh, sister. Tell this story properly.

Uh'oruu: There is no way to tell a story properly, Nkikima. There is only the way to listen properly. And if there must be sadness in this story why not insist on play too, eh? If they are listening properly, it doesn't matter how the story is told, they will understand.

Nkikima: But my way is better than yours, start with Mma'riama, neh? People are drawn to the stories that remind them of themselves.

Uh'oruu: You are here, no? Mma'riama is here? Here in this word, and the next that will be uttered. Is that not enough *you* in the story? The *you* who is not here does not belong to this story and this story does not belong to them. Let them go somewhere else.

Nkikima: Hya, hya, leave us to start.

Uh'oruu: Hya, hya, we have already started.

Nkikima and Uh'oruu: We are here, in the string of clouds surrounded by expansive sky cities that do not know what a bottom is and have not cared to look beneath them.

Uh'oruu: It is true, they say, "Below is for the feet and not the eyes." Once you are dead, you know more than when you are alive how words are magic, how proverbs turn our memories, twist our perspective, play catch with our understanding of ourselves in the world. Young Mma'riama has never had a chance, neh?"

Nkikima: A memory catcher and word player? Tsk tsk. Sister, she is your descendant and we were mad girls in life. The twisting of the child's mind began in their mother's womb. This is why they have always looked down, even being born to a people who rely on their ability to keep looking ahead and up. It is how they know how to survive as themselves.

Uh'oruu: What is mine is yours. Our descendant, Mma'riama, does not get to decide who she is born to. So she is born to Furah-Furah, and Mwaninimwa Li'Ochi, two women who left their closed-minded villages, and brushed by each other in the crowded city of Ma'juu on Órino-Rin. Furah-Furah had a grandmother from the outskirts of the city, and Mwaninimwa did not have any family she could trace her lineage back to. When they met, it did not matter what came before.

Now Ma'juu, being the city that it is, on the outskirts of a people who do not look down, the past is easily forgettable, thrown down to the bottom of the glassy molten volcano that catches what does not prosper Ma'juu citizens.

Uh'oruu: But we are evidence, are we not, sister?

Nkikima: Yes, yes, sis, I am getting to that part. Yes, we are evidence that the past does not like to be thrown away.

Uh'oruu: And Mma'riama?

Nkikima: Mma'riama was called, invoked even. In the womb of Furah-Furah Li'Ochi, Mma'riama started turning and twisting with memory that lived in her mother's blood and, when Mwaninimwa kissed Furah-Furah, Mma'riama swallowed some of her history too. When her mothers made love, Mma'riama inherited some of their preoccupations. The girl was born sad.

Uh'oruu: Not sad sister, something else, something more full than empty.

Nkikima: Now who is telling the story, you or me?

Uh'oruu: Us, just because you were dead before me does not mean you get to hog the storytelling. Ehe, now it's my turn. You have taken us back to back then, and it is taking too long to bring us back to the now.

* * *

Mma'riama swats the mosquito that attempts a second bite at her arm as she grabs her communication device from her backpack. A bluebird's call sings in her ear sending tingling serotonin down her spine. Two fireflies play with each other above her head and she watches them dance all around her, wondering if they are lovers or sisters.

"Upe'po," she whistles, and her partner, the large flying reptile, responds with wings and thundering claps that beat the air.

Collect this sample, she signs.

Upe'po pulls at the singing hibiscus bush gently. Mma'riama has taught him how to tug at only what the plant wants to give. Relational research is foundational to all of her work. She knows too many raevaagis – bearers of history – who caused harm reducing living beings to objects to be prodded, analyzed, and discarded. Upe'po screeches, then barks, offering his beak to Mma'riama's cheek.

"I'm fine," she whispers, her voice soft as flower petals. If she is being honest with herself, she is terrified but more excited than terrified... She quietens and signs, *What was that? Did you hear it?*

He lifts his beak to the air, sniffing. The sound is almost non-existent. Mma'riama has learned to rely on her other senses more than, if not just as much as, her ears. Her mothers educated her themselves, not trusting the public education to protect and teach a half-sound with her abilities. Maa' Mwaninimwa, whose past remains secretive to most of their Ma'juu community, taught Mma'riama how to defend herself if she ever needed to. Mma'riama needed to. For all of their ideas of their own progressiveness, Ma'juu citizens still held on to prejudice masked under paternalistic "flattering" curiosity. Mma'riama luckily or unluckily grew up suspicious. Mama Furah-Furah taught her the art of diplomacy. Wear masks. Smile to cover up your fangs, listen to hear what people are saying underneath the words they speak, and take up only as much space as is necessary for you to protect yourself and yours. Always leave room to disappear when you need to.

Mma'riama learned to listen to the tingling of her skin, the prickling hairs that stood up to warn her of potential threats. She now knows how to pay attention to the vibrations at the tip of her fingers when she kisses the ground with them. This is how those untethered survive. The surface of Órino-Rin is not solid, but the mountains, dormant volcanoes, and sky cities are stable enough. At least that is what the ancestors hoped for when they declared the planet to be a safe haven for vagabonds and lost beings across the five planets, when they built all those cities of the sky, and made rules that banished the past.

The Maji'ima volcano is closer to the meridian than is recommended for extended visitation, especially without a skin suit, but Mma'riama does not like the way the suits make her feel. Blocked, not fully aware, like the medication they tried to fix her with when she was small. The suits were made for full sounds, another part of her world that makes her feel like an afterthought. She carries an air filter and trusts that's enough to keep her safe. She is also well-practiced at scaling cliffs and holding oxygen in. Before Mma'riama became a raevaagi in training, Maa' Mwaninimwa and Mama Furah-Furah would take her on exploration adventures. Their parenting philosophy demanded preparation and attention.

"Always know where, who, and what you are. Always know when, how, and who you are with. And if you do not know, ask ask ask until you know."

If she was not touching Upe'po's belly, Mma'riama would miss the low rumble that travels from her companion's tail up his chest. The volcano's cliffs, which have been sounding a low whistle, begin to howl. Mma'riama looks up to see, the way she has been taught to. *A sonic storm*. She counts the beats between lightning bolts to judge how long she has. If she does not leave immediately, it will find her and make sure there is nothing left to find for those who come after. She packs up her materials, and saddles Upe'po whose anxiety has not abated.

Mma'riama wants to calm Upe'po, but is not sure how to when she, herself, cannot shake the feeling of impending doom. A darkness bigger than the sonic storm.

"Sksss skss." She gives Upe'po the signal to leave. His wings spread wide, their tips falling to the almost soil substance that feeds the dome-protected fauna and flora. Mma'riama starts to shake. She can't control the movement of her body. *Not now.* She grits her teeth. *Not now*. But her body does not listen, and the sonic storm regarding her screech as a beckoning only grows louder and more ferocious.

We won't make it back, she signs, and Upe'po draws them to the dome barrier where she is close enough to activate the voice-controlled panel.

"Shut down all systems." She is audible, even though her voice is barely a whisper. A second barrier extends over the first dome covering, blocking out the external world. Mma'riama and Upe'po are trapped, but they are alive.

* * *

Uh'oruu: Mma'riama, the word twister and memory keeper. Mma'riama who has never learned to distinguish between ghosts and people, between years past and years now.

Nkikima: Tell them about the echo.

Uh'oruu: Sksks I am getting there... Mma'riama was three years old, when she saw the echo of herself. A past playing out on the tip of her eyelids. Previous lives like wind carrying her through a current of time before her present life. Then, in five breaths, she was three years again, appearing to the physical world as if nothing had happened. She was simply the quiet something-more-full-than-sad half-sound-child born to Furah-Furah and Mwaninimwa. Five breaths was enough for both mothers to realize what and who their child was destined to be. Before she was born they were warned about the signs. Warned about the women that came before who did not know how to only live in their time. Mma'riama's mothers were terrified for her, and for themselves, so they pretended they did not know.

Nkikima: Mma'riama has always seen people as they were before seeing them as they are. Every building, ship and outpost she walks into, carries the lingering scents, colors and movements of before. It overwhelms her senses, splicing her consciousness for five breaths, where she is lost in time, wandering through memories that do not belong to her. These worlds of the past are so loud, they beat at her eardrums until blood starts to collect, pooling too close to her brain for her mothers not to worry, even though they already know, even though they ask and ask until they have no choice but to be honest about how much they already know.

In her sixth year, Mma'riama's mothers take her to another Kawa'yida education center and, on the first day as she enters the classroom, she experiences the past versions of everyone in her class, including her teacher. She does not hear half of what anyone says to her. When those in the present insist on pulling her attention, Mma'riama fragments, her brain stretching further than it is meant to go. Mma'riama holds her ears and screams so loud, the other children have to hurry out of class so her sound does not break them. After that, her mothers say she must go to an uroh-ogi specialized in echo neurology and then one practiced in sound-therapy.

On most days before this, Mma'riama does not know how to speak louder than a whisper. After the uroh-ogi healers, she withdraws into herself, going many days without communicating to anyone but the voices of the past in her head. Her mothers stop, take a breath; grieve the idea of the child they thought they would have. They finally sit with the fact of the child they do have. They come to the conclusion that they will love her as much as they love who they thought she would be, and this grows them. Learning how to love whatever sadness has decided to make a home of her, knowing that it is bigger than them, bigger than her even. They decline all the recommendations to make her *normal* and take her education into their own hands. Furah-Furah and Mwaninimwa decided that Mma'riama will learn how to measure her attention and emotions on her terms, and how to attune herself to the silences she chooses.

Nkikima: Ayii, sibling, the past is not silent. Mma'riama has always been sounding, just in her mind more than from her lips.

Uh'oruu: Have I said something to contradict?

Nkikima: Many things, but no problem. We are a world of contradictions.

* * *

From the unspoken video "Journals of Mma'riama": *AI translated from signed dialect

The Uh'oruu dome 301 of Órino-Rin is located on one of the four lower cliffs of the Maji'ima Volcano. It is a trick, this parcel of semi-solid ground that grows some of the most terrifyingly beautiful trees and plants of all the five planets: purple and black barked boa'obas, bioluminescent rainbow eucalyptus trees, shimmering blue, and yellow striped fig trees, with every variation of wildflower imaginable. The long blades of grass sing the cicada's chorus, frogs croak in pools that coalesce as the humidity of the dome traps water in the air. It smells like the large rainforests that existed in many parts of Wiimb-ó many years ago. The Uh'oruu garden project is a whole ecosystem of color, sound, and scent, except for when it is Silent. It has been silent more often than not these past years.

Very little trustworthy information is available about the Uh'oruu project. It did not take long for researchers to learn the trick of Uh'oruu. More and more, it became unwilling to divulge information freely. More and more, it became a tourist destination. People traveled from all over to witness the Uh'oruu project phenomenon. The way the dome blocked out all light so the plants would glow in the dark, singing songs that felt something more full than sad.

Humans with their curiosities slip so easily into colonization. Researchers took samples; people used sound devices to tap into barks to understand root systems. They argued, "If people can understand the flourishing of the

Uh'oruu garden project it will benefit a whole generation learning to cultivate agriculture on planets without soil." As if we have not already taken enough from the universe, and taken enough from ourselves.

Before long, the plants began to bite back. Roots secreted poison into their branches and leaves. Researchers who entered the sphere disappeared without explanation, and the Uh'oruu project was abandoned. People could not eat any of the vegetation, anyway. It was not for them. And what was the point of studying something that did not directly benefit you. That is the stupidity of people, the ignorance of centering the universe around yourself. The most frustrating thing is I also understand why people people. How could I not?

Humans are always carrying all of their time with them. Time carried in the body is a multiverse in and of itself. I know this more than anyone. And I am just as stupid as they are. I must be, because I cannot get the Uh'oruu garden project out of my head. After the project shut down, we were left with gossip, rumors, stories of what once was. My research, which has mostly centered around collective amnesia, feels unfinished. I have seen images of the dome all my life. The technology that secures it from sonic storms is old but still theoretically stable. Enough time has passed that it doesn't look the way it did. I do not care if it greets me with silence. It is a language I understand. I have told Shem my plans. She does not agree. She says I have a death wish and, if I was to be honest with her, I would tell her I think wishing for death is the same thing as wishing for life, but I have not had the courage to tell her this. She does not understand what it means to move through the world interacting with ghosts. At the very least, I have sworn her to secrecy. I am not telling Maa'' or mama until after I return. However, I think they know more than they are letting on. They always do. I have been preparing for the last year, studying as much as I can in my spare time.

Uh'oruu calls to me, or I am merely projecting my own desires onto a world that does not care to know me.

* * *

Five breaths into the sonic storm.

Uh'oruu Garden Dome

Silence?! You greet us in silence?!

Mma'riama's ears ring, the pain, a knife slicing the skin off her scalp, sharp and slow. The scream inside pulls itself up her pancreas through her kidneys to the back of her throat. The vines outside curl around her ankles growing thorns and drawing blood. Mma'riama can see the bones beneath the soil, the bones that have fed the Uh'oruu garden's plants and vegetation. The garden's memory infused into her five breaths like a torrent of feelings, images, sounds, and moments.

**THE MEMORY*

"Faster! Harder!" The soldier is a man with uniform colors that Mma'riama cannot distinguish. The people mine cobalt, copper, diamonds, and minerals. Two girls, siblings. One coughs, she is smaller than the other and slightly more frail. She falls and is picked up by her sister.

The air is thick, so thick, Mma'riama coughs until she spits. The cave is dark, the shadow of a night that will not end. Hammers strike metal and hoarse voices sing to call forth the minerals that have hidden themselves deep within the rock.

This does not look like Órino-Rin. Mma'riama forces her eyes open to the memory though they sting. This is Wiimb-ó, where most of her ancestors are from.

Why would the Uh'oruu project have a memory of Wiimb-ó?

The guards have sonic guns. They threaten to shoot anyone who is not working hard or fast enough. Every once in a while, they pretend to pull the trigger at nothing in particular, as a joke. Every guard has earplugs as a security measure. The longer they hold down the trigger on the sonic guns, the higher the frequency of pitch. When they get bored enough, they play around with the different frequencies.

"Vagrant buffoons!" They laugh at their own jokes.

One of the sisters, the smaller one hides something she picked from the ground when she fell. Mma'riama can see all of it play out, but she cannot touch it. She is a ghost of the future so she cannot speak, cannot change, only watch. Mma'riama follows the siblings. Something about their facial structure and demeanor piques her interest. They attract the attention of one of the guards too. The one who made the jokes that made the least sense. He follows the girls as they walk deeper into the caves.

Mma'riama's heart attempts to flee her chest as her frail sister trips over a stone, almost drops the secret thing she picked up, but then catches herself just in time. She hides it in the lining of her underwear. The guard notices and grabs her roughly.

"What is that? Stupid ingrate!" he yells and the girl doesn't answer.

"Wordless, are you? I saw you hide something! Where did you put it?" he yells again, yanking at her clothes, tearing what refuses to come off easily.

No. No. No. Mma'riama has been in traumatic memories before but, over time, she learned how to control when and how they come more. She has created a wall, a barrier between herself and the feelings that are too hard to do more than bear witness to. This one, however, is different. This one is like the first time she was taken into years past. It overtakes her, a five-breath history that crawls into every cell that makes her body what it is, so the small girl whose autonomy is being violated is right here right now, a breath away, and Mma'riama can do nothing to save her. She wants to scream, to attack him, but she can't actually change anything.

The guard reaches for the secret thing hidden underneath the small girl's panty lining. Mma'riama shakes with fury and despair. The girl's sister screams. Her sound is so loud, Mma'riama holds her ears shut as the guards reach for their sonic guns clumsily. The ones at a distance who are not immediately debilitated by the scream pull their triggers in the first girl's direction, assuming the scream is hers. She falls, and so does the man with his hand on her waist. The fallen girl's arm is outstretched reaching for her sibling whose scream falters, falling into a guttural cry.

"Nkikima!"

It is a name that is a memory-harmony, invoking familiarity, recognition, kinship. Mma'riama tastes the blood in the back of her throat, being yanked back into the searing pain of the present.

You are not supposed to be here and you came.

Mma'riama's nose drips blood, her ears ringing with the memory of the girl's scream. The thing Mma'riama has learned about being a half-sound raevaagi who cannot control when the past decides to visit is that the only way to survive is to count time in breaths. Count breaths in tension, desperation, pleasure, disgust, patience, restlessness, anger, fear. They will try to convince you that you do not belong to yourself, you do not belong to the present. You belong only to the gods of time, the ancestors of what was and what has been. Count breaths until the five that are taken from you, the five that are stolen by the thing, person, or place that has infiltrated every cell in your body is nothing but another memory of a memory. No matter how real it feels, let it go or you will not survive.

You are ours, child of the past. You do not belong here. You know you do not belong here, but you came anyway.

The five breaths of time-past hold Mma'riama captive. The voice jolts her off the back of Upe'po with its force. Catching herself with her palm, Mma'riama twists her wrist in the process. Her neurons fire, adrenaline rushing through her bloodstream. The memory has not let her out of its grip and now she has no way to leave. She is stuck in the past years of the "Uh'oruu project," known by another name long before; a true name that a human tongue cannot sound, a name angrier and more ferocious than something as precarious as freedom. She is trapped, just like the girls in the cave. The raging sonic storm outside travels through the barrier of the Uh'oruu dome as a whistle. She counts her breaths, sorting through the history she has been jolted out of.

The blood-thinning roots, poisonous barks, and biting flowers are as real as the cave and the sisters and the guards. Upe'po nudges Mma'riama's neck, trying to bring her attention to the present, trying to shield her from the attacking flora. Her wrist is on fire, and the flowers, the bushes, the boa'obas…

Are those teeth?

She signs. Upe'po whines.

The name that cannot be spoken by a human tongue invokes fear. Deep seeded, terrifying paranoia. The scream that was not hers still echoes in her muscles. Suddenly, she is six again and the voices in her head are indistinguishable from external voices. The past of this place… it is cursed, it must be. This is why the scream gathers in the pit of her belly. She holds it at bay.

I know what you are, she signs, pulling herself onto her knees as the bright red and purple bougainvillea vines reach for her thighs. Upe'po chitters and clicks, baring his teeth at the garden. Multicolored petals fall off trees like quick rain, and the semi-solid ground rumbles as if it is to become undone. The atmosphere around Mma'riama gets thick like the caves.

In the Memory: Nkikima's sister pries open her dead sibling's outstretched hand. In it, embedded into her palm, is a seed.

You are Nkikima's seed. Mma'riama signs.

* * *

Silence.

Nkikima: I found the word for something fuller than sad, dada. Anguish: the grief of a people who have forgotten how to check the wound. A people who only look up and forward and not back. This is what the girl carries: not just the pain of the past, but also the wound that has been covered, and ignored as if it does not exist, ripe for infection. You know?

Uh'oruu: Yes! You name a kin feeling. I lived my life with the wound of you, Nkikima. I know anguish well, I dance with grief. I carved the loss of you into a heartbeat passed down from parent to child to parent to child until it unfurled in Mma'riama's chest while she was still inside her mother's womb. We are each other's stories. Mma'riama knows this as true as every life she has passed through, as every history she has lived in to escape her own wounds, but now we must let it breathe. This is the payment for her life, the story of her pain.

Nkikima/Nkikima: Is there no other way?

Uh'oruu: Ask them, the one listening to the story and, if they do not respond, remember that silence too is an answer. This story must come, this story must go. The silence has decided. The man whose name Mma'riama has not whispered or signed since she made the decision to forget him was named Onesi'ni. We give you his true name so he may be shamed, even into death. He was her research advisor in her first year of training, a raevaagi himself interested in controlling memory. When he met Mma'riama he immediately recognized in her big potential that existed because she was half-sound and not in spite of her being half-sound.

Mma'riama would sit in silence listening to him theorize the feats that could be achieved "if we got to select our memories." She was captivated more by his effects, the ways his arms waved exaggerating his points as he spoke, the passion so deeply embedded into every syllable he sounded, the kindness that still softened his facial features, even though the world had been brutal with him. She knew this because he made sure to tell her, every chance he could get. When she first met him and was flooded with some of his past, she recognized in him the loneliness she had felt but could not explain.

Onesi'ni affirmed Mma'riama, praising her brilliance and offering her the attention and acknowledgment she would never admit to craving as a woman who walked through the world spoken over by most other people. Onesi'ni nodded emphatically when she signed and whispered her way through her own understanding of what she was curious about and why. He was the one who named for her *collective amnesia* as a subject of potential study. She wanted to know the moments in time when a society decides to forget.

Where does the collective memory go when they put it down? What are the ways it is passed down from generation to generation without even knowing?

Nkikima: Tell them why she was interested in those things. That is more interesting than that stupid man. No wait, let me tell them, dada. Those stories that Mama Mwaninimwa used to tell Mma'riama when she was small were stories of our people, miners who had learned how to sing songs that the rocks understood. Remember, dada? Remember how mama told us those same stories too, before we even knew what the word profit was? Before those soldiers made our lives what they became. This was before the corporations realized the gems our people had access to could create technology that would make interplanetary travel faster. The volcanoes told us their secrets, the caves sang back and told us where to find water, they—

Uh'oruu: I know what you are doing, dada. Yes, some memories are easier to sit with than others, some pasts make the present less painful, but we cannot escape hard truths by skipping over them. Those soldiers, Onesi'ni, and the person I became after you were taken from me, all of these people need to be greeted if we are going to save Mma'riama.

Nkikima: Then let her tell it, neh? Let her tell it how she wants. Onesi'ni is not the point, Mma'riama is, so this one she should tell for herself.

* * *

Mma'riama tries to push herself up with her still-working hand. She claws at the soil, but she is weak. She forces her muscles to relax, counting her breaths, demanding clarity. *Clear vision, clear thoughts*. The vines slither around her, the boa'oba branches stretch out, and acid maggots fall from the cracks in the barks of the eucalyptus trees. When they touch her, they burn her flesh. She imagines this is how they died, all those scientists and researchers that were never seen again. Upe'po swipes the acid maggots with his tail. They burn the hard exterior of his scaly flesh. He claws at the vines that attack Mma'riama, and they shoot thorns into the exposed skin between scales. He screeches and uses his wings to protect both him and Mma'riama from the sharpened earth blades. Mma'riama grabs onto his leg, and he tries to lift her but the vines wrapped around her torso have an unshakeable hold. They climb, reaching to pull him down too.

You are not from here either. Mma'riama signs to the haunting garden as the frogs croak and moan the death chants of ghosts. Two fireflies hover over her trapped body and land on the vines. They retreat, scuttling back to the base of bushes that released them. She immediately knows who they are. The sisters that have been telling her story.

A case has been made for your life, and more than one case has been made for your death. We are a fair judge, tell us your story.

* * *

From the unspoken video "Journals of Mma'riama Li'Ochi":

***AI translated from signed dialect**

The truth is I know the name of the lead researcher assigned to the Uh'oruu garden project. He was my advisor. I have listened to the oral document where he is named over and over and over again. The Mother has a cruel sense of humor. He was researching the memory magic of the garden. He found a new mineral that could only be mined from the Maji'ima volcano at the exact spot where the Uh'oruu garden project was. The organic matter of the first seed that expanded into the rocks of the volcano created a mineral that attached itself to the hippocampus. It could be fine-tuned to different frequencies, slowing down, or speeding up memories. Subjects tested with the slowing properties of the mineral were known to live so long in a memory that it became the only reality they trusted, while subjects whose memories were sped up lost any ability to recall the memory that traveled too fast in their brain for them to catch it. It wasn't control but it was close enough.

There were two ways to access the mineral: Extraction of nutrients through suction pipes connected to the barks of the trees. Over time, the mineral would slowly be pumped out with other life-sustaining nutrients for the dome. It would take time. The second option would be to unearth the garden and take what is underneath it. This was something Onesi'ni never thought the masses would understand, so he crafted the narrative that the Uh'oruu garden project was merely for agricultural purposes.

I am the evidence that it was not. He assaulted me. There, I said it. I trusted him and he betrayed my trust, then he... he made me forget it. We were in his lab. He had organic samples from the Uh'oruu project, it sounded familiar, sparking the memory of a story Maa" Mwaninimwa told me when I was younger. I gave consent only to test his serum, not for anything else. I believed him when he said that this would heal all of us. I wanted memories to slow down, not speed up. He was smart. I signed my consent so when I woke up with a fuzzy memory sped up he said I had agreed to it.

I have not screamed since my sixth year, but I could feel the boa'oba's bark inside my stomach roiling. I could not remember what happened, but my body knew. I screamed so loud the straps that held me down came loose. I screamed so loud his ears started to bleed. Then I ran, I found Upe'po and left. That is when I decided I would come here. My body knows extraction and violation, so does Uh'oruu.

* * *

Uh'oruu: Uh'oruu was the name I chose after Nkikima died, the name that insisted on something else for our people. I wanted to murder them, the soldiers who called us beasts on two legs. Instead, I became one of them. I believed the only way I would have any power to stop the atrocities of our people was to rise up their ranks. It is no surprise that I found no freedom in my assimilation. Many years before Mma'riama, many years before her mother Mwaninimwa, I was sent to Órino-Rin as the sky cities were new and developing.

Nkikima: We came, sister. I was always with you, just like we are with her.

Uh'oruu: But we could not protect her. Just like I could not protect you in life. How do we accept this role of witness without falling into despair?

Nkikima: We plant what we find, what we see, what we learn. We plant and watch it grow the way it chooses to.

Uh'oruu: That is what I thought when I saw the Maji'ima volcano. Something about the molten rocks millions of years old reminded me about our caves. When I landed on Órino-Rin I knew I would not leave. I planted the seed I carried with me since Nkikima's death.

Uh'oruu, namesake, hear me now. You are my sister's seed, born from the mines of Wiimb-ó many many years ago. Mma'riama, she is my seed, the descendant of those who descended from me. The ones who have hurt her are the ones who have hurt you. When we came to you we made a deal. If you find our story just, you will let Mma'riama go. You have listened, now

Let. Her. Live.

* * *

The dome rumbles and shakes, loud as an earthquake. The two fluttering dragonflies Mma'riama observed earlier fall, their stories complete. The vine's thorns retract, and the acid maggots melt. It rains. The large ceiling of the dome condenses the water in the air.

Your ancestors have spoken for you.

The voice sounds broken, defeated. The fat drops of rain slap Mma'riama's skin and, as much as Upe'po tries to shield her with his wings, she still gets utterly soaked.

Mma'riama's scream travels up her body and out her throat, transforming into a low long deep wail. She does not need the memory mineral to remember and grieve. Mma'riama wails for herself, for Furah-Furah and Mwaninimwa, for Nkikima and Demwa'w, for Uh'oruu, for all the grief in Maa'juu that has not found a home.

Mma'riama, the word twister, the memory-keeping grief catcher. Mma'riama, the half-sound something more full than sad wailer of Uh'oruu still breathing and counting all her breaths until morning comes.

The Sounding

J. Umeh

infernal ringing
warped creature concocting pain—
horrid silent scream

An ancient creature writhes into the present in ***J. Umeh****'s body horror story. On Wiimb-ó, specialist healer Jhuma-Riah is preparing for a make-or-break career assessment when a dramatic encounter with a young patient puts her work – and her very existence – at risk. Voices spewing gibberish, long-forgotten rituals, tell-tale trickles of blood…*

Welcome to "The Sounding".

I. The Happening

THERE IT IS, that persistent ringing sound. The hairs on the back of Jhuma-Riah's neck stand erect as goosebumps form down her arms. She is barely awake when tremors start to work their way through her body. An infernal ringing that just won't go away. It is slowly getting louder, a rising sound that swallows the usual chorus of domestic animals and neighbors.

The tremors increase and become jerky vibrations that course through Jhuma-Riah's entire being. It feels like she is being strained through a sieve. Her hands try to grasp her iri're pendant, which usually helps her calm down and voice the chant for bodily control, but the pendant between her breasts may as well have been on the moon. Her fingers are tightly curled into fists, which start to pound the sheets. Her arms tense as her body arches up, only her neck and heels touching the bed, her face a rictus of torture gazing unseeingly at the ceiling, and she voids her bladder.

Then, just as suddenly as it started, the ringing stops. Jhuma-Riah's body flops back onto the urine-soaked sheets. Her eyes are half closed and her lips move on their own accord, mouthing a soundless prayer.

As Jhuma-Riah begins to regain herself, a plaintive sob emanates from her still-moving lips as it dawns on her what just happened. Slowly, she peels herself off the bed to a sitting position. All those years of training as a sound healer for patients with mental illness had not prepared her for dealing with anything like this.

Jhuma-Riah gets up on shaky feet, ears burning and head thumping. She makes her way to the bathroom to wash up and prepare, Mother help her, for another long day at the clinic. Jaw clenched and lower lip set to maximum stubborn, as her father used to tease her, Jhuma-Riah starts her morning ablutions. She is resolved to get to the bottom of this and not let it affect her ability to do her work, at least until the Ishiteteh.

Then she looks through the window and sees that the light is fading. It's not morning, but evening, and she has slept the whole day away.

II. The Beginning

(Two days ago)

"Ajhuma, Jhuma, the wonder maker," sings the smiling voice of Den-Dirio as Jhuma-Riah enters their clinic and shared office space. "Did you stay up all night again?"

With a cheerful face, bright, intelligent eyes and a mischievous grin, Den-Dirio has a boyish look and charm that can be mistaken for immaturity, but beyond it lies a gifted sound healer, loyal friend and colleague.

"Deni, Deni, healer of many," she responds playfully, as is their custom. "How are we today, and when are we expecting to see the assessor for the Ishiteteh ceremony?"

Ishiteteh is the ritual in which she and Den-Dirio will be assessed as uroh-ogi specialists in using sound healing to treat mental illnesses, and Jhuma-Riah is a little anxious. She has, in fact, been spending nights at the clinic in preparation.

"I think he'll likely come when we least expect it. I heard he once presented as a patient to test another practitioner," Den-Dirio says with a slight smile that makes it difficult to tell whether he's teasing her.

"Well, in that case, he better not be my next patient because I might just 'treat' him to a real mental illness," says Jhuma-Riah half-jokingly.

Den-Dirio snorts. "Speaking of which, I believe your next patient is waiting. It is a family, so be gentle; our reputation may be riding on this one!" He chuckles as he walks away to his healing chamber.

Jhuma-Riah peers into her reception area at the family of three. The parents are deep in hushed conversation, and she can make out what sounds like an argument between wife and husband, before passing into her office to drop her bags and put on her regalia. She makes sure her iri're pendant is securely in place and mouths a quick prayer before heading out to the family with a smile.

"Greetings, how may I bring Our Mother's healing to you on this day?" She can tell from their clothes that they are not local. Perhaps they are from another side of Wimbo-ó.

"Thank you, oh wise healer," they respond in unison. "May Our Mother guide your healing efforts."

The father continues, in a heavy voice. "My name is Dokwa-Nna, and this is my wife, Dokwa-Mma, and our son, Dokwa-Obichi," gesturing to the worried-looking woman and rather subdued pre-teen boy. "Our son has a terrible condition which is getting worse. We can't take our eyes off him in case it happens again, Mother forbid!" Dokwa-Nna clicks his fingers twice to ward off any such occurrence.

Jhuma-Riah beckons to them sympathetically. "Please come into my healing chamber and you can tell me all about it."

They follow her. A large round mat with cushions lying around its edge dominates the center of the chamber. An ornately carved kalabash gourd, suspended by a nearly invisible thread, is hanging down from the ceiling mid-point above the circular mat. They settle down on the cushions.

Jhuma-Riah reaches to touch the gourd as she intones a prayer to Our Mother for a successful session.

Jhuma-Riah twirls the gourd so the ornate carvings seem to take a life of their own. "Tell me, when did your troubles start?" she asks.

"Three days ago," Dokwah-Nna starts, speaking quietly. "We knew something was wrong as soon as we arrived in town, didn't we, Mma?" He glances at his wife.

"Yes, Nna," replies Mma, staring at the rotating gourd. "We hadn't even finished unpacking our belongings when Obichi began to flail and shake like a leaf, speaking such strange words." She looks accusingly at her husband. "Why did we have to leave your last job near Osasala and come here? You and your esoteric nonsense about semi-mysterious maragates and antique sound concentrators – who knows what our poor Obichi may have picked up by coming in contact with your dirty tools?" Turning to Jhuma-Riah, she implores, "Oh, wise healer, please help our boy!"

Jhuma-Riah studies them all carefully. "Of course, I'll do everything in my power to help."

She settles herself on the cushion and observes the boy still staring intently at the now barely moving gourd without expression, apart from the slight movement of his lips, as if in silent prayer. He hasn't said much since they arrived.

"How are you feeling, Obichi?" Jhuma-Riah asks the boy. "Will you tell us what is happening to you?"

Obichi turns, eyes staring vacantly at a point above Jhuma-Riah's right ear. His lips, still mouthing silent words, now start to move faster, uttering unintelligible whispers. Jhuma-Riah leans in closer, straining to hear what he is saying.

"*Hrrmmgrb llbrg swxayf]afj asbf krsb arkwn blzgrb, frsbr frsbr frsr fgrszztr...*" Obichi whispers. The words spill out of his mouth and start to take visible form as wispy, smoke-like tendrils emanating from his lips. He turns to stare at the gourd which starts spinning in reverse, picking up speed as the words continue to form smoky shapes, darkening in color with flashes of amber-hued fire within.

"Mother help us!" gasps his startled father, wide-eyed with worry as he turns to Jhuma-Riah for assurance.

She is already chanting protective incantations, her eyes fixed on the gourd, willing it to stop. But the gourd only spins faster.

Dokwa-Mma is hunched over crying and calling her son's name. "Obichi, Obichi, why are you doing this to me?"

"Ashf krsh arkwn blzgrb frshr frshr frsr fgrszztr hrrmmgrb llhrg swxayfjafjh..." The boy barely pauses for breath, smoky shapes obscuring his face. The spinning gourd speeds up, keeping pace.

Jhuma-Riah continues to chant, occasionally tapping her iri're pendant and slapping her hands together as if killing a zizingha fly. The crack of her palms coming together slows the spinning gourd and partially disperses the sinister haze in front of Obichi's face, but it doesn't last.

Finally, Jhuma-Riah utters a powerful chant in the ancient tongue, claps her hands loudly three times and grabs the stalled gourd with both hands.

Obichi throws his head back and sneezes explosively, expelling the last trailing tendrils of smoky word shapes which coalesce to form a hazy cloud above his head.

The cloud spins and expands into a mini vortex. Various small objects start to fly and skitter across the chamber as though caught in a silent whirlwind. Apart from the muffled sobs of Dokwa-Mma, whose head is buried in her husband's chest, and the quiet incantations of a trance-like Jhuma-Riah, everything happens in complete silence.

Obichi screams suddenly. An invisible hand lifts and flings him across the room, stopping just short of crashing him into a wall, before he slides unconscious to the floor. Then, slowly, the silent storm abates. The dark shapes dissipate like smoke in a cleansing breeze.

Dokwa-Nna and Dokwa-Mma rush to Obichi and he stirs, staring blearily at them.

"What happened, Nna, and why is Mma crying?" asks the bewildered youth, as his parents both gasp and embrace him, overjoyed to hear him speaking normal words again.

"Oh wise healer, may the Mother be praised!" Dokwa-Mma cries out.

"Our son is back again!" exclaims Dokwa-Nna, happiness written all over his face as he turns to look at Jhuma-Riah who is still holding the gourd with both hands, eyes locked on its carvings.

She finishes her chanting. Exhausted, Jhuma-Riah stands shakily on unsteady feet and makes her way to the huddled trio. “Let me see him.” She looks at the transformed youth, who gazes shyly back at her as if meeting for the first time, eyes tired but bright and intelligent.

“What happened? Am I in trouble?” Obichi asks, looking searchingly into her eyes. “I had the most horrible dream!”

“No, you are not in any trouble,” Jhuma-Riah replies, “and you sound much better.” Carefully placing her hand under his chin, she tilts his head to one side and sees a small trickle of drying blood from his right ear. “Are you in any pain?” she asks, peering into the ear.

“No. I’m fine, thank you,” Obichi replies shyly. Turning to his mother, he says, “I am hungry, Mma. When can we go home and eat?”

Dokwa-Mma just beams back at him, clearly bereft of speech.

“I think you can go home.” Jhuma-Riah smiles, as she dabs Obichi’s ear with a piece of cloth. She can see he is getting restless. Turning to his parents, she says, “But since I’m not yet sure what caused this, please listen out for any changes in his speech and let me know as soon as possible.”

“Mother forbid it comes back,” the Dokwas reply, fingers snapping in unison.

“We can’t tell you how grateful we are,” says Dokwa-Mma. “May Our Mother continue to guide your practice.”

“We will tell all our friends and relatives – this has been such a miraculous day,” Dokwa-Nna adds as they usher Obichi through the alcove to the reception area.

“Thank Our Mother that I could help you today. Go well and be well!”

Jhuma-Riah watches the family disappear through the door, then she turns to stare pensively at the mat and disheveled chamber. “Oh, this is going to take some cleaning up,” she mutters to herself, as she bends to wipe off a small dark stain on the mat, just below the swaying gourd. She feels a slight, sharp pain in her right ear, followed by a tiny trickle of warm liquid. She touches her ear and her fingers come away bloodstained. Baffled, she gets up, swaying slightly, and then she buckles as darkness engulfs her.

Jhuma-Riah wakes in her healing chamber, shocked to realize that she fainted. She struggles to get up, her body so tired that every movement is a chore. It must be the stress of the imminent Ishiteteh; she knows she has been overdoing it. Well, she certainly can’t continue to see patients in this condition.

"Deni," she calls out, emerging from the healing chamber, "I'm going home to rest for a bit. Can you reschedule the rest of my appointments today?"

He comes out of his own healing chamber, looking not the least bit surprised. "Didn't I tell you that you need more sleep? Go, I'll see you tomorrow. And if I pass by later and find you practicing for the Ishiteteh, there'll be trouble!"

She smiles but feels uneasy as she packs her things and makes her way home. A slow ringing is starting in her right ear, making her wonder if she has a headache or is perhaps coming down with some illness. By the time she reaches home, Jhuma-Riah is so tired she barely makes it to her bed before dropping into a deep sleep.

III. The Whispering

Jhuma-Riah walks groggily into the clinic the following day. She is wrapped up in thought and nearly stumbles into a tall, well-dressed and scholarly-looking man.

"Excuse me," she says, an apologetic smile on her face. "How may I help you, sir?"

"Not at all, my child." The stranger smiles. "My name is Samfa K'naah, and I'm here to see Jhuma-Riah and

Den-Dirio, the clinic proprietors. Would that be you by any chance?" he asks in a warm, rich voice.

Jhuma-Riah can see he is not as young as she originally thought. Laughter lines around the eyes juxtapose with deeply etched worry lines on his forehead, giving him an air of a wise, experienced but kind practitioner of the healing arts. This must be the assessor. Dear Mother, of all the times for him to turn up!

"Yes, my name is Jhuma-Riah," she blurts out nervously. "Please come this way." She leads him to the office.

"You seem a little peaked," observes Samfa K'naah. "Was it a tough session with your last patient?"

"Er, they were not too bad." Jhuma-Riah straightens up in an attempt not to appear as exhausted as she feels. That ringing in her ear is back. This is no time to be ill, she admonishes herself, then turning to Samfa K'naah, she says, "Here is my colleague, Den-Dirio," just as he rises to greet the assessor.

"Greetings, wise healer and assessor. We have been expecting you." Den-Diro points to a chair and continues, "Please sit down and let me get you a drink."

Samfa K'naah waves off the drink but sits on the proffered chair. "Thanks, young man. There's no need for refreshments as this shouldn't take long. Please sit."

Jhuma-Riah and Den-Dirio take their seats, looking at Samfa K'naah expectantly. He smiles reassuringly and launches into a well-rehearsed description of the assessment process and what to expect at each of the three stages, including thc final Ishitctch ritual. They both nod their acknowledgement, subdued.

Samfa K'naah tries to break the tension by asking, "Why don't you tell me about any interesting cases you havc comc across recently?"

Den-Dirio says, "I don't know that we have an excessive list of 'interesting' cases or clients." Smiling wryly he adds, "We plan to build a reputation that can expand beyond this town, so we're not seeking any undue excitement or challenges at this time."

Samfa K'naah nods wisely in agreement, then turns to the pensive figure of Jhuma-Riah. "Perhaps Jhuma-Riah can share her experience with her last patient. It seems to have taken its toll and I'd be interested to hear about it."

Jhuma-Riah does not want to talk about it, but realizing that this may well be part of the assessment, she decides to tell the full story of her encounter with the Dokwas. She concludes with a slight frown, "It was like something had taken possession of the boy and a very different child left the clinic than the one that came in."

"Hmmm," mutters Samfa K'naah, who had been studying her closely as she was telling her story. "It certainly sounds like a possession of some sort." He leans forward, a quizzical look on his face, and continues, "You described a hazy mist of shapes spewing from his mouth, right?"

"Yes, I believe it was caused by the sounds he was making." Jhuma-Riah's forehead wrinkles with the recollection. "It was forming into a small vortex just before I was able to stop it with the kakaskaarid reverse-curse. At least I hope that is what shut it down," she adds as she rubs her right ear.

"Oh, I'm sure it had a part to play," responds Samfa K'naah. He frowns. "Is something wrong with your ear?"

Alarmed, Jhuma-Riah quickly lowers her hand. The last thing she needs is for him to think she has some sinister condition. "Water went inside during my ablutions, that's all."

"I see," the assessor muses, then goes on. "The kakaskaarid chant is potent on many levels, so it's important to be sure of the underlying cause of this event to determine whether it is truly gone." He pauses, apparently searching for the right words. "I don't mean to alarm you, Jhuma-Riah, because I believe you did well to vanquish the symptoms without the help of a menigari, especially one that is spiritually attuned, but did you say there was a trickle of blood from his ear without any visible injury or impact on his hearing?"

Jhuma-Riah tries not to think about the ringing in her own ear. "Yes, that was puzzling to me, as he didn't appear to have any ill effects from the episode." Frowning, she asks, "Do you think that had anything to do with the illness?"

Samfa K'aaah replies carefully, "It's hard to tell. The boy may not have been suffering from a mental illness or spiritual possession at all." He steeples his long fingers and stares off into the distance, continuing in a softer voice, speaking almost to himself. "It can't be possible, no one has ever come across it in our lifetime, or many others before us, yet, maybe..."

Samfa K'naah sighs and shifts his gaze from one to the other. "Let me tell you a story from ancient times when silent spirits walked freely among our people. According to the raevaagi who compile these legends, there was a creature known as Intigitih, whisper worm, which enabled our ancestors to hear these spirits and communicate with them. Only those with great strength of mind were able to withstand the voices of these spirits. For others, it was like a demon had taken possession of the poor souls, driving them mad and feeding off the cacophony of jumbled sounds, broken thoughts, and jagged whispers in their frenzied minds. Sufferers would go as far as ripping off their ears, or poking through their eardrums with sharp objects, in a bid to stop the whispering."

Jhuma-Riah and Den-Dirio lean forward, listening raptly to his words. Jhuma-Riah, shaken, resumes rubbing her tickling ear.

Den-Dirio mutters incredulously, "But surely you can't be suggesting that this creature is back from antiquity! And even if it was, what could it possibly want with a young boy and how would an obscure kakaskaarid reverse-curse stop it?"

Samfa K'naah strokes his chin. "The raevaagi say that Intigitih, which has no voice of its own, seeks to possess those with pure hearts and take their voices.

If left untreated, Intigitih will eventually take over the person's mind and spread to others. Legend has it that only the fabled soul screecher bird could overcome Intigitih; its loud screeches would drown out all the whispering as it plucked and ate the worm straight from the victim's ears!" He stops speaking as he sees the horrified look on Jhuma-Riah's face. "But who knows how much of that is truth or fantasy? No one has ever seen a soul screecher."

"Thankfully, as you said, such creatures no longer exist," says Jhuma-Riah, trying her best to be defiant. "But even if they do, there are sound techniques we can deploy to deal with that and many other phenomena these days."

Den-Dirio adds, "We also have noise desensitisers and silencers to cancel out any kind of sound."

Jhuma-Riah cuts in suddenly; an urgent thought has just struck her: "I hope this isn't a topic for assessment, as it isn't in the syllabus even under rare occult illnesses and symptoms."

"Not at all." Samfa K'naah smiles as he waves away the thought. "We already know what we have to do next for the assessment but if, for any reason, the things we've discussed bother you, I'm happy to come back another day."

"We're fine to start now," Jhuma-Riah replies, conscious that Den-Dirio is also watching her closely for any residual ill effects from her encounter with the Intigimajiggy thing Samfa K'naah was just describing.

"In that case," Samfa K'naah says, "let us begin."

IV. The Assessment

Four acolytes stand around the edges of the central mat, horns pressed to their lips and cheeks puffed out, as they blow the notes that signify the start of the Ishiteteh assessment. Jhuma-Riah and Den-Dirio stand nervously on a mat in the center of the large assessment chamber in the Uroh-ogi Hospital in town. Samfa K'naah, the head assessor, stands before them. Two other uroh-ogi are at the other end of the room.

Samfa K'naah, Jhuma-Riah and Den-Dirio link hands and fix their gaze on a large, ornately carved kalabash gourd suspended from the ceiling without any visible means of support. The gourd starts to descend until it is at eye level with the trio at the center, then stops and starts to rotate slowly.

They all stare at the kalabash as its ornate carvings come alive, depicting scenes meaningful only to the observer. Samfa K'naah lowers his gaze, joins Jhuma and Den-Dirio's hands together and exits the circle, returning to his seat with the other uroh-ogi to observe the session.

Jhuma-Riah peers into the kalabash to elicit the right question for her partner. It goes wrong from the start. She can't make anything out of the images on the slowly rotating kalabash, and it seems as if the more she peers, the less focused her impressions become. Oh, wait, perhaps there is something...? She begins to speak, hesitantly.

"I am come to Eh'wuaizo... Come to, to Eh-weh... Eh'wauizo..." Jhuma-Riah's voice trails off as she stares at the spinning gourd. Is it picking up speed? She continues speaking, faster, as if to keep up with the quickening pace of the gourd.

"Eh'wuaizzzzo... hazzz come to me after zzzenturies of outzzzide and inzzzide. You are zze one. Zze ozzzers are uzzzlesss," she proclaims, with an unnatural rasp to her voice and a semi-puzzled look on her face.

What is that infernal buzzing sound? Perhaps a small fly entered the chamber without notice to torment her? Or is it the work of ancestral enemies trying to displace her?

“I do not know where that came from,” she says with her normal voice, turning to the judges. It slowly dawns on her by the look on their faces that everything hinges on this last part of the assessment.

Den-Dirio bravely attempts to save the proceedings. “I hear you are from beyond the spirit realm, but can you reveal more about how you want to help people?”

Jhuma-Riah is only too grateful. Turning back to the gourd, she starts to respond, but her mind won’t obey her or form the right words. Instead, she feels that dreadful familiar tickling in her ears. “*Bzrthfd-whchsirttzz-fcrskfjish-wneh-dhg-skll-aczsh...*”

The unintelligible sounds tumbling out of Jhuma-Riah’s whispering lips make her look at Den-Dirio with fear-etched eyes and, as he realizes what is happening, he signals to the uroh-ogi that something is wrong.

But Jhuma-Riah is too far gone. Her eyes roll wildly in their sockets as she continues to mumble incoherently. A trail of misty shapes emanates from her lips.

The sounds of the acolytes’ horns, which until now have been in melodic synchrony with the ceremonial songs, become a jumbled cacophony of screechy, guttural, disjointed noise increasing in volume and pace in line with the chaos within the circle.

Samfa K'naah springs into action, raising his hands and chanting an ancient chorus to counter the entity taking hold of Jhuma-Riah. The two uroh-ogi watching in wide-eyed amazement quickly join him.

The spinning kalabash responds with increased velocity, accompanied by Jhuma-Riah's words, which are getting faster, louder and more tangible, fortified by the reflective noise of the horns blowing by themselves. The acolytes stare slack-jawed. Objects and items twitch and tremble as if fighting a strong urge to jump and fling themselves across the chamber.

Then Samfa K'naah lowers his hands abruptly and yells, "INTIGITIH! YA'YN! UMBRAH-HRANEH!"

A purple haze descends over the center circle and the spinning gourd stops. Still chanting in strained tones, the other two uroh-ogi also lower their hands and utter the same phrase in unison. The noise stops and the objects freeze in place. Jhuma-Riah screams, holding her ears, and falls into Den-Dirio's outstretched arms.

He gently lowers her to the mat. Her body is rigid, eyes staring at nothing in particular, and her lips moving without a sound.

There is a heavy atmosphere in the chamber. By calling out the entity's name with a command to desist in the old tongue, it is now clear that Samfa K'naah is locked in battle with something both old and dangerous.

With a sigh, he says to his two colleagues, "It is just as I thought. We must make preparations for the Sounding, or else this creature will spread and cause untold suffering for us all."

V. The Sounding

"Somebody has to exorcise the Intigitih and we use the Sounding to bring it forth..." Jhuma-Riah recalls hazily the words the renowned menigari Mma M'gama spoke, the one Samfa K'naah brought in to help with her case. She'd also said something about how exorcising an Intigitih was not a task for the faint-hearted, even for the few practitioners and raevaagi who might remember how it was done.

Yet here she is, Mma M'gama, standing in the chamber, closely watching Samfa K'naah prepare the largest of four deep, bowl-shaped resonating stone crucibles.

Jhuma-Riah feels thankful, albeit a little alarmed that the menigari is even interested in her case. Is that a good thing or bad? She is not sure. All she has been able to do, in her semi-awake state, is clutch her iri're pendant and try to stay quiet as she observes the flurry of activity around the chamber.

Samfa K'naah casts a careful gaze into the largest stone pot while feeling its interior surface, fingers searching for any cracks, bumps or pits on the smooth inner surface. Satisfied with his inspection, he gives the pot a light tap with a small crystal rod from the collection of items hung around his neck and listens to the sonorous tone that resonates across the healing chamber.

He surveys the chamber one last time, then turns to Mma M'gama. "Shall we begin?"

Mma M'gama nods and adjusts her wrap, which seems to be in a perpetual state of coming loose. She is a stout, heavy woman of several decades, with white ceremonial markings on her face as well as on her bare shoulders and arms. She wears rings of wood, iron, string, rubber and crystal on her fingers. Her assured movements give her an air of authority.

Quickly snapping her fingers, she summons the two uroh-ogi back into the chamber to take up position behind two of the sound pots. She moves behind a third, opposite Samfa K'naah and the pot he'd just been inspecting.

Jhuma-Riah groans as she slips between clarity and haziness. In those moments of semi-lucidity, she can recall what is happening to her, but only from a distance as though she's observing herself outside of her mind. No, she thinks, it's more like an unwanted guest in her mind, needing to fight for every scrap of intentionality in her thoughts and words.

Den-Dirio is at her side, but he might as well be across a vast canyon. She glances at his worried face and tries to call out to him but the words just won't come out right, only soft mumblings and groans. A thousand fingers are poking holes in her mind and she would give anything to make it stop.

Samfa K'naah's voice sings out loudly into the healing chamber, "Ra'khwa! Ya'yn! Khwa'ra!"

The exhortation to the Mother signals the start of the Sounding. Everything is quiet. All attention is focused on the central mat on which lays listless Jhuma-Riah, with Den-Dirio gently cradling her head as the ritual progresses.

A haze descends again over the mat, bathing those ensconced within in a purple glow. Mma M'gama's voice joins the song, raising the crystal rod high above her head.

"Tonda'ririh!" exclaims Samfa K'naah, and they all strike their crystal rods against the stone pots, ringing out as one with a strong clear sound. A visible radial ripple spreads from each pot. Each time they strike, new ripples join the previous ones to create a lace-like pattern of illuminated sound.

Jhuma-Riah notices that the patterns are contained only within the purple haze. It is getting more difficult to hear as the tickle in her inner ear becomes a wriggly, whispery sensation in reaction to the sonic wall of sound.

The haze brightens like a halo around her head. Den-Dirio can hardly hold her now. Jhuma-Riah's head whips back and forth as if trying to separate from her body and run away from the all-enveloping sound. She is sweating profusely, eyes shut tight, and her lips muttering incessantly.

Mma M'gama's voice rises above the others as she communes with spirits of healers past to return the Intigitih to its rightful place outside the physical realm it has somehow found itself trapped in. Even the horrific Intigitih is merely a warped vessel of that same Mothersound which infuses and binds everything in existence, including the spirits.

Mma M'gama now taps her stone pot repeatedly in a hypnotic three-three-four pattern that makes Jhuma-Riah feel both sadness and a deep longing to drift away in its cadence. It is so beautiful, so... *brtzk txstri schzt zkzzt krbpldrj kafhkenro hygsg...*!

Jhuma-Riah screams as her body tenses, arching and contorting with wracking pain throughout her entire being. Her brain feels like it is being ripped apart by a calloused hand squelching around inside her head trying to grab something wriggly, and squirming desperately as it tries to escape by slashing and shredding anything it touches.

There is no respite from the onslaught.

Jhuma-Riah meets Den-Dirio's tearful gaze as he helplessly watches her, as she undergoes this torturous process.

Finally, eyes bulging, mouth agape in a horrified silent scream, Jhuma-Riah's ears bulge and burst with a gut-wrenching sound, like air escaping from a punctured bladder. She flops back down on the mat and something warm and bloody, with a thick, fetid ichor, oozes out of her right ear.

It is the Intigitih! Unbelievably long, with tendril-like tentacles matted around a mass of jellied blood and specks of brain matter, the creature's head is pitted with many whispering mouths. The horrific mass starts to squirm in an attempt to crawl away from the all-enveloping sounds.

On seeing this, Samfa K'naah utters the dread spell, "INTIGITIH! YA'YN! UMBRAH-HRANEH!" again to bind the creature.

Then all the uroh-ogi and Mma M'gama redouble their efforts to weave a blanket of concentrated sound around the writhing creature. The Intigitih's many mouths stop their whispering and start snapping at the strands of sound before they form a cocoon from which there is no escape.

But it is too late. The last strands enclose the creature completely, and additional layers start to form almost immediately to immobilize it. Once fully encased in the thick sound blanket, Samfa K'naah scoops the cocooned Intigitih into an ornate, sound-proof casket, in which it will remain until it can be safely disposed of.

The room gradually falls silent as the wall of resonant sound abates.

Jhuma-Riah stares wide-eyed around the room in wonderment. How peaceful silence can be! But her relief slowly turns into uncertainty, tinged with fear, as she realizes that not only can she not hear, but she cannot speak, because her mouth is sealed.

The soundproof casket before her looms with menace, and Jhuma-Riah lets out a silent scream, its resonance lost among the many whispering voices of the Intigitih's countless mouths, one of which is hers.

Naguu-Àll, Echoed in Moonlight

Moustapha Mbacké Diop

rustling at midnight
solstice thrum of sacred drums—
perverted auras

***Moustapha Mbacké Diop**'s heroine Khami'sissa longs to find the Great Beast of the ancestral realm so she can ask it questions that lie deep in her heart. A seer of deep sensitivity, she has been sheltered all her life on the planet Wiimb-ó. Now Khami'sissa is ready to break free and make her own way in the world – but she has no idea what fearsome shape her freedom might take…*

Welcome to "Naguu-àll, Echoed in Moonlight".

IT BEGINS as a whisper, stroking her temples with ghastly fingers. Her breath stops. The pressure grows

tangible. A clap resounds, snatching her eyesight from her, replacing it with an ocean of sound.

The black sound is of a deep humming. It is heavy, its might otherworldly. It is a promise of drowning.

The silver ones slither with laughter and passion, up and around and inside her. They flutter close enough to her ears to reveal their names, but she cannot breathe. So close. They skim her eardrums and...

Khami'sissa gasped for air as whiteness erupted around her in a paff sound. In her panic, she had blindly fumbled with one of the pa'affatan pods out of her leather pouch. She'd felt its grainy texture, crushed it between her fingers, and released the characteristic sound, equalizing to all frequencies, that soothed her nerves and had drawn her from the vision.

As the Summer Solstice approached, the visions were occurring more often, with more intensity. "You are a special one," her father had always whispered, his voice trembling with worry. As a toddler, she played and argued with things unseen. She was submerged in trances whenever masked musicians would play the tambi'ibinn during celebrations; so, she was forbidden to attend any. In her town, there weren't any known menigari: spiritually aligned individuals who were in touch with the ancestral plane. Dô was a market town of butchers and hunters who never stayed long enough to require spiritual guidance.

Baaba intended it to stay that way. His wine-tinted lips set in a thin line of silence every time she asked about her abilities. Khami'sissa could ask no one else. She'd lost her mother early to an unknown epidemic, had no friends. Unless a hat or opaque glasses covered her eyes, she was barely allowed to go outside! The other villagers didn't seem to care about Baaba Diarr'aja's homebound daughter. Everyone was minding the business that sustained them: it was only her and Baaba. His fear for her was overbearing, worsened by how unsettling the visions became. Now, Baaba was on his way to another town, two days away from theirs, to get her more pa'affatan.

"Please stay home and sleep early," he told her yesterday as he left, leaving a kiss on her cornrows. "I don't want you outside during the solstice."

Khami'sissa mumbled a reply and crossed her arms, looking away – she lost that battle long ago. But her father nudged her shoulder gently, adjusted his worn leather cap on his bald head, and shut the door behind him. Silence crept in the space he left, as it always did before the visions struck.

"Tonight," she whispered to the empty house. The visions were an itch she couldn't quell. A secret, bound for her ears only, that she had to unveil.

All would make sense, at last, on this night of the solstice.

The physical moon, Javuiili, was beaming, heavy and glorious, in the midnight sky. Pearly white, she cradled the mortals' sorrows in her bosom. Khami'sissa knew of Javuiili's sisters, the spirit moons. But despite being a menigari, she had never been able to see them. She'd never told Baaba, even though her moods fevered up and quieted as they waxed and waned, invisible to her eyes. It confused her. Now that she began seeing her moonblood, she felt their pull haunting her in a way she couldn't explain.

It would be her first solstice as a woman, not a girl any longer. Tonight, it was relentless, tugging at her cool brown skin that had grown too tight.

Khami'sissa also knew of the arrival of a greater being. It would draw covetous hunters deep in the grassland, perhaps to their deaths, searching for the power it was rumored to carry. The cost was steep. Few would attempt the journey: they'd seldom come back alive as, every solstice, the spirit was said to incarnate into physical form to prey on humans.

This time, it was Khami'sissa who needed to find it. *Her*.

Leaves of the bush she took refuge in pricked her cheeks, grounding her in the present. The tall grass felt alive, swaying despite the absence of wind. Cold, ominous waves emanated from the ground and through her shoes. She was certain there was something observing her, deep within the shadows.

Khami'sissa shook her head and dispersed the remains of the white sound before it gave away her position. Heart racing, she inhaled a second time, straining her gaze under the moonlight. Her palms grew sweaty as she grasped the bronze saber protruding from the pouch at her waist, waiting.

The hunters had stopped. None looked in her direction, thank the Mother, but they huddled around one of their own, crouched on the moss-covered ground and rubbing his fingers together.

"Baay Badu! You're wasting our time. It's not a regular animal that can be tracked!" the weasel-voice one said, nostrils flaring in impatience.

There were four of them. A somber boy, slightly older than Khami'sissa, with a fade that left braided hair on the top of his head. A middle-aged woman whose dark eyes darted about, made sharper by the scar across her cheekbone. The one that spoke in that annoying voice, feet pounding the ground and betraying his nervosity.

Silently, Khami'sissa crawled closer to them to see what the one named Baay Badu stained his fingers with. His thick curls verged on gray, and he had the cold eyes of a man who had seen – and done – much.

"Spiritual beings leave spiritual tracks when they interact with our world," he spoke, in a raspy yet soft voice. There was a wet indigo substance splotched across the ground underneath his zebuskin sandals. Khami'sissa thought she heard giggles, fresh and airy.

"What is this?" The woman tilted her head downward, then looked back in Khami'sissa's direction.

Since nightfall, Khami'sissa had followed them as they entered the rustling grass, but now it was as if they were going back on their heels. She cursed herself for being so close, and almost clamped her eyes shut in fear that their violet glow would betray her. These weren't like the hunters she'd come across in her Baaba's shop, who had a certain air of wisdom about them and held respect for every animal they hunted. This group exuded danger, making her skin crawl with unease.

"Munn'umm sprites. They populate the bottom of rivers and seldom leave the water."

"How are they of any help to us?"

"These sprites go to her when she comes, for she is their patron deity. They will guide us straight to the Great Beast."

A soft gasp slipped from her lips. There was such confidence in the way Baay Badu spoke. It was as if...

Was he another menigari?

Khami'sissa shook her head. She was convinced she would feel it, somehow, if she were in the presence of kin.

He sounded like he knew so much. Experience shone in the way he followed the path of shiny blue across the leaves.

Again, she held her breath, but the sharp-eyed woman didn't see her through the foliage, focused as she was on keeping up with their leader. Khami'sissa was grateful that her skin was dark enough to allow her to blend in. Amidst the sprites' giggles that faded as they left, Khami'sissa waited there for a full minute.

Something fluttered at the corner of her vision, and she felt a breath behind her neck. A new, intrusive presence. Goosebumps erupted all over her arms as she looked over her shoulder.

This was how she felt when a vision was incoming, but it had never been so… tactile.

She shuddered, scurried away from the bush louder than she'd have liked, and promptly followed the hunters.

They all carried identical crossbows, Khami'sissa noticed after slinking closer. Already armed with machetes, thick metallic spears of various lengths and a Géréwiig club for Baay Badu, their fingers kept reaching for the small weapon as they scanned their surroundings. The weapon was unusual for the hunters around these parts, who favored intricately carved Géréwiig bows and arrows, each personalized to the wielder. It was as if they were a special kind of assassins. Their crossbows held bolts coated with a bright yellow substance she couldn't recognize, nor smell from this distance.

Something else caught her eye. An open bangle bracelet, seemingly made of bone, tightly cuffed the woman's wrist. They were all wearing one, too snug for comfort. She frowned, trying to recall if any hunter guild identified themselves by bone bracelets. But she didn't get to ponder.

Khami'sissa heard the rush of water against water as they approached a clearing in the tall grass. Young boa'oba trees and massive rocks steadily replaced the tall grass. A wave of humidity dampened her face as the sound of water drowned that of the party's footsteps.

Hiding behind one tree, she rubbed her hands against its bark. They'd reached a waterfall: clouds of fog bloomed from where the cascade turned into a small river. Croaks and bubbles merged with the roaring noise and created an abnormal cacophony. This place stormed Khami'sissa's senses, driving up her nervousness. The hair on the back of her neck stood at the spiritual surge that swirled all around her.

Yet the trail of Munn'umm sprites was gone, and their presence, which she could sense earlier, had faded. There was no sign of the Great Beast. Annoyance filled the faces of the crew as they looked around, then back at Baay Badu's impassive gaze.

Ignoring her own labored breathing, Khami'sissa looked up at Javuiili and mentally calculated her course across the sky, as her Baaba had taught her. Twisting her insides, her anxiety grew as she realized it was well past the middle of the night. The solstice would be over soon, and their only lead had gone dry.

Could the Great Beast have come and gone already? Was she back in Eh'wauizo, the ancestral plane that Khami'sissa had no idea how to penetrate?

An icy breath behind her ears. The edges of her eyes darkened as veins twitched and dilated across her temples. Fervently, Khami'sissa willed her heartbeat to slow. She was too exposed. She could *not* be having a vision right now.

She was so focused on calming her senses that she almost missed it when the weasel-voice hunter lunged at Baay Badu, grabbing the collar of his tunic and lifting him up.

"What game are you playing?" the hunter sputtered in Baay Badu's face, eyes wide with fury. The others twitched and their hands flew to their weapons, either to stop the man or back up his violence. "We should have killed that thing by now and be gone with its horns! You promised us you could find it!"

"Ado'olo is right," the boy with the braids growled, finding his voice above the waterfall's uproar. He squinted and pointed his spear at Baay Badu. “We’re not leaving without the horns, and if we don’t find the beast…”

For a moment, his threat left a heavy silence between them. Baay Badu seemed tranquil, but the lines creased in his forehead and his hand tight around the handle of his club said otherwise.

Her own pulse grew restless. Alarm rendered every one of her muscles stiff, because, for the first time, she realized she didn’t know what to do. Even if the party eventually found the Great Beast, there was no way Khami’sissa could slip under the noses of such honed fighters and talk to her. She had, vaguely, counted on her ability to go unnoticed, quiet and merging with the shadows. But that was out of habit. It would work against neighbors that never paid her any mind, not against these people.

It scared her, how they were so prone to turn against one of their own. How violence electrified the air between them as they began arguing, with no care of being heard by predators. How easily they could wield that violence against her…

The vision pressed her eyelids shut, demanding to be beheld. It constricted her throat. It didn’t bulge.

Out of fear, she bristled and scoured her backpack for the remaining pa'affatan pods…

She had moved too much.

A hand grabbed her shoulders. Sharp fingernails dug into soft skin. Still wrestling with the vision, Khami'sissa opened her eyes and met those of the woman, dark and focused.

"Who in Yikoh are you?"

Holding Khami'sissa by the back of her hair, the woman dragged her against the hard stone to where everyone stood, their attention fully directed at her.

Tears swelled in Khami'sissa's eyes for the bruises she was collecting and the pressure building between her temples. Fear sealed her lips shut – feigning bravado was useless. The harsh truth was that she was only a frail girl in the face of danger. Alone, away from her home. She wished she'd heeded Baaba's words. Now, he was too far away to protect her.

"Answer the question, girl! Why are you here?" the one named Ado'olo asked with spittle flying from his mouth. His breath stank of beer, filling her with nausea, and his brown eyes were bloodshot.

"Look at her eyes," the other boy said before her silence.

Baay Badu scrutinized her, and shivers burst up her spine. In his gaze, Khami'sissa read curiosity, first, then resolve, as he decided what he was going to do with her.

"She is menigari," he said. "She is in tune with the spirits, so she will know where the beast is."

The older man grabbed her chin with his thick, sweaty fingers and she yelped. "Tell us! Where is it?"

"I… I don't know!" Khami'sissa croaked. She was so dizzy that she wouldn't be able to stand, even if she could. From her blurry eyes, she saw the other boy emptying the contents of her backpack. He discarded the precious pa'affatan pods, a pouch of water, and fiddled with the saber she'd stolen from under her Baaba's bed.

"You lie!" Ado'olo jerked a sinewy arm behind him as if he was going to slap her, but Baay Badu pushed him away. He snatched the saber from the boy's hand and crouched, pressing the bronze blade against the pulse in Khami'sissa's neck. A droplet of blood trickled down the blade and his sneer reflected on it.

"Tell me, girl," Baay Badu whispered, "or I will make you regret wandering away from your mother's wrapper."

Tears cascaded freely down her scarified cheeks. She was crying out of fear, of anger, of the pain now ringing in her head and her helplessness.

They should have been wary of harming her. But superstition didn't weaken their determination, and Khami'sissa couldn't pretend she was sacred and close to the spirits. Even on a night like the solstice, she couldn't sense the Veil or summon the beings that inhabited it. She knew nothing. She was useless.

Baay Badu was as hopeless as she was. He wanted to use her to find the Great Beast in light of his own failure at doing so; it was his own way not to lose control of his crew. If it meant maintaining the respect they had for him and their goals' achievement, he did not fear violence.

No one was going to save her. She'd have to save herself.

Timidly, her own resolve built up from deep within her bones. Khami'sissa was doing this to prove to Baaba that she wasn't fragile, that she deserved answers about the anomalies that tormented her. She didn't need to bridle or mask them: they were a part of *her*.

She deserved to be free to embrace them.

When Baay Badu's crew twitched on their toes and yelled at him to force answers out of her, she sensed his fingers harden on the blade and shift it toward her eyes.

But when the vision bucked against her temples, Khami'sissa shrieked as it flared the pain up to its paroxysm and drenched her eyes in darkness. Despite the agony, she let it stop the breath in her lungs. She let it drown her in the sounds that were familiar, now.

The answers were within her all along, and she let that symphony carry her, far, far away.

* * *

A hum settled in her chest as Khami'sissa opened her eyes. She was floating in a buzzing void, which had no beginning and no end. Filling her with vertigo, glacial currents swam up and down – threads of this world's fabric that disobeyed any physical law she knew. To her, it smelled like the spicy thiouraye that Baaba had once bought from a wandering merchant – Baaba would burn the fragrant incense on special occasions, like her birthday.

This was Eh'wauizo, plane of spirits and ancestors. It had called her for so long, but she was too confused, too *afraid*, to allow it to welcome her.

Facing her was a woman. Tall, thrice her height, dressed in dark leather that molded over her every muscle. Short, thick locks framed her round face, cheeks scarred like her own, and eyes the color of secret gold.

That woman. She was the Great Beast.

Twin shadows shimmered at her sides. They observed Khami'sissa also, radiating with quiet amusement.

Khami'sissa knew who they were.

"Diarr'aja." The woman greeted her in a booming voice.

"Keita'ka."

The woman's last name had flown out of her lips, so naturally.

"Diarr'aja." The Great Beast greeted her again.

"Keita'ka," she answered.

"Diarr'aja. I have called you three times."

Her voice struggled to rise from her throat as Khami'sissa basked in her might, shaken by all the power leaking from her in waves of deep sound.

She trembled in fright, for an even greater shadow hovered over the woman: four-legged, with long horns growing straight from the sides of its head.

Revealing themselves, the smaller shadows turned into light. Two women, identical in the mischievous smile curling up their lips, in the silky black curls pouring down their back, and in their silver-hued skin.

"Keita'ka," Khami'sissa finally said. Her voice grew loud, steady, as the sound fueled her confidence. "Great Beast. Daughter of the Buffalo Woman. Mistress of the Arcane Sounds. Esteemed Companion of the Spirit Moons. Ko'lon'kan."

Khami'sissa genuflected as best as she could, with no ground to support her feet, saluting Ko'lon'kan, Vuiili-ku and Vuiili-ki. "Naguu-àll, Echoed in Moonlight."

They were pleased, all smiling brightly at her. Drawing her gaze, the spirit moons seemed to taunt Khami'sissa. Their skin rippled in magnetic waves, enthralling her, forcing her to perceive their elusive beauty.

"Daughter, you are in danger," Ko'lon'kan suddenly said, her gaze softening.

Khami'sissa bowed her head, yes, her stomach heavy.

"They're going after you." She blew a quivering breath. "For your horns."

Ko'lon'kan looked over Khami'sissa's shoulder, silent for a moment. The shadow behind her bristled as if chasing away insects.

"Do you know what they want them for? Have you listened to their hearts, menigari?"

Flinching, Khami'sissa wrung her hands together. The spirit moons swam, elegant and swift as if underwater, and exchanged places, their black eyes never leaving Khami'sissa.

"Great Beast, I'm not really good at being a menigari. I don't know much, my Baaba keeps me secret, I..." Words cascaded out of her lips, troubling the deep sound around her. "I'm alone. Baaba doesn't want me learning more about menigari ways. He wants a normal life for me, he wants to protect me, he—"

"What do *you* want, Khami'sissa?" the spirit moons said in unison, a soft, eerie voice that resonated inside her mind. A touch of knowing, a touch of passion.

Khami'sissa still couldn't breathe, but she realized she didn't need to. She couldn't speak, but her thoughts, her desires, were now clear in her eyes.

Conjured out of nothingness, they handed her a tambi'ibinn. The wood-carved flute was longer than her forearm, warm to the touch. She caressed its alabaster surface, lifted it to her lips.

She played the tone that her soul dictated, alive with the emotions at her core. What she couldn't put into words: her loneliness, how she longed for a mother whose face she'd long forgotten. The love she had for Baaba and the surety of his arms, no matter how suffocating they could be.

Khami'sissa lay herself bare for them to see: her insecurities, her fears, all of it.

It unlocked something.

Realization dawned on her as she pulled her lips from the instrument, feeling how another part of herself was now uncovered. She was not only menigari, in truth.

She was *more*.

Her heartbeat went feral as the spirit moons circled her lanky frame and Ko'lon'kan laid her forehead against hers.

Then Khami'sissa found herself gifted new knowledge. Waves and waves of deep and shrill sound infused in her aura, pouring from sacred kalabash to parched host.

She wasn't alone anymore.

* * *

When Khami'sissa awoke, she kept her eyes shut for a moment. Instead of listening to the hunters who loomed over her and kicked her sides so she would wake, she found a way through the sound that Naguu-àll, Echoed in Moonlight had graced her with. It was the one from her visions, which she'd run away from for so long. Now, it was hers.

She listened to their hearts, and what she heard made her muscles tremor with anger.

These four weren't hunters. Their bone bracelets marked them as Sâkoukou: a secret guild of assassins whose ancestors had once lived on a now dead planet. Led by Baay Badu, this particular group acted on its own.

Khami'sissa parted further through their sound auras, as if plucking the cords of a musical instrument. She heard the crackle of long tobacco pipes as they lit, the rustling of fabric as hands wrapped a headscarf around a regal head. A guttural voice, singing, intertwined with the beating of sacred drums, generated a visceral magic that was key to her people's prosperity. The singer had iridescent, purple eyes.

Understanding flooded her as she tugged the song back into herself. These people wanted Ko'lon'kan's horns so they could target the chief of a secluded tribe, far up north, who was also a menigari. They would use the horns to harvest the chief's aura – her voice, her *life* – and use all that power for themselves. Doing so would kill her, certainly, but none of them cared.

Their leader had done it before. All he'd committed perverted his aura. Like poison, he'd infiltrated the inner circles of chiefs and regents, time and time again. She quivered as sounds lingered around her eardrums: the swift slashing of a knife against a child's throat, another gasping for breath as poison curdled their blood inside their veins... Baay Badu had been around, killing nobles and their children, framing rival groups for the murders so perfectly that no one would ever suspect him.

Khami'sissa opened her eyes. They must have radiated revulsion so strong that the Sâkoukou took a step back, then frowned. A metallic tang coated the inside of her mouth and when she spat, it was a lump of blood. Like a newborn calf, she staggered upward, uncertain of her legs.

She knew they could sense the strangeness all around her, but they seized their spears instead of fleeing. They surrounded her, bent forward in offense. Baay Badu bared his teeth like an animal and swirled the club in his hand, but Khami'sissa was unfazed.

Her fear of them, of what she was, was gone. She relished in the taste of the familiar humming, rolling it over her tongue as it bubbled up her throat. She braided the silver songs around her larynx and knew that, back in Eh'wauizo, the spirit moons were watching.

Khami'sissa hunched low and grunted, inhumanely, as pain exploded through her temporal bones. Her opponents didn't realize, at first. With their spears, the three of them charged her – Ado'olo and the woman, out of violence, the boy, also out of fear.

Their leader stood back as a bellow exploded out of Khami'sissa's throat and sent them flying, landing on the wet rocks with a sick crunch. Her own bones cracked and twisted in new shapes, and unspeakable agony tore through her every limb. It was a glorious torment, befitting the rebirth of her true self. She bellowed again, so loud that the waterfall stopped its course and receded up from whence it came.

Long, silver horns curved up and away from her elongating face – now growing into a snout with fuming nostrils – and illuminated the clearing, interwoven with streaks of energy. She landed heavy hooves on the muddy ground, blowing hot air from her nostrils and shaking her head. Blood shot from the sides where the horns had pierced outward her skin. She set her gaze on the shape of Baay Badu before her, kneeling not in submission, but to avoid being blown away. His shoulders tensed with menace as he looked back at her, at the slick oil of her coat and the horns, buzzing with power.

Khami'sissa *was* the Great Beast. She embodied her Sound, floating alongside it like the white and yolk of an egg. Ko'lon'kan's might was hers.

And her rage, oh. It was screaming to strike.

Too fast for her to process, the assassin raced forward, leaped, and thwacked the tender spot where the horns emerged. She stumbled backward, grunting and dizzy, as she loomed over him. Khami'sissa flapped her ears in anger and opened her muzzle to bellow, but the sound cut short.

Hints of yellow flew past her head and buried themselves in her flanks. Swinging her tail, she kicked where last Baay Badu stood, but he had moved already, holding his crossbow with one hand. A sickening grin twisted his lips as pain bloomed all over her body. Unlike the headaches she endured as a human, this one burned and flayed her nerves, her muscles. She could not allay it.

She fell to the ground and rolled in fury, but the poison only worked faster through her veins.

"Akakikikaka venom," the spirit moons hissed in her mind, their voices overlapping.

"He means to make you suffer before you die. The horns would hold more power, then," they said, as the burning intensified, blinding her.

"It's too much!" Khami'sissa and Ko'lon'kan both screamed.

"Spirits know nothing of pain," they answered.

Fur began to rot, exposing turgescent flesh across her rump. Flat teeth bit through her tongue, hard, and she tasted blood again. Her eyes rolled in their sockets as she rose and bucked, trying to trample her attacker, but he kept evading her, chest heaving and eyes haunted. She wanted to gore him, to make him suffer as much as she did. "But humans know it all too well. Khami'sissa, you must tame the pain!"

Their command brimmed with urgency. The luminescence cracking across her horns dimmed. The Sound inside of her was dying – she couldn't let it. Instead of releasing the Sound like a weapon outside of her parched throat, she gathered it in her lungs, let herself swallow the pain as she had done before. Guided by the spirit moons, she delivered small pockets of sound to each of her cells. Like her pa'affatan pods, the humming strained out all corruption, leaving her breathless, bleeding.

Malice shone in Baay Badu's eyes as he shook his curls and pressed his fingers around his machete, mistaking her stillness for defeat. When he came near, she waited until he lifted his arms, ready to strike, and shot her legs forward, hitting his chest and pinning him to the ground.

His ribs cracked under her hooves, as they dug on either side of his upper abdomen. She inched closer than she wouldn't have dared at the beginning of this night, her muscular body rippling with waves of hatred for the scum that trembled beneath her.

Baay Badu opened his mouth. Energy cracked within the silver horns and scattered through her brain, settling in her vocal cords...

Khami'sissa released the Sound in a thunderous bellow, until the earth rumbled and the rocks cracked. His skull exploded, like a ripe fruit, and his skin peeled clean off his flesh and shattered bones.

"Breathe," the spirit moons said, flatly.

Brain matter coated her muzzle. She wanted to scream again, to release the newfound violence she felt burning in her. She looked away from the corpse and toward the other criminals: their chests rose and fell despite their wounds. She wanted to hurt them more, quivered at the thought of allowing the predator within her to fully take control...

Vuiili-ki and Vuiili-ku appeared simultaneously, leaving a trail of Eh'wauizo's winds behind them.

"They have yet to take a life," one began.

"And you will find them, if they ever do," the other finished.

Their touch was soothing against the fetid sores that the poison had left on her. Through thin lips, they whistled a spell, their eyes pleading with her to repeat it.

Other beings materialized all around her: tiny creatures with midnight skin, eyes round and doll-like, their small feet facing backward. Their giggles rose in the air as they fluttered across her body, splashing it with cooling water and washing away the rest of the poison.

Khami'sissa hummed in lower frequency, matching the tune that the spirit moons were teaching her and directing it at the human shapes before her. In Eh'wauizo, they'd shown her the truth about herself: her Sound's innate frequency had always matched Ko'lon'kan's own. If activated with the right humming, which she'd have to find out by herself, it would allow her to shift into buffalo form. Only during the Summer Solstice would she be able to tap into Ko'lon'kan's spiritual power, to tamper with sound auras as the Great Beast did.

Kiy-soppiku was what the spirit moons had named individuals with her ability. Another part of her, perhaps the truest, that she couldn't fear.

The horns buzzed once more, fueling her with energy, as Ko'lon'kan receded and let her emerge forward, feeling the auras of the remaining Sâkoukou like strings against imaginary fingers. Shifting, adjusting, here and there, she thought of the rage that the spirit moons radiated and hummed a parcel of it. She detached and played with the memories embedded in their auras as they began to wake, holding their heads between their hands and watching her in horror.

The horns cracked, emanating one final blow of light when she finished reshaping their auras.

All sounds faded, and pain burst anew as the horns disappeared under her scalp. Under Javuiili's dimming light, her bones broke, and found replacement. Fur recoiled back into skin and Khami'sissa lost consciousness as Naguu-àll, Echoed in Moonlight departed the physical realm.

* * *

It ends with an embrace, cold against her skin. Ko'lon'kan's humming has settled in her ribs. She wears the fury in twin crescent tattoos over her mastoid bones, so they can keep whispering their names into her ears, so she doesn't forget. Knowledge rests at the base of her skull. Sitting before the waterfall, she hums it as she rinses the assassin's blood from her hands. The others groan awake, exchanging confused looks at each other and at the woman who is ignoring them. They ought to make new memories, so that good deeds can replace the evil Baay Badu had drawn them into.

Khami'sissa will be watching them, and all the Baay Badus in this world. The Summer Solstice will come, inevitably. Again, she will become the Great Beast, and she will be their doom.

Separation

Stephen Embleton

voiceless, i can't scream
a maze of caves and tunnels—
silence is monster

*In **Stephen Embleton**'s tale of silent terror, the enemy is not quite as it seems.*

Wezébuizé is trapped in a prison he can't see, hear or feel. He has fallen prey to the dreaded rá'shnururu, a monster that has taken many of his people on Órino-Rin to their deaths. Separated from his wife and child, he fears he will never leave the monster's lair. He hangs mid-air, slowly dying, as the rá'shnururu siphons his sound. And then he discovers the creature is not alone...

Welcome to "Separation".

I.

YOU DON'T need magic to know when you're not alone. You don't need to be a seer to know when something's watching. Though blind and deaf to the world, you still know it's not the temperature shifts that chill the hairs on your body. You feel it as an extra sense.

I feel it as terror, beloved Dzébelele. Not for what detestable, invisible entity holds me, but for the uncertainty of whether I, Wezébuizé, your husband, will return to you three, or hold you again. Terror at the thought of what you're suffering at this moment. I don't know where I am, or where you and Hmbalele are. Were I to wrest myself free, where would I go in this dark maze of caves and tunnels?

Dizziness comes in waves. I know I am tethered like the tarp over our decrepit saltshack whipped by the desert winds, but feel myself drifting away into the vast blackness of this echoless, subterranean world. It's not from the lack of water. I managed to gulp, choking and spluttering, from the small rivulet running not far into the cave. I had our two kalabash gourds filled when my world went utterly black with pain.

All hope of bringing any water to you both is lost in this hollow earth.

Speaking to you as I am, silently in my mind, could be my deepest soul-sound telling me the inevitable, the unimaginable: that you have passed over into Eh'wauizo to be with our ancestors.

How long will this tormenting beast hold me captive here before I meet you there?

The sensation returns. It sets my heart racing.

As a predator, I have watched prey. The communion between Our Mother God, the beasts and us in the ritual of the hunt is far more thrilling than the toil of the salt mines of our laboring nation. Our arrows are meant for food; we are not a warring or defending people. Who would want our barren, saline realm?

My senses are attuned. Something is watching.

I shudder, thinking how it stalked me as I wandered through these caves. Now, here I sit as prey, ensnared and vulnerable and waiting.

The Soundless is far more than I ever could have imagined, Dzébelele. I am immovable in this void, barely able to draw breath.

No sound. No vibration. Unnerving and dizzying. I have stopped biting down in the hopes of hearing my teeth crunch through my aching jawbone. No sensation of my heartbeat – the pressure of the Soundless engulfs my heart's dull pulsing in my ears. Soundless but not painless.

Voiceless, I cannot scream, *Pain be damned!* Nor can I utter your name, to hear the magic of your word and the warmth it brings, rising from the depths of my body.

Dzébelele!

* * *

I am grateful to Our Mother that you're not here with me in this black, black cave of silence. Only on those rain-drenched nights of the monsoon, out on the salt pans, do we ever come close to this coal-black darkness. If not for a dim sliver of light falling down the rockface from an unknown fissure in the earth, growing noticeably brighter since I woke, I would be convinced I was no longer in the realm of the living. A soul hanging in Eh'wauizo, unsure of what happens next.

For all my unbelieving, even ridicule at times, at our people's superstitions, here I am, entrapped in the Soundless by what I can only imagine is a wretched rá'shnururu of our folklore. A god or demon, depending on who tells the tale or what moral they want to impart.

* * *

I awoke for the first time with the remnants of a nightmare, or memories of a scream so loud my ears were bleeding; a terror so real my shoulder muscles jerked as I tried to thrash about, wrench myself free of the monster crawling through my mind. But something held me fast. A throbbing pain washed over me, and I sensed I had been unconscious for only a brief time.

Now, the smell of water on rock fills the air. Without sound I cannot tell how close it is. How deep am I snatched from the surface?

The creature has bound me in what, I cannot fathom. Unknown restraints, like nothing I have ever felt before, grip me as if between boulders. Mud-molded and enveloping every inch of my body, pushing. The drying, white-gray mud of our salt pans after the rain ceremony can hold an object immovable. This is the same. Aching jaw, neck, back. My entire body, frozen in a contorted pose, is pain and discomfort submerged in a packed, unyielding mass. Breathing is an effort.

I shift my gaze with all the effort I can summon, but my head is immovable. My right shoulder is in view, but none of my bonds. The throb intensifies, bringing echoes of when the blackout hit. When something hit me.

I recall that brief instant of pain.

The sound before the pain.

My brain is trying to catch up, trying to make sense of everything while something squeezes it from all sides.

I keep seeing things. Flashes in the dark. I wish someone was coming to deliver me. But nothing comes of it. No sound reaches my ears. And yet, I sense something out there, something coming.

It could be my mind playing tricks on me in this otherworldly cave. These curved walls with sweeping striations from the darkness above, all the way down below, give it a strange, mesmerizing pattern, as if a giant, clawed creature has scraped away the rock and granite.

Below my right shoulder, where I know my hand and arm are stuck, I summon the strength to pull and push with all my might. There is a minuscule give to my restraints, but I relent, wheezing for breath. I try again. The pale tips of my salt-stained fingers come into view. My hand is there. A little bit more…

Our Mother God!

The sight overcomes me. Disbelief and exhaustion.

How is it that nothing holds me? An invisible force grips me suspended in mid-air in this chamber. My breathing is labored and a cold sweat covers me as I fight the fits and impulses of my muscles to be free.

If I move my arm, like pushing against a boulder, some invisible magic pummeling from all sides slowly impels me back again. I am drained.

What I thought was light, those flashes in the dark, are behind my eyes. Like rubbing them too roughly, pushing on my eyeballs, sprouting dark patches and swirling light bursts. The Soundless must be a force, a magic so primal, from the birth of our worlds, which holds me by invisible tendrils like a web of kalabash ropes. It is the very Soundless holding me.

I wish I could wield my spear, summon our magic, compel some power, any power, and free myself now. But, in this soundless void, conjuring sound magic is impossible. Brute force is not an option.

With this knowledge, as I grow accustomed to my fate, I would have hoped the dread would subside. In truth, beloved, I am ashamed to say, at the slightest sensation, a hint of hidden motion in the dark void of the cave, anticipating what comes next holds its own terror.

The air in the dark chamber shifts.

Give me a face! Show me something! Any hideous monster is more bearable than what I hold in my mind. My imagination breeds the most terrifying: scales, claws, fangs, blood, eyes of hate and fire.

The monster is the silence.

Pressure, like a fist or elbow, presses down on my right shoulder so forcibly it will dislocate. Another on my left forearm. Now others on my thigh and ankle, my lower back and neck. A seventh on my forehead, and finally my jaw clamps shut. Something is on me. A disembodied force.

I am indelibly connected to this animal, touching it, touching me. Does it read my pulse, anticipate my movements, sense my thoughts?

Though insubstantial, I expect it to leap out into reality in some unspeakable, savage form.

My eardrums press in.

A quick shift in the atmosphere compresses the wind out of me. The soundless is holding me tighter. No, it's the creature holding me, a magic grip so tight my blood is turning to stone.

An icy dread overcomes me.

Something, a warmth, cups half my face, and then the draining sensation comes with a new darkness, enveloping me.

II.

I wake once more, with a sense of depletion and the after-image of a nightmare lingering: our sweet boy, Gwa'jaja's body covered in dry, white sand. Our rock rabbit, not yet eight years old.

My head rigid, I reflexively glance up, eyes straining, imagining his shallow grave above me now.

This strange chamber is becoming darker, the pale patch of filtered light dwindling like my hope. That retching sensation rises at the thought of more time passing between us, beloved.

Have you yet forgiven me for trying to stop you feeding our daughter with your milk?

I remember how tears streaked dark lines down your dusty, pale face as you screamed you would allow her to feed off your dead corpse. You uttered my name – *Wezébuizé* – in disbelief and disdain, adding to the heart-wrenching impact I still feel, and the courage I didn't possess.

Here I hang, useless, something slowly eating me. Not skin from flesh, or flesh from bone, but my soul-sound essence. Whatever hope of using magic to escape these bonds, to put this creature down, is ebbing out of me. I will be no more than an echo, an empty vessel that once held my soul-sound.

I think of our elderly, succumbing to soul-sound sickness, their feeble minds and vacant eyes glossed over and myopic, staring off into the hazy horizon.

As I wait with dread in this hideous noiselessness for the relentless rá'shnururu's return, I wonder what shriek or moan my soul-sound will emit as it depletes? Is this predator replenishing its own soul-sound with mine?

It may be a fitting end to my questioning mind. I wanted to be more than a salt miner at the mercy of the gods of rain. I couldn't wait for another season for Our Mother God to piss down on us a trifling water nourishment for our meager crops.

I was reckless in my assertion that our small family could make this trek. My father's protests fell on my unhearing ears as we left our people for something better. My stubbornness led us to this. Gwa'jaja is in the ground, and you and Hmbalele are out there, exposed.

The nightmare after-image of our son's body covered in dry, white sand persists. Along with it the tingle of my raw fingertips, scraping the stony topsoil away as deep as I could dig, while you nursed Hmbalele at your breasts.

And in that moment, as I buried our son in that barren earth, I hoped I would never have to bury again. Here I am, one mind telling me you're no longer here and I'll not get to bury you, after all. I long to hear your sounds, any sounds, all sounds. The good and the bad. Sound engulfing me. My senses alive. The sounds of life and even death are better than nothing.

Days after our water ran out, you, beloved Dzébelele, whispered a hoarse plea for me not to go to the caves. All the fresh water we could imagine? I had to try.

For what, in the end? When you pass below the dusty horizon into Eh'wauizo, will you pass by me down here? Will you grant me a glance of pity, and look upon the shame I hold in my eyes?

My fingers ache the feeling of scratched earth. Could I claw my way to you from this cave? I must get free. It may be too late, but I must try.

As I fade, as nightmares overcome me, I hope for guidance from our ancestors in their realm. If only to redeem myself and fight to get water, cupped in my hands, back to you both before it is too late – because another mind tells me you're still alive and waiting. I have called on Our Mother, begged for aid, and my mind is flooded with doubts and insecurities of whether this monster is an aspect of Her? Is it Her who I have irked beyond reason in this life?

My mind is boundless. My tormentor when the monster is not around.

* * *

Wait!

Something is thrumming in my ears.

Is that a sound? Impossible. Perhaps my blood shifting pressure around my body. The sound is familiar.

A pall of sweat cools my skin. Hairs bristle. I am lightheaded from the exhilaration, and attempt to catch my breath.

Again! A shift in the room's atmosphere, but this time to my left.

I flex my arms and legs, ineffectual but something gives. As if in response, the pressure around my body intensifies in a bone-crunching instant and I freeze rigid. Can't breathe. Something constricts me like a monstrous snake every time air expels from my body. Nothing coming back in.

I am fading again. Just as my body gives in, as that oppressive darkness threatens to envelop me, the pressure abruptly falters.

I wrestle for air, blinking in the gloom. Whatever that held me in a death-grip, released its hold on me before I suffocated.

It knew!

With slackened restraints I glance around. There's nothing to see, the spherical chamber barely discernible.

Just then, the constriction hits once again, and in that brief, familiar moment before I black out, there's the depleting sensation, coupled with that thrum in my ears.

* * *

Blood pounds through my veins, beating my eardrums with a torrent rippling through me, its power coursing steadily; the rhythm wanes, almost imperceptibly, then builds like distant drummers.

My breaking point came on the last ceremony we attended as a family, while the first monsoon inundated our salt pans. Laden with as much water as we could carry, I took the four of us out of our people's territory. I separated us, extracted us.

"Salt courses through us. The mud is part of us." My father's words echo in my mind. I remember how he pulled me around by my arm. "We are the one constant which cannot be detached from this land, Wezébuizé."

"Our time is running out, father!" I hissed in his face, wet with rain and tears. I raised my fist between us and shouted over the incessant storm. "Our hands toil the shallows of the ground. Our magic separates the water. Our feet carry our loads. It's an endless cycle!" I shoved him away and picked up my bundle.

"You chose to turn your back on the magic that resides deep within you, my boy." He watched me, helpless.

"For what purpose?" I shouted to the raging night skies. "I have witnessed far too many of our people, whether from old age or our grizzled existence, burn on our pyres under the stars, noticing how our hands and feet are the last to catch fire and incinerate up to the heavens and Our Mother. The white mineral dust,"

I rubbed my fingers together, "so fine, hardened over years on the salt pans around our most primitive of tools in this world."

"Our Mother's bounty—"

"No." I stopped him. "Every year, emboldened by Our Mother's *merciful* bounty, we add more to our people's numbers, more than succumb to the Great White Tsadiri'Tdidi – this salt pan that's a living thing and it consumes. It consumes *us*. Yet we expand. It's little wonder we've become more reliant on the southern traders to survive, when they dare venture into our inhospitable lands."

Fantastical knowledge from the traders consumed me. I yearned to hear more, to see more, reach for the other planets and the wider universe out there. Even the planet with the soundless regions like ours.

Father was always wary, distrusting anyone he perceived to be looking down on us. "The traders think we are backward, yet they come to us," he said defiantly.

"Arrogance," was the last word I said to him as I led us towards the stormy horizon.

* * *

That thrum again, shifting. My dark world swirls as I fight memories but hold onto sounds.

Two ceremonial drummers stand in the near distance in the gloom, their mud-white skin on fire with light and sound as they slam their palms against the rain-wet drumskins of the hollowed-out giant kalabashes. One of our Great Separation ceremonies has begun.

In the monsoon-drenched salt pans we gather, the tsamanărari and those skilled in the sound magic that separates the water from the salty mud. Collectively we separate, to quench us all.

Mingling with the thrum of the kalabash drums we chant: “Sa’xhamimi.”

“Our people’s fresh waters.”

We repeat the word, *Sa-xhaa-mimi*, and it rings upward in rhythm with the drumbeats.

Sa’xhamimi.

The drummers are closer. I am younger, smaller than their lean, towering frames full of muscle as I step forward for a better view. The woman, thick hair flailing down around her shoulders and bouncing against her thighs, moves to her beat.

I laugh with my friends, caught up in the maelstrom of the rain celebrations, as downpours fill the salt pans.

The spectacle of the tsamanãrari magic is alive to me, to every villager, transcending time and connecting with our ancestors before us.

We stand in the milky, briny mud, our black skin and matted hair rich with the mineral-rich soils. Young and old sway to the drumbeat, twirling, chanting, and raising the magic into the twilight skies.

Two drummers flank either side of me, and pound the same beat on their giant kalabashes, transporting me, for a moment, into a silent realm.

The rain, the mud. Writhing black and white bodies. Magic sparkling in the air. And yet silence like a thick mud in my ears.

I stare, bewildered, at the drummer to my left, her thudding pounds through my body, soundless. Echoing this sensation, the soft, rising mud ripples around me with the impacts of the beats, but with an eerie stillness. Was the sound too loud for my ears to discern? No. It was something else altogether.

I panic, startled and lightheaded. I stumble backwards, wide eyes flitting from one drummer to the other, moving away from their silent void.

In an instant my world engulfs me in a turbulent roar as my senses readjust to the recognizable sounds of the ceremony.

Now, the memory of it all wells up in me, as if the rains filling the salt pans are bringing with them a rising tide of memories and understanding just out of reach.

The white mud is rising, engulfing, hardening each time I wiggle. A mass oozes through the soil towards me. Closer it creeps below the surface. The constricting grows. A torrent blasts my skin, raindrops sharpened like a thousand arrowheads.

I wake in the darkness, out of breath and frozen.

* * *

Something is vibrating the space around me.

A single drum beat itches in my ears.

My mind races. The odd markings carved into the cave. I think of the pale mud rippling around me, and the sound waves emanating from the drummers… just like the striations on these rock walls!

There is sound in this soundless cave.

This is no region devoid of sound. For how long has sound pulsed within these walls, pounding, etching and carving its patterns into this unyielding rock?

I now know the rá'shnururu is creating an emptiness to focus its feeding of my soul-sound. A near-perfect defense mechanism in a world of magic. Oh, beloved Dzébelele, our people have believed we are weaker, feebly at the mercy of these cunning fiends.

How many lost to the wilds of the caves, desperate to find these sweet waters, captured as victims of the rá'shnururu, unable to return to us? I will return. If not to you, my love, then to my father and our people to tell them.

The silence is not real.

In here, our arrows are useless. Bone and muscle are useless. But not our magic, after all, if only I can summon it.

What did our tsamanãrari teach us on our first day?

Our true magic is in the chest and throat, children, not in utterances of elaborate words and complex phrases, from forgetful mouths. The least effort, beyond the mind, within your body.

From the pit of my stomach, my rage seethes and boils and retches. A guttural sensation rumbles in my thrashing gut. It builds and moves into my chest, hovering like a sonorous stone in my throat.

Father!

Light flashes behind my clenched eyelids.

I am looking at my father. He's younger than I am now. Skin dark and taut against his lithe frame. A young father to a boy so stubborn.

I am a child, maybe three or four years old, holding his hand. Bounding along and waving to my friends eager to see the watermancers for the first time.

Only at the right age did we receive our first experience of the magic that helped our people survive for so long.

I'd forgotten, dear Dzébelele, how truly magical it was. Is.

I struggle in my restraints, pushing, pulling.

I'll be different with Hmbalele.

Is she…

A force leaps into my world, striking me bodily in my restraints.

I thrust with all my might and, rather than that oppressive pull and smothering, my fist connects with something material; invisible but substantial.

This is no god! Neither an ungodly creature. It is real.

As if in response to my thoughts, it's upon me again.

The shock of it stuns me. My arm shifts enough to claw at the force crushing around my neck, my throat, threatening to snap in on itself. What I touch is, at first, a coolness. Yet it is a live, rippling texture, but with a warmth emanating from within. I reel inside my rigid body, nauseated by the idea of a strange monstrosity in my grasp.

The moment's hesitation gives the primeval force time to drain me of my consciousness.

The monster isn't the silence, I think as I fade. The monster is *in* the silence.

III.

My chamber is a formless, impenetrable darkness. All light has left me.

Dizziness comes in waves. I am fading again. In my mind, a scream.

You scream, dear Dzébelele. Twice. You screamed each precious child into this world.

That sound reverberates in my ears. Moving. Behind me.

A primal scream building and shaking everything around it. It's the sound of a creature giving birth.

* * *

Light. A day has passed. Time I cannot get back.

There is a strange, vague warmth to this cold, damp place. Not from the light, but things around me.

It is all clear to me in this dark place, that I am surrounded by infant rá'shnururu ready to be delivered.

This creature is surviving, as you did, beloved, as a parent fully ready to sacrifice herself for her own offspring to survive.

* * *

My father released his firm grip on my hand, and I darted to the front of the crowd to my friends, settling down on our haunches. Adults shushed our boisterous noise. We waited in elbowed-silence, eager for the spectacle of a recent graduate tsamanārari, a watermancer.

I was transfixed. At first by the familiar sound emanating from her. Then by the crackle of the magic she so effortlessly wielded.

The tsamanārari placed two wide alabaster bowls on the dusty ground and stood with flourish. The splashing, milky water in the left bowl subsided. The other bowl was empty. A gentle hum rose in her chest. She inhaled whispery whistles and exhaled booming growls, though her mouth barely moved. Her fluid-like fingers twirled and swirled in a circular motion. On the ground, the bowl with the water rippled and stirred in a single direction. The first signs of a whirlpool, the center point rising up.

The water tubed itself upward, arcing waist high to the empty bowl. The liquid emulated the tsamanãrari's spiraling index finger and undulated in time with her vocalizations. She was controlling the water, its shape and direction.

Twinkling white sparks. Above the hum of the tsamanãrari's magic, the crackling sounds grew louder. The sparks splattered out of the water-column, and fell into the swirling water below. The single spiral-arc thickened as more water flowed into the filling bowl. Water dwindled in the one bowl, rose and became more translucent in the other.

"Salt!" shouted a girl, and someone scolded her.

A murmur of awe reverberated through the small crowd.

"Sa'xhamimi," whispered someone nearby.

Then another, "Sa'xhamimi," louder this time.

I leaned in and whispered to myself, “Sa’xhamimi.”

Sure enough, the sparks were salt crystals extracting from the water, magically exuding back into the drying bowl.

Rather than the exuberant chant of the Separation Ceremony I would witness in the years to come, the crowd maintained a low, respectful tone for the graduate. Within moments, as the tsamanărari hummed, the last of the water plopped into the clear bowl, and dry salt crystals cupped the other bowl.

I was proud of my people. Proud of our magic. In awe of the tsamanărari, our sacred teachers.

* * *

The tsamanărari words whisper in my ear.

The least effort, beyond the mind, within your body.

For too long I have felt alone among my people. But it was a self-imposed aloneness. I wanted to find myself by leaving, when instead, I can find myself anywhere.

I must exist for a purpose.

Movement. Something has entered the chamber.

A rush of energy flushes me. My senses are alive. Blood pounding in my ears, its rhythm within me hammering like firm, dusty hands on kalabash drumskins.

The creature's movement is fluid, gentle, caressing. It's a mother's movement. Her innate instinct. Like her, our magic is survival.

We hold sacred the relationship between predator and prey.

She spirals closer.

Let me take your soul-sound to the spirit world! I scream in my head.

My rage rises once again, but this time I suppress the retching, convulsing sensation and bile threatening to burn my throat. I allow the guttural sensation to rumble up through my body, deep within where her dulling force cannot penetrate.

The outer silence persists. I can feel my sound.

She is on me with a staggering force. She compresses me from all sides, perhaps by her invisible limbs or her overwhelming magic.

My own sound magic builds and moves into my chest. It hovers in my throat for only a moment, a sonorous stone that's a reverberating rock, a booming boulder. It rams over my tongue and behind my gritted teeth.

It's primal. Unrefined magic from my core.

Beast against beast.

Inwardly buffeted, I feel her consuming me.

The word is forming in my throat.

Sa'xhamimi!

My sound bursts out, volcanic and brutal. It shatters silence.

The pressure on my skull is excruciating. Light flashes behind my eyes and visions swirl. She is defending herself. Defending her young.

Cracks of sound all around, jarring screams and swirling, ungodly caterwauls. Every tendon is flexed, each chord in my throat humming my magic outward.

Pain flows like a deluge.

In this cold, grim darkness, warmth. I feel sublime.

Another recognizable sound, beneath the wailing. It's your song, Beloved. The one you sang to our children. It was the magic you uttered to them. It was solace and sanctuary, swaddle and hold. Are you here with me, beloved Dzébelele?

My magic feels different. You are gone. I am diminished without you. Our magic conjoined on the day we fell in love. This day, now, it is separated.

In this bedlam, I cry. I am separating from her bonds. A glow fills the cave and I see the glimmer of my tears.

Scent of blood in the air. I collide with the rock-hard ground beneath me. The pressure on my body, the force pummeling me, is gone. Sounds rush toward me all at once. I am rising from a depth, the sound of water is not imagined. My spherical prison roars with the rushing of fresh cave water.

I know it is too late for you, my Beloved.

A blaring whine rises and falls. The haunting call I first heard when the creature took me, moments before I went unconscious. It's the sound of my nightmares.

As sudden as the rush of cacophony, her sound is gone.

Beloved. The monster is silent.

Sound Healing

Miguel O. Mitchell

The wind sang despair
Its tears filled the ears of a h'rumamah'ru
One who walks the Path of Pain
Her whole body an emotional antenna
finely tuned to distress stations

Anulaluna swam in the ripples of grief
as the spirit moons hummed into her nafsisinaf
the core of her being
She exhaled their grace
Wound sound sleeves eaves
Wiimb-o'o wawa ponyaji'yaji
Zuung'usha'sha na'fungafun'na
Wiimb-o'o wawa ponyaji'yaji
Zuung'usha'sha na'fungafun'na
Song of healing bind fast
Swirl and lock o!
Song of healing bind fast
Swirl and lock o!

Barefoot she walked through the forest
Distance measured in units of misery
Elevated anguish mapped as contours
A colorful kasukukasu bird flew above
  her mocking
"Foolish girl! Foolish girl!"

She arrived at a village of the broken
World-shaping voices stolen
Prisoners of the Silence

Screams swallowed by the void
Dressed in rags and mud
Mouths distended like panting dogs
Eyes bulging with insanity

Their wailing wavefront had escaped
the death throes of this black hole
But bring her compassion too close
their sickness would suck her dry

Only a god could shout down this emptiness
but she knew another way another way
Echoing through her core her core
find the *wiimb-o'wezi wiimb-o'wezi*
song thieves song thieves

Trek through days and nights blurred
Feet raw and crying for relief
Anulaluna dropped to her knees and wept
Child of the Forest Folk
City rich called them the witches that whine
Klii'amchawiwi of Wiimb-o'o
Worthless primitives
Her beloved people

She pulled the chords down down
The spirit moons sang her to her feet
Swaying but up
A single sweet note filled the air
A tall tand'lamkubwa appeared
Spirit deer smelling of ozone and majesty
His spiral horns changed the breeze
  to helical light
His furry ears tilted to hear the
greater whispers
"You are righteous, child," thundered his voice
"and the righteous shall ride"

Folding his hindlegs to lower himself
Anulaluna climbed the sacred beast
Astride they flew across the woods
Where hooves struck the ground
tiny stars exploded without heat

The camp of the wiimbo'wezi
Magic-gorged human ticks
Bellies swollen with bloodsong
Their own tunes tasted sour and petty
All six came out of their tents

Muffler clubs and voice nets at the ready
Laughing and pointing at the threadbare girl

The tand'lamkubwa blew away
A mass of butterflies
"Make your stand, daughter"
Anulaluna raised her head and proclaimed
"By the secret light of Vuiili-ki and Vuiili-ku
I smite you with my power!"
Her hands stretched forth
Sound tethers connected her arms to the thieves' bellies
They tore in frustration at cables of air

H'rumamah'ru kuzaaku h'rumamah'ru
Mamiv-u lao-vao nii mamiv-u yao-vao
Nkukua'an-i! nkukua'an-i!

Empath begets empath
Their pain is your pain
I curse you! I curse you!

Writhing and moaning
Evil deeds tore their insides

Sins strained for release
The thieves got on their horses
Raced to the Silence
Vomited the stolen songs
Justice shattered the void

Wiimb-o'o na'arudi-rudi wiimb-o'o na'arudi-rudi
Song homecoming homecoming
Her people's joy vibrations crested at
their healing
The waves crashed over Anulaluna
She gave voice offerings to the hidden spaces
A paean to the spirit moons
They loomed above her with pride

Ripples in the Blood

DaVaun Sanders

fraught journey here
dance of blood splatters to life—
true name is power

***Panaagi**, the heroine of DaVaun Sanders' tale, steals her way onto the Adza'Kurei space station. Severed from her people and her magic, she seeks a new home and new allies. Delegations are arriving on the station to help plan the Boãmmariri, an interplanetary gathering meant to unify the five planets. When a stranded ship delivers harrowing news, Panaagi leads the delegates on a rescue mission... but none of them anticipate the horrors that await.*

Welcome to "Ripples in the Blood".

PANAAGI SLUMPED over in the pilot's seat, head teetered at a disquieting angle. That simply wouldn't do. The woman rested a practised finger against Panaagi's neck. Her rhythmic, obstinate pulse lingered. A moth's whisper of breath fluttered about her lips. Perhaps the arms positioned, just so, on the console? Feigning a nap? Case of vertigo?

The woman had only moments. Storage cubby? Would it smother the inevitable groans, the pleas for help? What other choice might the Mother send, so close to the station's mooring quay? Deep space. The shuttle's airlock safeguards could be manipulated to muffle the presence of Panaagi's still-warm body – the woman had done it before.

The airlock hissed open. Damnation.

"Panaagi?" An overly cheerful voice rang through the shuttle interior. "Welcome to Adza'Kurei Station. I am Kisasi, and honored to—"

"You've pronounced my name wrong." The name of the woman's last sacrifice had grated her ears. She offered a thin smile to Kisasi while the attendant stammered her way to a more suitable arrangement.

"You've no pilot?" Kisasi sounded shocked.

"Budget cuts." The woman – *no, Panaagi, she was now Panaagi,* her new identity, she reminded herself – offered a world-weary sigh.

"Disgraceful. Here, I'll help you myself."

The new Panaagi waved a dismissive hand. "No. I've been given more than either of us can carry alone."

So. The cubby would have to do. One firm shove. The former Panaagi's vertebra snapped. One threat suppressed, though ten new ones heckled her in its place. Names held so little meaning for her anymore. There was only her work. The *who* and the *how* could be stripped away if the need arose. Misgivings over such truths simply wasted breath.

"I'm the first to arrive?" Panaagi's assumed name settled in easily, a freshly sliced fillet on a crackling hot pan. The rest of her guise needed more seasoning. "Are arrangements in order?"

Kisasi's demeanor wilted as she gestured Panaagi into Adza'Kurei's depths. "Yes, although I'm hopeful more will come. The station itself performs admirably in this… eddy between our suns. But journey here can be fraught for poorly outfitted craft. We assist with more than our share of strays."

Panaagi nearly missed a step. "Is piracy a problem? Even with Zezépfeni's protection?"

"Yes and no. They present obstacles and opportunities."

Intriguing and troubling. Panaagi worried her lip, debating how to play this. "Kisasi, are Adza'Kurei personnel amenable to my… presence? I've heard rumors that Zezépfeni's delegates resent meddling from other worlds."

A delightful laugh exploded from the attendant's lips. "Please! Hosting a renewed Boãmmariri for the federation is all we've talked about on Adza'Kurei. This place deserves to matter."

Hmm. Pride, attachment, stubbornness. Unexpected. "Walk me through the layout? I've always been a more… tactile planner."

Kisasi blinked. "But other delegates may come late. Plus other station personnel arrivals. Instrumentation here is inconsistent—"

"Kisasi. No one cares about this place. You know this, yes?"

The attendant's smile almost cleaved away. Did her eyes flit to the cubby? "They'll envy your eagerness one day."

Ahh, ambition. This, Panaagi could use. "So convince me."

Nothing like Adza'Kurei existed in all of the federation, beholden to none and accessible by all.

So Zezépfeni's government claimed. Three tiers of interlocking rings nestled within the embrace of the twin suns, Zuúv'ah and Juah-ãju, apart yet intertwined. An impudu-pudu's maddening nest from one vantage, a fractal ouroboros in the next. Panaagi had glimpsed some of the structure's undulations on approach, once her namesake stopped struggling.

Kisasi delved through Adza'Kurei, constantly checking over her shoulder for Panaagi's approval. Pride swelled in her voice. The designers – craftsfolk from every corner of the federation, Kisasi was keen to point out – imagined the station as a place of accord, respite, and deep insight for the gift of Mothersound. Each tier reflected this intent. Kararatu, for study. Shi'iru for silence. Ibada, for worship. The melding of gravity fluid tech, magic and inspired intention was not lost on Panaagi. She held in her marveling with an effort. Adza'Kurei could be vital to her designs in a way she hadn't realized. And not just because she needed a place to be rid of a dead body.

Panaagi no longer counted the years since her long-ago banishment. Her Severing. She had wept plenty over the broken kin ties, and her loss of the Mothersound. But the station offered more than recruits to her vision. Adza'Kurei might serve as a base of operations. A new home.

Kisasi paused at a juncture of walkways. Nooks and crannies pervaded the surrounding metal's curvature, reminiscent of an inner ear of some wounded prowling thing. Or perhaps the bisected shell of the beings theorized to inhabit ancient Mahwé. Panaagi's skin itched, tantalized by unseen needles, a vestige of the magic she could no longer grasp. A glance showed that Kisasi mirrored Panaagi's distaste.

"Why have we stopped?" Panaagi asked.

"Listen."

One of the wall's hollows pulsed, not an arm's length from Panaagi. *How…?* The blue-green metal rippled like a boil of wrawling fever poised to burst. A thrumming, musical hiss reverberated through the walkway. Panaagi backed away inadvertently as the surface groaned.

"*Journey here can be fraught.*"

"*We assist with more than our share of wayward craft.*"

"*Is piracy a problem?*"

More voices flooded from the wall. Whispers, laughter, quarrels, a brooding tapestry flayed their own stolen words. "*They present obstacles and opportunities.*"

"Are Adza'Kurei personnel amenable..."

"Anything to be pulled out of obscurity."

"Yes and no."

Panaagi's lip curled at the violation. "We're being... monitored?"

"Yes and no." Kisasi's taut laughter ruptured the air. The whispers fled as suddenly as they arrived. "Hmm. How often do I use that phrase? I'll have to be mindful." She traced a finger along the curving wall as she set off again. "The echo chambers pervade this place. I thought a demonstration would work best. The original design cohort intended a tribute to the Mother, a place where worship and song could be looped, layered. Infinite."

"I'm surprised we don't hear more."

"They come and go. Once Adza'Kurei's personnel realized their everyday moanings might be captured indefinitely, well..." She flashed her teeth. "People are selective with their words. Or silence."

A space of wonder devolved into a place of secrets. Panagi could do very well here. "How long can a whisper last?" she asked softly. "Forever?"

Kisasi shrugged. "The designers worry over the same thing."

Panaagi's brow furrowed. "They're here?"

"Oh. Yes. And many others with thoughts on the matter. At night when I sleep. Every damn waking moment when a breath of peace is all—" The attendant cleared her throat. "I forget myself. They can't answer your questions, not directly. The latest generation has been dead for fifty years."

Capturing words? Panaagi's gorge rose at the prospect, and how easily designs intended for worship felt like an affront to the Mothersound. Capturing sound itself, against the speaker's will? What horrors might such inventions birth? Adza'Kurei deserved to kiss one of the twin suns until the station burned to ash. Yet, she could use it. Her mind shied away from the hypocrisy. Nothing about her purpose here required morality. Kisasi crossed her thoughts. Could the attendant receive Panaagi's purpose?

They progressed to the Kararatu tier. Kisasi explained how gravity's push–pull between Zuúv'ah and Juah-ãju allowed Adza'Kurei to remain at a fixed point in space. "Maadiregi debated about the Sisu'um in this space. Could it spread, or do the suns somehow contain it?"

"Sisu'um." Panaagi inhaled sharply. "These esteemed designers of yours knew, and still built this place near an accursed pocket of silence?"

"In theory. The maadiregi never did quite agree."

"And what do you think?"

"Adza'Kurei remains the ideal retreat for contemplating Mothersound. Allow me to show you."

"That won't be—"

"How did you describe yourself again? A tactile planner."

Panaagi followed the attendant reluctantly, deeper into Adza'Kurei's ever-weaving guts. Could a Silence affect her... condition? Had it already? Asking further would only risk revealing her secrets. More than a year's worth of plotting to embed herself on this station, realized by the Mother's accord. She couldn't turn back, though every step into Adza'Kurei's central mass felt like surrender. Devourment.

From one breath to the next, Panaagi's skin splayed tight against her bones. The thieving recesses and gleaming eddies of the echo chambers fled from new, impassive angles crafted of a lusterless, bone-like material. Her fingers stretched forward reflexively. Instinct screamed at her to snatch them away.

"Welcome to Shi'iru tier." Kisasi's voice shrieked through her smile. "Sound can be contrary here, beware of any reveries."

Reveries?

She led Panaagi into a spherical chamber inset with thirteen indistinguishable doors. The chamber itself rotated slowly. The door directly ahead would eventually flank them. Panaagi pivoted uneasily to keep the exit from twisting out of her periphery.

"Never close the door behind you," Kisasi said softly.

"Contemplation chambers?" Panaagi asked.

"As close to a place of perfect silence as could exist in all of the federation. Agony, or ecstasy. Depending on your point of view. The early Adza'Kurei personnel swore they could experience the space between the Mother's words if they endured long enough. They stitched kitchen mitts to their uniform sleeves, to keep their cartilage intact." Kisasi made a clawing motion over her ears. Panaagi clasped her hands behind her back, failing to hide a shiver.

Muffled weeping tickled her ear, steering her to one of the doors. A figure stirred on the other side of the viewing portal, ragged and hollowed out. Panaagi blinked. "I know a prisoner when I see one, Kisasi."

"You have a keen ear. It's a shameful use of this place," the attendant admitted. "This one is afflicted with… an aberration of the soul."

What did this small woman know about aberration? "A murderer, then. A vicious one, to be locked away like this."

"Yes. It was thought that time in the Silence might bring about a healing. A correction of his soul's disharmony, the uroh-ogi proposed. But—" A chime sounded. Kisasi inclined her ear, eyes widening at the melody. "More dignitaries! This might not be a wasted year yet. Ah… no offense."

"None heard. I'll be right behind you."

The prisoner's blank eyes sharpened as they regarded each other. A guttural, rasping breath shuddered from them both. Sudden vertigo overwhelmed Panaagi. "What is this?" she hissed.

A certain despair creased the man's face. Panaagi knew the expression well; whenever she acknowledged the void within her, the drowning silence – given breath and blood and bone – forcibly shoved into her being. Nameless. Deprived of a maadiregi's gift, her rightful magic. This is what it meant to be Severed.

"We're kindred, you and me." A gravelly semblance of a voice shuddered from the man's lips.

"You're not from Órino-Rin. The lilt in your voice, the tilt of your gait."

"You know what I mean. You've been Severed, too."

A complication she did not need. Panaagi's nails dug in her palms. "I'd heard rumors that we might… sense each other. Little good it does us. You, especially. Encaged in this place. The whole station terrified of you, surely."

An ugly, bitter laugh. "They'll be terrified of you soon enough."

"You're not wrong."

"The void's gnawing never stops. The Mother's ears must bleed from all of my pleas…" he whispered. "How… have you survived this long?"

"Purpose. Shall I share it with you?"

The man straightened. "What must I do?" he rasped.

"The things that got you into this place. What you do best."

"But… why?"

Gift or threat – she couldn't decide. Panaagi regarded this Severed man, her kin, for a long time. "The Mother requires our hands."

* * *

"We have a problem," Kisasi announced as Panaagi rounded the walkway returning to the station's mooring quay. The attendant stopped exchanging chime commands with Adza'Kurei's systems and began pacing. "I've chimed the last shuttle for entry permission, but they've ignored the sequence. Instrumentation resonates with no errors, we may have a medical situation."

"Mother send us warmer songs than that," Panaagi murmured.

"Mother send," Kisasi agreed fervently. "I'm overriding their shuttle."

They stewed for long moments until the airlock achieved a secured meshing clamp. Kisasi prepped medical drones. Adza'Kurei itself chimed a release sequence for the shuttle's inner door. It hissed open. Kisasi rushed through the craft's empty cargo hold, striding for the corridor adjoining the pilot's nest. She stopped so suddenly, Panaagi nearly ran up her back.

A man sat in the pilot's seat. Tendons strained on the back of his hands as he gripped the armrests, face slack and breath rasping. A woman perched above him, muscles knotting and unknotting in the smooth skin of her exposed back. Her rhythm summoned an undignified moan from deep in his belly. She cast a glance back at Panaagi and Kisasi. Her hips stopped swiveling. “Oh. We’ve arrived,” she murmured. “Experiment’s over.”

The man’s eyes popped open. He nearly fell out of his chair at the sight of Kisasi and Panaagi. “I didn’t— How are— What—”

Kisasi coughed delicately in her hand as he scrambled to clothe himself.

“I’m A’rra’ya Tra-balu’gah.” The nonplussed woman dressed casually as if ending an evening at the harmonic pools of Órino-Rin. “Ambassador from Zezépfeni, and delighted to share Boãmmaririri preparations with the federation, as a proud ally in bringing a renewed continuity to our worlds. My colleague is Bomehi Deseramba.”

“A maadiregi,” the man choked out, somewhat less rehearsed. “Here for – that is…”

Panaagi held her face smooth with an effort. “Kisasi, can you show the ambassador to her accommodations?”

The woman blinked at the clear command. “Of course.”

“Bomehi, might we speak?”

The man started, falling in reluctantly beside Panaagi. “Diplomat, I’m more than embarrassed over my improper actions. Chagrin isn't the word. By the Mother, I couldn't be less..." She allowed him to whinge until his apologies burned themselves out, gliding along until echo chambers undulated on either side. The station was ready for his secrets.

"Tell me of your work," she said.

"I..." he peered at her intently, a hooded, defensive light in his eyes. "My research involves... Mothersound. The intersection of magic and, well, ecstasy." Panaagi arched an eyebrow. He continued hastily. "If physical joining results in harmony, where does that converge with magic?"

"Interesting, yes, but—"

"Which leads us to ask, where does Mothersound meld with love? How does—"

"So it was an experiment," Panaagi interrupted. "I see. I'll join you with the others."

Panaagi spun on her heel and left him gawking, grimacing over the future of any poor young research protégés lured into his study. She doubted his ideas struck any chords with her own vision. Should she ignore her first impulse and spare his life? Or trust her intuition, shattered as it had proven itself time and time again?

She needed time to think. Snarling to herself, Panaagi walked down the corridor alone, praying for the Mother's forgiveness as she listened to Adza'Kurei's secrets.

* * *

The reception for the visiting dignitaries was housed in the station's central dining hall. Adza'Kurei personnel in crisp green uniforms mingled with a scant handful of visiting delegates, all from Zezépfeni. No other worlds had taken the station's offer seriously. The goal of a united Boãmmariri celebrated across the federation was still a future whisper.

Panaagi spotted Kisasi chatting amenably with one of the guests and caught her gaze. The woman nodded, inclining her chin toward a tucked curve of the space, furthest from the refreshments. As Panaagi picked her way over, the Zezépfeni ambassador slipped an arm through hers. "I was bored," A'rra'ya said simply.

Panaagi didn't break stride. "I don't care."

"Don't you want to remove me from this little gathering now?"

"Far from it." Now was as good a time to start as any. "You're exactly the kind of people I seek. Bomehi, too, maybe."

A'rra'ya swept a stray loc behind her ear. "Oh?"

"Free thinkers. Unconventional wisdom seekers. Unless I've misjudged, and you're merely here to slither your way into chasing power."

The woman snorted, lifting a fluted glass to her lips. Panaagi noted that she did not drink. "Boredom is why I've been cast out to this… esteemed gathering." She spotted Bomehi and crooked her finger. He extricated himself from conversation and reached Panaagi at the same time as Kisasi.

Panaagi took a deep breath. *Mother send me the truest words*. "Kisasi. How many people were invited from across the federation?"

The attendant winced. "Just under a thousand."

"How many from worlds besides Zezépfeni?"

"Just you."

"Just me." Panaagi eyed each of them in turn. "My government instructed me to spy. Steal tech if possible." Lies came so easily to her now. "Boãmmariri was… an afterthought."

Bomehi barked a nervous laugh. Kisasi muttered

angrily under her breath and stalked away. "Why tell us this?" A'rra'ya asked finally. "I could mute out your entire existence if I repeated one word of this back home."

"Don't I know it," Panaagi said wryly. Carefully, now. She couldn't unspool everything she meant to share. Not yet. "The federation needs a network of... goodwill. Beholden to no lurking group, no one leader save the Mother herself. Zezépfeni's government is secretive—"

"All worlds hold secrets—" Bomehi started.

"And mine is corrupt. Ekwukwe harbors vile experiments in this place – I've seen one up close. Where does it end?"

"Here," A'rra'ya snapped. "Boãmmariri planning is *simple*. Keep our glasses filled until we all go back to our wretched lives and praise each other's work with our superiors. And get some damn music in this stinking sculsh pit." Her voice rose irritably. "Someone...! Kisasi?"

Kisasi stepped forward hesitantly. "Forgiveness, ambassador. Another craft approaches. This one is—"

Panaagi let air hiss through her teeth as the Zezépfeni folk conferred. So much effort to reach this place, this moment. And her words had failed her. *Mother send me strength*. Her only true connection was with the Severed locked away in Adza'Kurei's bowels. What did that say about her? No… she wouldn't entertain that sort of thinking. She needed to try a different tack.

"Ambassador, I'm sorry if—"

"A moment." A'rra'ya frowned as Kisasi relayed sonar imaging of the incoming craft.

Panaagi edged closer. "That's no shuttle. It's an escape skiff." The craft was barely fit for planet hopping – old, retrofitted beyond recognition. Tremendous damage caked the hull, new wounds atop old scars.

Kisasi kissed her teeth. "Ambassador, forgive me but the station is obligated to—"

"By the Mother's bleeding ears, spare us the ridiculous spewing over protocol!" A'rra'ya snapped.

Panaagi reached past them both and enabled the communication chime. "We're standing by to assist. Adza'Kurei recovery drones are en route."

A haggard voice crackled to life on the responder. "I don't know who you are, but thank the Mother for you!"

Don't thank me yet, Panaagi thought silently.

Kisasi departed to oversee the escape skiff's recovery. There was nothing for it but to wait in their own stew. The remaining delegates meandered out, ushered off by station personnel. Bomehi muttered to himself, eyeing Panaagi as though he wanted to speak further. He flinched when A'rra'ya directed a single scowl his way. She sipped her drink serenely and waited.

Kisasi returned, hauling along a bedraggled individual wearing a burned red-silver uniform and permanently dazed expression.

"This is Jalaan," Kisasi announced tersely. "A maadiregi from Zezépfeni."

"We've been limping here for weeks." Jalaan described his journey in a hushed whisper. "I've taken asteroid samples dozens of times, but we were attacked—"

"By what world?" A'rra'ya demanded sharply.

"No world…! Our navigators reported a strange creature burrowing into the hull right before the planetary defense system targeted us. Our own world! We barely made it to the skiff before the hull breach ruptured our tier… it made no sense." Jalaan swallowed. "The Li'ishe crashed somewhere in the World. We played dead, many of us, and let our skiffs drift. It was either here or Mahwé, and… the Mother smiled upon…" He trailed off.

Another station attendant appeared at A'rra'ya's elbow to fill her glass – she swatted the man away.

"If he's been drifting as long as he claimed, we would have heard of the rescue *well* before we departed!"

"Mother send," Bomehi murmured. The man looked ready to pass out.

Jalaan peered at A'rra'ya' abashedly. "Can the federation help?" he asked. "Our own world betrayed us. I don't know what else to do. Our friends may still be alive."

"Doubtful," Panaagi cut in before the ambassador could answer. "But perhaps an... alliance, rendering aid where the worlds cannot. Or will not."

They locked eyes. "We must leave at once."

* * *

Panaagi fought exhaustion on the shuttle bound for Zezépfeni. Kisasi, still eager to make a name for Adza'Kurei Station, insisted on accompanying them with a small contingent of personnel to assist with the rescue. Panaagi had allowed it on one condition – the Severed prisoner's release. Of course, Kisasi protested, but ambition won out.

The Severed sat across from Panaagi, slowly flexing and unflexing his hands.

Panaagi smiled at him as she rose. He didn't return it.

In the shuttle's navigation nest, Jalaan bordered on hysterics. Kisasi attempted to calm him. Panaagi understood the commotion immediately. Zezépfeni's defensive weapons dominated the upper half of their viewing pane, massive and glinting and trained upon their shuttle.

"They won't fire on us." Bomehi let out a long breath. "I don't think. They've accepted my credentials, such as they are." He laughed bitterly. "Too obscure to cause concern."

A'rra'ya laid a hand on his arm. "Their mistake is our blessing."

A collective sigh of relief sang out as the shuttle swept toward Zezépfeni without incident. Panaagi stilled her breathing and focused on the distant blue speck, just brighter than the dull glimmer of nearby asteroids. The world gradually grew kalabash-size, swelling until nothing else filled their forward viewport.

Jalaan muttered the entire time, honing in on the crash site with Bomehi's help. The engine vibrated, humming as the craft skimmed into the world's atmosphere. A warning chime sounded, then ceased. In moments they broke through the steel-gray clouds, descending rapidly.

A'rra'ya frowned through the portal. "We're close, aren't we?"

"Nearly on top of it," Jalaan confirmed.

"I…I can feel it."

Kisasi nodded worriedly. "As can I."

The dozen personnel stirred and muttered as well. Panaagi felt nothing. She allowed the ache in her chest to pass. The landscape beneath them was devoid of human settlement, although thick overgrowth and greenery had reclaimed impact craters, a rash sweeping to the horizon. Some deep enough for waterfalls and starfall lakes in their depths, others no more than a dip in the tree canopy.

All save one.

"Mother's cradle," Kisasi breathed.

The fresh impact site carved an ugly gouge just beneath the saddle of two mountains. Smaller than Panaagi expected, and far enough away from settlement for Zezépfeni to explain it away as a simple meteor. Parts of the remaining ship still smoldered.

Jalaan circled the site, transfixed. "Someone could have made it."

Kisasi leaned close to whisper in Panaagi's ear. "Is this what you wanted?"

"Yes and no."

The attendant snorted. Jalaan set the shuttle down near the upper summit of a crater beside a copse of blasted trees. Everyone exited the shuttle, Kisasi directing wide-eyed attendants to unload the recovery drones, calibrate them for atmosphere and complete a grid sweep for survivors. Jalaan and Bomehi whispered intently together for a moment and set off in a direction through the ruined forest.

Panaagi motioned to her Severed kin. "Take lead. Try to keep them alive."

"What's out here?" he asked.

"A threat to us all," Bomehi called over his shoulder. The man grew more agitated by the moment. "We must be swift."

A'rra'ya withdrew a weapon from her belt. "I'll go with him." She hesitated. "I've heard… whisperings of what doomed that ship. The planetary defense was just a formality."

Still more secrecy – would it ever end? World after world, the same mistakes. Submerging what should be exposed. "More reason for us to investigate."

The terror that filled the others in the sky finally revealed itself to Panaagi as they pressed after Bomehi and Jalan. She couldn't feel magic, but the fallout of its corruption showed plainly on every side. Sound itself seemed to beg for an end. The utter life and joyous bustle of survival that clung to any ecosystem was somehow festering. The aberration was evident: here a copse of trees with bark twisted and leaves curled as though sunlight were poison. A noise like agony ghosted through the misshapen branches at the smallest ghost of wind. There, a bird fallen from its nest, squawking piteously until the mother flew close for rescue. The fledgling ripped a hole in the mother's gullet and began to feast. The Severed crushed it beneath a boot.

Panaagi pressed a hand to her stomach.

"It will be worse," Bomehi moaned. "The closer we get."

Kisasi gasped and pointed beyond Panaagi's shoulder, further down the rocky slope. "By that rock face, beneath the setting suns – I saw someone!"

"Effico." A'rra'ya swore. "There shouldn't be *anyone* here! Not settlers! Not..."

"Survivors," the Severed suggested.

"No. We saw the crash site. We need to find what's being hidden in this place before the forest eats it." Panaagi led the way. They soon passed a crude settlement beside a slow-moving creek. The water curled around a dislocated boulder, flowing deeper into the forest. An emaciated woman floated face down, twirling slowly with one arm stretched out as if to reason with Panaagi. Another body bobbed beside her, and another, all caught in the eddy. Kisasi made a mewling sound.

This place… Panaagi's own Severing had nearly ended her. But this place? The forest around the crash site echoed her own pain, a tortured hymn she couldn't imagine before this moment. It was not just an absence of Mothersound – it was a turning away from it. A rejection. A mockery. Nothing here should be possible, yet it existed. Urgency, and a desperation to act warred with her fear – whether redemption awaited her here or not.

Her group climbed steadily. Smells of decay and char deepened around them. Animal howls cut through the twilight, intermixed with song and prayer.

A campfire beckoned ahead, tucked next to the rock face Kisasi identified. A bare-chested man stood, peering at them. "Ah. I knew there would be more to come."

Panaagi forced herself to meet his gaze. Wetness dripped from a cavity just beneath the man's ear. One of his eyelids was gone, and blood stained a once crisp uniform now smeared with dirt and offal. "You are hurt," she said finally.

"No, *you* are hurt." He peered up at the wall. Unnatural markings marred the surface – angular slashes of char. Foul, sweeping stains that wrinkled her nose. Layer upon layer, twisting her eye. Residue from the asteroid? It screamed of wrongness. "I have nearly done the impossible."

Bomehi edged forward cautiously. "You are... Farchol?" He scrambled to one knee briefly. "Of the Susu Nunyaa! What has happened here?"

"My name doesn't matter. Names don't matter. Words don't matter."

Something cold pressed deep into Panaagi's chest.

"We've seen people," A'rra'ya pressed.

Farchol's eyes flickered to Panaagi. "It's all meaningless. Let me show you. What is your name?"

The question stripped Panaagi bare. "*Ho'oyo.*" Her true name tore from her lips, compelled. She staggered, hands grasping her throat in disbelief. A true name meant power over her. Her secrets unfurled for the worlds to see. Her shame.

"Now that's something different... You resisted."

The man gestured suddenly.

Energy seized Panaagi and flung her toward the rock. "Release me—!" The force of the impact drove the air from her lungs. She crumpled to the ground before the rock face, head spinning.

No one moved. The man stared at the mountainside intently. "Now this… is powerful. Not begging, or a soundless scream, or gibberish. A command, pure and true."

He traced a finger along the rock where Panaagi struck. Her blood glistened on the surface. He stared at it as though nothing else existed, ripping a wide leaf from one of the tortured tree's boughs. Panaagi gasped in pain as her Severed kin and A'rra'ya helped her rise.

Farchol dug a finger into the leaf, hard enough to bruise and rend it without punching through. A delicate mutilation. He held it up proudly after a few moments. "Don't you see? I've captured it. This changes everything. What a tremendous gift."

In the dying light, Panaagi recognized the resemblance to the splatters of her own blood upon the rock. "What is this?"

"Your *sound*, of course. Don't you recognize it?"

Panaagi stared. Memory of the station assailed her, the last time her sound had been stolen from her throat. *Journey here can be fraught*. This man had done it with…

a pattern. A blood ripple pattern conjured through sound itself? The implications sickened her. "You must die."

The Severed slipped smoothly from behind the tree and hooked both arms around Farchol's, pinning him. Restrained, the man still grinned. "Say it again. With your chest."

Jalaan snarled, snatching A'rra'ya's weapon from her hands. "You must *die*!"

Farchol inclined his chin. Jalaan sailed into the campfire in a crash of sparks. He screamed as the fire consumed him. Madness licked Farchol's eyes. "I must have this." He breathed deep. "*Release me*."

The leaf beside his feet crackled with energy. The pattern of Panaagi's blood splatters danced to life upon it. The Severed's arms flew behind him with a snap of bone. He fell to his knees, howling. His arms flopped uselessly by his sides. Bomehi screamed and ran into the forest.

Kisasi gawked. Panaagi held a finger to her lips. Silence.

Farchol grabbed another leaf from the tree, peering urgently at Jalaan's burned remains. "Don't you see, Severed?" he asked Panaagi. "All that you've lost can be restored. Never to be taken again. The Nga'phandileh know life outside of Mothersound, and so can we. Blessed Silence upon all of the Mother's children."

Panaagi did see.

She walked slowly to the tree, past her moaning, Severed kin. She plucked a leaf of her own. She stood beside Farchol at the fire. This is what she had been called to do.

Farchol watched expectantly as Panaagi gestured A'rra'ya forward. "All that was forgotten can be said again forever," he said.

Panaagi nodded. "Forever." She met A'rra'ya's eyes. "You are mine and mine alone."

Farchol released a rapturous exhalation. "Yes! We need only create the proper… patterning to tear it from her lips."

A'rra'ya cowered, peering in the direction Bomehi had fled. Panaagi knelt and plucked a charred stick from the fire, hissing as it burned her fingers. She held it ready over her leaf. "A'rra'ya. Say the words."

"Panaagi. Please."

"Do it."

Kisasi clapped a hand over her mouth, backing away. The Severed kin stared at Panaagi in disbelief and horror. A'rra'ya squeezed her eyes shut. Farchol's energies swept her into the air, the words screaming free. "*I am yours—*"

Panaagi drove her stick into Farchol's windpipe with

all of the strength in her body. He sputtered droplets of blood over his lips and collapsed. A'rra'ya sank like a discarded prancing doll.

Panaagi drove her heel into the man's neck. To be sure.

She rushed to A'rra'ya's side, where Kisasi already knelt. A'rra'ya slapped her full on the face. "Thank you," she whispered. The three of them embraced.

Gathering Bomehi took some time, splinting the prisoner's arms enough for travel took longer. Afterwards they stoked a fire. Kisasi knelt to say Mother's blessing over Jalaan, but, again, Panaagi held a finger to her lips. They scoured Farchol's hut nearby the forest. He had likely been there since the asteroid fell. Every last plucked leaf that was tarnished with his smearings went into the fire. Then they took the embers and burned the settlement, what remained of the crash site, and the forest.

To be sure.

Only when they were leaving orbit, back aboard the shuttle did Panaagi speak. "The federation should know of this."

"Yes," A'rra'ya said quietly, sharing a resigned look with Bomehi. "But there would be chaos. We all know it."

"The question is," Kisasi added, "what are we to do about it?"

"Exactly. Perhaps now you will reconsider my proposal." New name. New home. Purpose surged in Panaagi's chest, as she gazed through the shuttle's front viewport, awaiting sight of Adza'Kurei. The sight of home. "We have much to prepare."

Endling

Nerine Dorman

crouching between wrecks
unalone in terrible creep—
sing we to the stars

In ***Nerine Dorman****'s "Endling", a monster haunts a space station, devouring bodies and chants. Divided, tribe against tribe, the station's inhabitants have no defense against the onslaught. The only hope lies with Auu'reti, among the last of their tribe, and Uya'Kwazi, a child on a desperate mission to save them all. Two people – a child and a youth from warring groups, sworn enemies to kill each other – must join forces... For the beast that hunts them is a far greater threat.*

Welcome to "Endling".

"Mortals are weak, they are bound by rules. They die, they are forgotten. But memories... memories never die." – "Hologhiri", by Akintoba Kalejaye

(*Mothersound: The Sauútiverse Anthology*)

I'M NOT ALONE in the abandoned agricultural chamber. Apart from the steady hiss of escaping atmosphere, and the ping-ping-ping of rapidly cooling structure near the breach, there's a shuffle, a sharp intake of breath. And something else... A dry whisper of leather on polished metal. It's so slight, I pause, draw myself up as small as I can into the shelter of an upended crate.

Lights flicker, die, and plunge the space into gloom, blood and ozone thick in my sinuses. My fear is a shard lodged in my gut. Each moment is a shattered fragment, a miracle or a curse. My teeth chatter from the marrow-deep freeze, my breath pluming before me as I press myself to the metal, try to make myself one with the shadows. To stay small, to remain hidden.

Not alone.

Whatever got Lu'phawu might still get me.

The staccato screams, the acrid stench of burning circuitry underpinned by the iron tang of life haunts me, turns every heartbeat fragile. Each inch I creep forward is another that takes me away. I'm alive. Lu'phawu is not.

We were the last. My people have dropped away farther than I can touch. Quicksilver through my fingers. It's not real. Or maybe I'm not real.

My nephew's empty, staring eyes will always watch me. I'm too late to save him. Too late to save myself. Grief must wait with its talons.

Yet, I'm not alone here, in the grip of a deep mammalian fear because *something else* shares this space. Its sound-signature tastes *wrong.* I cannot shape the sound on my lips and tongue. And it took most of Lu'phawu.

It can't be real, it can't be...

Until I shake whatever is creeping, sniff-snuffling, and echo-pinging after me, like carrion eaters from our long-lost motherworld, I'm not going to live to spite this great wrong. Life in the face of death. My hatred puts iron in my spine.

I wait, hardly daring to breathe. When I squeeze shut my eyes and reach out with the hum in my blood, I can almost hear the edge of my path, sliding and slinking between the aquaculture vats leaking their briny contents. Away from the horror. Away from what killed Lu'phawu, the last of my blood.

This nameless terror passes, is aware: I draw myself into a cold hard knot, so the shadow flows over me. Not even a whisper.

My limbs cramp as I gradually unwind and creep past the sorting tables where, only a few hours ago, Lu'phawu was dehusking oily mahilli berries. Until the thing came and finished what the Yokha'a tribe had well underway.

Blood-and-water puddles mingle, soaking into my torn leggings to chill my skin. Heavy with sorrow. I swallow my sobs, try not to breathe too deeply of the stench of voided bowels and death's sweet-sweet perfume.

So, when I round a tumbled workbench and run face first into a *living*, terrified boy crouching beneath the wreckage, I don't know who is more shocked. His eyes go wide, and he sucks in a breath. I'm on him, my hand clamped over his mouth. Like a praying longlegs, I wrap my limbs around him as he wriggles, but I'm bigger, stronger than him.

"Quiet," I breathe into his ear. "Not a sound. I'm not going to hurt you."

He tenses, but I don't relent, and then the fight goes out of him, and he becomes porridge. The child stinks of grease, carrion, and piss. I'm only too glad to release him.

We face each other, huddled beneath our flimsy shelter.

He's not one of our own, one of the N'yotha tribe. His ebony skin is not mottled, like mine. He has no markings at all. Not even the intricate ritual scarification patterns of our allies, the N'yashi. Which means…

He's one of *them.*

My anger blooms with sudden violence, and I ball my hand into a fist, as if I would smash him. But he's just a child, staring at me with those big, dark-gray eyes, his teeth chattering.

I reach out with my senses but cannot detect that nameless presence from earlier. It's moved on. For now. But it doesn't mean that I must stop my vigilance.

"What's your name, boy?" I murmur. "And be quiet when you answer. There is something hunting us."

"Uya… Uya'Kwazi," he whispers. He's clutching his left arm to his chest, and the blood stink hits me afresh. He's hurt.

He's just a child, no more than seven years old, if that. Those fingers haven't grown big enough to handle the short, stabbing v'hushalele – the spear. But he'll still grow up. He'll be taught to hate. To kill. To shape words that bring death.

Just a boy. No older than Lu'phawu.

Dead. All dead. The heavy veil drops over my vision, my chest grows tight. I'm alive. They are not.

Small fingers close on my wrist, and my numb skin doesn't at first register the touch.

"Auntie?" Those big, pleading eyes.

"I'm *nist*." It's an easy mistake to make – in a certain light I could be either. Or both.

"Oh. What's your name?"

I want to snap at him that I don't give my name to strangers, least of all to someone who shares blood with murderers, but… What harm can it do?

"Auu'reti." I wait for realization to sink in, for him to figure its tones are different from his precious Yokha'a, but he gives no indication that it matters.

"I need help," he whispers, glancing about wildly, his breaths staccato. "I need to get to transmission spire five seventy-three."

"You what now?" The nearest transmission spire

is in an area that's been off-limits to my people for more than a year – that's if it's the one he means. "Why ask me? Why not ask one of the warriors in the ii'mphis?" I want to add "those damned murderers" but stop myself. My grief has thrust its barbed harpoon through my chest where my heart used to be, raw and rusty. I'm an endling now.

"They'll stop me," he says.

"*Your people?*" What is he saying?

He reaches into his tunic and pulls out a loop of fiber. A clear crystal shard pendant glints like a tooth, as long and thick as my forefinger, the tip wicked sharp. "They want this."

"I don't understand. What am I looking at?" I frown. We need to go. Not examine baubles.

He opens his mouth to speak, but the lights go out.

We're plunged into a darkness so solid, even the air becomes like glue.

Uya'Kwazi hisses, and reaches out for my hand, his fingers cold and trembling.

I swallow back the whimper that builds in the back of my throat.

There it is again, that whisper of leather on metal. Shhhh-ssskkk. A heavy sound I can feel, taste, that leans down with an immense weight. We crouch together, caged in each other's arms, trembling, so very naked and exposed.

The Yokha'a enforcers love herding us into an enclosed space, then triggering us with whoops and yells bursting with terror, so that each wave crashes over you until you flee. They make a game of picking off the stragglers.

So, I hold, and I keep Uya'Kwazi from making that same mistake.

You should let him go, he's the enemy, my dark heart whispers. *He can be bait. Distract whatever that thing is hunting you.*

He's just a child.

We wait, crouched beneath the broken workbench, shivering and so very, very afraid.

Our breath turns gelid, our hearts thrumming so loud, I swear, they're drums in the dark, loud enough to hear clean across the habitat. Then, as quickly as the presence arrived, it's gone. Dim, green emergency lighting kicks in near the exits.

I exhale, sag, and Uya'Kwazi slides into a boneless heap.

"What was—"

I put a finger to his lips, shake my head, then motion for us to go.

Where, exactly, I'm not certain. We need to avoid the main thoroughfares, perhaps dive into the maintenance tunnels. I all but shove the boy ahead of me towards the corner where the grille is that leads to the drains.

Two years ago, my ma and I escaped a pack of enforcers that way and traveled across two sectors before we doubled back to our usual haunts. But thinking of Ma now brings a sweet pang of hurt as I fumble with the clips, then shove the boy in ahead of me, down into the drain.

You should leave him; he's a burden.

He's just a kid.

And yet there's an echo to him, a hint right at the edge of my hearing, of how this child of my enemy is a crosspoint. The Mother has laid Her hand on him, as much as I'd like to ask Her why She would favor this one and not Lu'phawu.

In the dimness of the drain, Uya'Kwazi's eyes are huge, reflecting the blue-green of the strips of glow-moss that fur the ceiling. Our feet slosh in the thick, slick sludge that's cold up to our ankles, bringing with it the brown stench of vegetative rot.

"We need to get to the transmission spire," he whispers.

"Why?" I ask, as I secure the grating that locks us in.

I huff out a breath of almost-relief at being ensconced in the scummy metal pipe. The air's warmer here, moisture-laden.

"We need to finish the Rite of Uu'donga'ah."

"Never heard of it," I say.

"It's why this habitat was first built, but…" He sighs and settles on his haunches, back pressed against the wall. "No one knows about the rite anymore."

"And you do?" I try to keep the waspishness out of my tone. Who exactly is this boy to talk about forgotten rites? But there's that echo again, as if the Mother is whispering, *Pay attention. Listen.* I shiver.

He nods. "Our habitat is dying, and we have lost our way. We splintered when we should have been singing in harmony." His face has gone slack, as though with a memory.

I snort. "It is the way things are now. Have been for years."

When last did I sing?

The creaks and groans from the superstructure punctuate this thought with their own threnody. I try not to listen to them.

Uya'Kwazi snakes out his hand to grab my wrist with a strength that belies his age. "You must help me. No one else will. They want the shard." His eyes blaze with a feral wisdom that echoes through me with its potentiality.

"What's so important about your shard?" I lick lips gone dry.

"It's a key." He reaches into his tunic to retrieve the crystal. "I took it from one of the reactors in Power Generation."

"You went *there*?" I scoff. "And you got out, alive?" No one breaks into that sector. Yet I don't sense the untruth in him.

"I was with Ene'dle'we, my… teacher. He—" Uya'Kwazi swipes at his eyes with the back of his wrist. "The rite is important. The Word of Breaking is unsung, so the Word of the Barriers cannot be uttered."

"Those are just old songs," I tell him, even though I feel like I am lying to myself saying so.

His face crumples in anger and disappointment. "Now you sound just like my people. No one believes me. They say, 'Uya'Kwazi, you are just a little boy, what do you know?' But I *know*!"

His eyes glitter tear-bright, and my heart twists in response. He truly believes.

"How do you know this?" I whisper.

"Ene'dle'we showed me. I am...*was* his apprentice. He was a Keeper of the Way but... He made the elders angry. We were in the Hall of Records – our job was to clean things. It was very boring." He sighs. "But I found something. There was that big quake when one of the ventilator systems broke."

I nod, because I remember this. They'd had to turn off entire sectors of the habitat, and we'd ended up having to move yet again because our territory suffered a catastrophic power cut. Even now, I don't know if that part of the habitat has ever been restored. Probably not – they don't want my people finding more hiding places. Not that there are any of us left now. The old pain crawls back up, and I glare at this scion of my enemy.

"What did you find?" I ask.

"It was a record crystal. A very old one. It was so old; it was cracked and very fragile so had to be kept in a box. My hands are small. I could get it where it fell in a crack." He holds up his hands for emphasis, as if this will validate what he has to say.

"What did the crystal sing?" I may as well humor him.

"He got it to fit in one of our tablets, and it whispered a rite – one that Ene'dle'we was learning about when he was my age. But he says… said… that, until now, we had only tiny pieces of the song. So, he got very excited. He even showed me how the words were chanted differently from the ones we use today. We need the crystal to finish it. That's what it sings in the rite."

Uya'Kwazi's excitement about this relic stirs a flicker of mystery in me. Over the years, we've found fragments hinting that our habitat once served a greater purpose, but when you're so focused on not being eradicated, thanks to an accident of birth, it's hard to set aside the resources to dig deeper into your existence – why we're here, isolated and drifting through a hostile, star-pierced vacuum.

I'm on the verge of asking him more when a loud clang and scrape a few feet behind has us both cringing. The illuminating strips wink out, plunging us in sudden, frigid darkness. Metal squeals, ruptures.

I grab a handful of Uya'Kwazi's tunic, and scrabble forward, my feet not quite gaining purchase on the slimy floor. It's behind us! Whatever *it* is, it's found us. My heart convulses as if it will collapse as a wordless wail tears itself from my lungs.

We're tiny p'aanya rodents fleeing from the wild tetekute feline, and our bright fear is sharp on my tongue as the shadow hurls itself after us. We hit a branch in the drain, this one plunging so fast we're sliding tail over skull, down, down, and around. I flail out with hands, feet. Uya'Kwazi whumps into me, his head colliding with my ribs so all my air whoofs out my lungs.

We splash into a pool of sludge, the sudden stop after slip-sliding at an insane velocity stunning. It's warm, the atmosphere redolent with decaying organic matter. Everything... glows with a bioluminescent green. We're in one of the digester sumps. It's not the worst place we can be.

I hold still, barely breathing, reaching out with all my senses while a quivering Uya'Kwazi clings to me like a disc-shelled uu'kwu sucker would a wall.

I freeze, expecting our hunter to have followed us, but when one breath becomes two, becomes three, I allow myself to relax. The boy is quivering, his head pressed against my chest as he whimpers.

"It's all right," I whisper, smoothing my hand through his crop of tiny braids. "It's passed us over." I won't lie and say it's gone. The Mother has intervened, given us a reprieve, and I send a silent thanks to Her.

The boy looks up, makes eye contact with me. "It won't stop, will it? Whatever it is."

I offer up a slight shrug. "I don't have the word for it. All I can tell is that there are worse things out there than the enforcers." Never have I believed I'd ever say this.

"We used to have songs," I tell the boy. "When we could still sing. Old songs, in a tongue that is shaped different from yours and mine, and the songs tell of the ones that lurk in Yikoh, the void, and how jealous they are of us. Where they are, there is only dark and nothingness, and a terrible, terrible hunger."

Speaking this resonates in my blood, my bones, and I know a truth is lodged in my words. I haven't dared to sing in a long, long time. I don't know if I still can.

"This is why we are here," whispers Uya'Kwazi. "In Ene'dle'we's record crystal it spoke of the Shadow of Shadows that will devour us all. The Unmade. The Unsinging. And for a while, we were all one people put here to stop them from ever bursting through.

But then, when there was no shadow for a long time, we turned on each other instead."

We haven't been one people for many years.

A chasm yawns beneath me with its accumulated blood debt.

He's just a boy telling fanciful tales. He could be Lu'phawu.

I shiver, and it's got little to do with the soupy mess of bioluminescent algae in which we are stewing. What if he's telling the truth?

"We need to get out of here," I tell him. "We don't have time for stories."

"We need to go to transmission spire five seventy-three. It was never finished. We finish the rite; we save our worlds."

As if in response, the floor shudders and, from deep within, terrible groans issue. Myriad ripples tremble on the scummy surface, sending out flashes of blue-green light.

"Come," I say to him, even as I disentangle the child from me. "We can't stay here. Something isn't right."

Parts of the habitat have died. Some have broken so badly they've fallen away into space. Urgency grips me by the base of my spine, and we slosh to the small, recessed stepladder at the far wall, Uya'Kwazi holding onto my hand so tightly, I fear he's going to cut off circulation to my fingers.

I could move faster without him and, by all rights, I should abandon him. I shouldn't feel the weight of his life wrapped around my heart the way his fingers curl around mine.

"Up you go." I push him towards the steps. "This should open in one of the maintenance tunnels. Stop before you open the door and listen. If you hear anyone or any*thing*, tell me. Only open the door if you're absolutely sure no one's there."

He jerks a nod, his teeth chattering as he begins to climb, all skinny elbows and knees. I follow, blinking in the gleaming liquid that drips from him. Fortunately, the glow from the sump fades quickly, and we're soon ascending in the gloom of the strip-lighting that comes to life when we trip motion sensors.

The habitat's rumbling shudders spur us on – whatever is happening in this sector cannot be good. Uya'Kwazi doesn't need to be told to hurry. We reach the hatch where, dutifully, he pauses to listen.

"Can you hear anything?" I say when he's been sitting there awhile.

"N-no."

"Can you feel anything… stranger, unnatural?" Everything feels out of place and wrong.

"No." He sounds more certain.

"All right. What are we waiting for?"

He sobs, and I can hear him fumbling with the latches and, just as I'm about to shove past him, he opens the door, and we tumble out.

We've spilled into a passage where the air is thin, and a faint whistling accompanies a stiff breeze. There's a rupture further down.

"Head in the other direction," I say.

Face drawn, he nods, and I close the hatch behind us. We hurry along, our footfalls strangely muted, our breathing labored. We've gone perhaps a hundred or so paces when the thudding of footfalls from the intersection ahead of us warns of trouble.

I'm too tired, too cold, too sad. I freeze, paralyzed by an overwhelming "what now?". Indeed. Inevitability sinks its claws into me. I cannot flee back the way we came – I'll run into certain death. Yet this death is bearing down on us so rapidly I can't act.

Five enforcers skid to a halt in the passage, bristling with v'hushaleles, traceries of energy charges crackling at the spearpoints. My dismay is sour. Uya'Kwazi grabs hold of my arm, as if I can do anything about these warriors. His fear layers over mine.

But this is not a Yokha'a ii'mphi – their braids are beaded with red and black. They're a sister-clan, the Ah'bui. Allies.

A tall woman steps forward, her v'hushalele lowered. "Identify yourselves."

I suck in breath but have no sing-scream that might buy me seconds to escape. Uya'Kwazi shakes his head, meeting my gaze briefly. He steps forward, strangely bold.

"I am Uya'Kwazi, apprentice to Ene'dle'we, Keeper of the Way. I have captured this spy tampering with one of our outlying servers, and I request an escort back to Sector Seven-Oh-Nine."

The woman grimaces and frowns. "That sector's off-limits right now. Show me your identification."

Not letting go of my forearm, he dutifully raises his left arm to expose his wrist. Warily, the woman approaches and brushes her own over his. Beads of light come to life on her bracer, and she nods.

"Fine," she says, "you check out, but we've lost contact with that sector. We're supposed to be looking for survivors and any… anomalies." She says that last word as if it leaves a bad taste in her mouth, while glaring at me. As if it's somehow my fault that entire sectors of the habitat are destabilizing simultaneously.

She glances over her shoulder at a glowering man. "Bring the restraints." She gestures at me. "Can't afford to let *that* be running free."

"It's fine," Uya'Kwazi says. "I have them under control."

"No offense, child, but…"

Uya'Kwazi straightens, squares his shoulders, which only serves to make him appear even more comical. "*It is fine*. They have made an oath."

"We won't have an unbound enemy among us."

"Then we will go alone."

The woman scowls, looking between me and the boy. "Something about this entire situation isn't right."

The floor shudders and bucks, and we are all flung to our knees. Lights flicker, and an acrid stench of burning components hits us. That old, animal panic claws its way up, and I want to spin around and run, but Uya'Kwazi holds me firmly.

"Don't," he murmurs.

Men and women cry out in fear and surprise. Weapons clatter to the ground and roll. Then gravity fails completely, and we float. The unexpected weightlessness has me sliding off what used to be the floor, turning end over end, clutching in vain at handholds that remain out of reach.

A horrific screech of metal sings through the passage, then an ominous clanging, like deep bells – the sound distorting as if the air has grown thick. My breath mists before my face.

The Ah'bui patrol leader flails in our direction, her mouth drawn in a rictus of horror. Behind her: choking darkness that spreads.

Uya'Kwazi grips onto me, twists, and pushes off the wall with his legs so that we hurtle away from the approaching nothingness. Behind us, a short, sharp shriek cuts off. I don't look back. Instead, the boy and I have become one, gripping each other while using whatever protrusions – light fittings, exposed pipping – to propel ourselves along. We're cut, bruised, scraped.

In one of our mad rotations, I glimpse the Ah'bui woman explode into a red mist before the shadow expands and that part of the passage vanishes.

For now, whatever is in the darkness is content to boil and fret behind us, and the screams die down as we ratchet around a corner into a side passage where, without warning, gravity snatches us, and we slide and skid along until we come to rest against a tumbled pile of debris.

An alarming smear of scarlet marks our passage, as if we've been dipped in ink and dragged across the floor. I'm panting, the air stinging my lungs. Uya'Kwazi lies far too still, but he's breathing. Faint screams and muffled thuds reach us, sparking up a fresh wave of terror. Tears prick at my eyes, but I dash them away.

"Boy." I shake him.

He mumbles, shudders.

Another gut-churning shake of the habitat has the gravity fading in and out.

Uya'Kwazi looks up, grimacing. "It hurts."

"Come, sit up," I tell him. A glance at his left side makes me wish I didn't look. He's been punctured, his lifeblood leaking out too fast. Too much.

I shrug out of my tunic, take my knife, and rip through the bottom of the garment so I can make a strip for bandaging. The rest I wad and press against the wound.

"Push down on it, like so," I tell him.

He whimpers but obeys, and I work to secure the makeshift bandage that quickly soaks through. The iron tang of blood invades my senses, overwhelming and rich. He needs a maadiregi who is skilled in singing the body together.

I open my mouth, breathe in. Try to feel my heart to bring up the song, but all I do is croak. I knew it wouldn't work. My eyes blur with frustrated tears.

"It hurts," he whimpers.

I was too late for Lu'phawu. I failed him just like I'm failing Uya'Kwazi now.

But what about justice? Does Uya'Kwazi deserve this death any more than Lu'phawu did? I don't know how to answer this, save that I don't want this child to die.

Lights in the passage perpendicular to ours wink out, our breath mists, and that primal sense of something bigger that hungers, weighs on my heart.

I drag Uya'Kwazi to his feet.

He opens his mouth to protest, and I clap my hand over his lips.

"Not now," I mutter. "We go."

Leave him here, my cruelty whispers. *Save yourself*.

One look into those wide, frightened eyes, and I can't. I hunch so that the boy can clamber onto my back, then I carry him as if he's a much smaller child. My skin is instantly wet and sticky with blood where his wound presses against me.

We need help. He needs help. He's dying.

Why do you care?

I break into a shambling trot, and I can hear he's doing his best to suck in his painful whimpers with each jolting step. Why do I keep running? No one can help us.

Gravity gives as we reach a hallway that may once have been a waiting area. The floor is the ceiling then the floor again as we rotate gently. The superstructure releases a tortured scream. Lights flicker. Grow dim.

Everything normalizes again, but the ground is vibrating in a way that warns things will get rough. We're not going to make it.

I run until my breath tears through my lungs and bright spots dance before my vision. Blackness nibbles in from the sides. I don't know when I last ate or drank. Uya'Kwazi is a dead weight, and I need to rest.

We keep fleeing until we fetch up in a forgotten suite. Once, this may have been a home, but judging by the jumble of boxes tumbled across the floor, it's been used as a storage space for these past few years.

I lay the boy down, and his eyes are glazed, the lids barely lifting.

"I'm thirsty," he rasps.

"So'm I."

A silence stretches between us until Uya'Kwazi grips my wrist, hard. "You need to finish it."

I stare at him, uncomprehending.

With his other hand, he grabs the shard on its string from around his neck and presses it into my palm. "Finish it."

"How?"

"Get to the transmitter. Sing it into place."

I want to tell him my voice is broken, but he's peering into me, hard, so that I don't have the words.

"That thing hunting us, that's what we need to stop. It's what we. Always. Must protect from. Finish… the rite."

His eyes drift shut, he exhales, then slackens. He doesn't breathe in.

Just like that.

I rock back on my haunches. How can he be dead? Everyone dies.

Fierce anger blooms in my heart, sends its black flames licking through my veins.

Am I predator or prey? I grip the shard hard, so the edges bite. Stupid boy. Why has he gone and died on me? And yet, as that shard pulses in my grasp, the potential of its echo reverberates through my blood, my bones.

This is an object of power – all the lines converge here. All the enforcers in this habitat can shake their v'hushaleles all they desire, but I am small and quick. That greater darkness from beyond the void – now *that* frightens me more.

"Stupid boy," I mutter at the dead child. "This was supposed to be your burden."

I rise, the shard clasped as if I might wield it as a weapon. And it *is* a weapon.

Outside the door, I read the numbers, calculate as the habitat's layout unfolds. The Mother has smiled on me. I am two levels below and one sector across from where I must be. Unencumbered, I run. I am a little shadow, always beneath others' notice.

The habitat groans and cries out, shaking and shuddering.

Death comes for us all. Death cast its shadow already since I was enfolded in the womb, and it began stalking me as soon as I breathed air – whether it was the Yokha'a, the Ah'bui, or any of their allies. Death might strike if a sector suffers catastrophic decompression. Death might creep upon me with a sickness that turns my insides to muck.

I lose count of the ways in which Death can take me. I'm fooling myself if I make claims of immortality.

What matters is *how* I choose to embrace death and return to the Mother's arms. It's awful that I've only had twice as many juzu on this habitat than Uya'Kwazi ever had. If anyone can claim how unfair life is, it is he.

Thirst, hunger and exhaustion gnaw at me, whisper that it is easier to lie down and wait for this *other* thing that's slunk in from the outer darkness, a symptom of a greater evil. We have eaten too much of each other's hate, and now we have run out of time to make peace.

Reaching transmission spire five seventy-three is surprisingly easy when you're small and you know where you're going. The gravity this far out from the habitat is gone, and I pull myself along, hand over hand along icy metal rungs that burn my skin.

The air is thin. And it's cold. So very cold. Sound travels strangely here, bringing with it tortured creaks and groans.

I can no longer feel my extremities and, in many ways, this is my entry into a birthing canal, my entire existence narrowing to a single point within the tube as I follow the thin strip of lighting that vanishes into infinity.

Fear is at my heels, and I can't look back. My heart wants to squeeze itself right out of my chest. Everyone must die; it's the time and manner of one's choosing that is the blessing.

I'm too young to die.

I'm going to die anyway, but on my own terms.

I choke on my sobs.

Someone must finish this.

Why must it be me?

Fool. Did the child of my enemy doubt himself when he took up his burden?

The shard is heavy against my chest, cold and hot simultaneously as a ferocious hum thrums through the spire. Too heavy, so that my teeth ache and warm liquid that isn't tears seeps from my eyes and brings the salt of an ocean I'll never see to my lips and tongue.

A screech ululates up the spire behind me.

The lights plunge into instant darkness. Thick darkness.

I drift.

Am I far enough?

This must be. I bring my hand to my chest, numb fingers barely feeling the shard.

That nameless dread has found me. Unlike death, this thing has no name.

I can't breathe. Can't shape the sounds.

It's coming…

I don't have the words for this rite, I don't have the sounds, but if the antithesis to this great hunger exists, it is love – the love of life. The offering of hope.

Mother, take this from me. I give this to you. I give you the completion.

There, beyond my heart lies the spark, my song, an endling spark of the Mother. A linchpin in a crystal lattice just beyond my reach. All it needs is that tiny fire – not so much the correct rite but rather the intent. For that, the Word of Barriers has been waiting a long, long time.

I grip the shard in both hands, with fingers that don't want to work.

A corresponding tone, like a wet finger on a crystal singing bowl fills me, spills out so that my veins light up like a twining um'diliyah vine about to send forth fresh tendrils. Warmth radiates outward. Star stuff, star seed, pushing back the sucking darkness that squeals and screeches, like nails on metal. It is right that it fears.

I'm overfull, spilling out, a lock without a key.

It will only hurt a little.

The crystal is sharp, and it presses past cartilage and bone with ease.

Mother, I am coming.

I ignite, and for one limitless moment, I can sing down the stars.

About the Authors

Dare Segun Falowo is a writer of the Nigerian Weird. Their work draws on cinema, indigenous cosmologies, pulp fiction and a lived surreality. Their short fiction has appeared in the *Magazine of Fantasy & Science Fiction*, *The Dark Magazine*, *Baffling Magazine* and others. They have also contributed to the essential anthologies of black speculative fiction: *Dominion* and *Africa Risen*. Their lysergic science fiction epic, "Convergence in Chorus Architecture" has been translated into Italian and was longlisted for the British Science Fiction Award for Short Fiction. Their first collection of stories is "Caged Ocean Dub", out on Android Press in the US, and Tartarus Press in the UK. Dare lives in Nigeria, where they are trying to find their truth in text, symbol and Spirit.

DaVaun Sanders is an author and editor based in Phoenix, Arizona. He's the publisher and executive editor for the Hugo award-winning *FIYAH Literary Magazine of Black Speculative Fiction*. His middle-grade novels include

Keynan Masters & The Peerless Magic Crew, the first book in his debut fantasy series, and *Minecraft: The Tournament*. His adult short fiction has appeared in Fireside, Uncanny, Podcastle, and elsewhere. When deadlines are scarce he enjoys exploring the world with his wife and twins, cheering himself hoarse for the 49ers, collecting new injuries in Muay Thai, and any DIY project that requires outrageous new power tools.

Ishola Abdulwasiu Ayodele is a creative writer and an educator. A finalist of the 2023 Isele Magazine Short Story Prize and winner of 2022 Ibua Journal Continental Poetry Prize, his work has been featured in or is forthcoming in magazines such as *Iskanchi*, *Brittle Paper*, *African Writer*, *Isele Magazine*, *Omenana*; and in anthologies such as the *Year's Best African Speculative Fiction 2022* and *Spacefunk!*

The creative director of the 2021 Artmosterrific Residence Program, he has been a creative writing mentor for Sprinng Writing Fellowship since 2020.

He is the founder of Firefly Initiative, a nonprofit dedicated to inspiring his community's students. He enjoys mysticism and psychology, and occasionally blogs at imoleitan.substack.com.

Jamal Hodge is a Bram Stoker & Elgin Award-nominated poet, a multi-award-winning filmmaker, and a member of the SFPA and HWA. He earned Rhysling Award nominations in 2021,

2022, and 2024, with his poem "Colony" winning second place at the 2022 Dwarf Stars. His debut poetry collection, *The Dark Between the Twilight*, debuted as the number one hot new American Poetry Release on Amazon (June 2024), while his debut anthology, *Bestiary of Blood: Modern Fables & Dark Tales*, launched as the number one New Horror Anthology Release. His new collection, *Everything Endles*s, is a collaboration with SFPA Grand Master Linda D. Addison. www.writerhodge.com.

J. Umeh is an author, blogger, record producer and film reviewer. He lives and works in the UK as a technology consultant and responsible AI strategist. As a creative artist, technologist and former biologist, Umeh's interests span the confluence of technology, art and humanity, and this is a theme he explores in his first speculative fiction work "Kalabashing", published in the inaugural Saúútiverse anthology ***Mothersound*** (2023). Umeh is passionate about the co-evolutionary tension between emerging technology and intellectual property (e.g. copyright), and he publishes and speaks regularly about these topics, in various blogs, journals, magazines and international conferences.

Kofi Nyameye is a preacher and minister of God who writes in his spare time. His work has appeared in ***Asimov's Science Fiction Magazine***, ***The Manchester Review, Science Fiction World*** and ***The Best of World SF Vol. 1*** anthology. He currently lives in Accra, Ghana.

Linda D. Addison is an award-winning author of five collections, including *How to Recognize a Demon Has Become Your Friend*. She has been honored with the HWA Lifetime Achievement Award, HWA Mentor of the Year and SFPA Grand Master of Fantastic Poetry. She is a member of CITH, HWA, SFWA, SFPA and IAMTW. Find her in anthologies: *Blood Games: A Vampire Anthology*, *Playlist of the Damned*, *Weird Tales: 100 Years of Weird*, *Enter Boogeyman*, *Folk Horror*, and *Bestiary of Blood: Modern Fables & Dark Tales*, including *Everything Endless*, a poetry collaboration with Jamal Hodge. Her website is: lindaaddisonwriter.com.

Mazi Nwonwu is the pen name of Nigerian journalist and writer Chiagozie Fred Nwonwu. He is the co-founder and managing editor of *Omenana Magazine*, a leading platform for African-centric speculative fiction. He was part of the Lagos 2060 workshop, which produced Nigeria's first science fiction anthology, and he contributed to *AfroSF*, Africa's first pan-African science fiction anthology. His works have also appeared in publications such as *Brittle Paper*, *Saraba Magazine*, *Sentinel Nigeria*, *Jalada*, *Africanfuturism: An Anthology* and the anthology *It Wasn't Exactly Love*. Through his speculative fiction he aims to project Africa's diverse culture into the future, offering a unique narrative that blends tradition with the futurescape he creates. His first collection of short stories, *How To Make A Space*

Masquerade, was published by Narrative Landscape Press in 2024.

Miguel O. Mitchell, PhD (he/him) is a speculative poet, science fiction and fantasy author, visual artist, and retired chemist living in Maryland, USA. He has published poems in *Amazing Stories*, *Eye to the Telescope*, *FIYAH*, *Scarlet Dragonfly Journal*, *Scifaikuest*, *Space and Time*, *Star*Line*, and the anthology *The Year's Best African Speculative Fiction* (2022). He has published two poetry collections, *Periodic Table of Alien Species: Elements 1–86* (Barnes & Noble Press, 2021), and his scifi novel-in-verse *Surrealia* (Gnashing Teeth Publishing, 2024), the latter book nominated for the 2025 Elgin Award. Miguel was editor of the 2025 *Dwarf Stars* anthology, a collection of the best speculative poems of one to ten lines published in 2024, and was co-editor of the 2023 *Dwarf Stars* anthology with David C. Kopaska-Merkel. He is also Editor-in-Chief and Co-founder of *SpecPoVerse: An International Journal of Speculative Poetry* (specpoverse.org).

In the areas of science fiction and fantasy prose, Miguel has published the flash fiction story "Trading with Monsters" in *Fantasy* magazine and the short story "The Revenant Saga" in *Scarlet Leaf Review*. Find out more about Miguel's poetry, prose, and visual art at his website: miguelmitchellsart.com.

Moustapha Mbacké Diop is a medical student and writer living in Dakar, Senegal. His writing mainly explores African spirituality, grief, and colonialism through a darker speculative lens. He has been published in *Omenana*, *Agbowo*, *Haven Spec*, *The Magazine of Fantasy and Science Fiction*, as well as anthologies: *Africa Risen*, *Blackened Roots*, *The Year's Best African Speculative Fiction*. Moustapha is a finalist for the Nommo Awards 2024 in the short story category. When not writing, he can usually be found daydreaming, watching animated movies, and/or procrastinating. You can find him on X at @/mdmoustaf.

Nerine Dorman is a South African author and editor of science fiction and fantasy. Her young adult science fiction novel *Sing down the Stars* won the Sanlam Prize for Youth Literature in 2019 and the Percy Fitzpatrick Award for Children's and Youth Literature in 2020. Her novella *The Firebird* won a Nommo for "Best Novella" in 2019, and her YA fantasy novella, *Dragon Forged*, was a finalist in the Sanlam Prize for Youth Literature in 2017. She is a founding member of the SFF authors' co-operative Skolion and curates the South African Horrorfest literary component, Bloody Parchment. An active member of the African Speculative Fiction Society, she is represented by the African Literary Agency.

Shingai Njeri Kagunda is an Afrosurreal/futurist storyteller from Nairobi, Kenya, with a Literary Arts MFA from Brown. Shingai's work has been featured in the *Best American Sci-fi and Fantasy 2020*, *Year's Best African Speculative Fiction*

2021, and *Year's Best Dark Fantasy and Horror 2020*. They have work in or upcoming in *Omenana*, *Fantasy* magazine, *Fractured Lit*, *Khoreo*, *Africa Risen*, *Baffling Magazine*, and *Lightspeed*. Shingai's non-fiction appears in *Afro-Centered Futurisms in Our Speculative Fiction* and her debut novella *& This is How to Stay Alive*, published by Neon Hemlock Press in October 2021 won the Ignyte Award for best novella in 2022. Shingai is the co-editor of *PodCastle Magazine* and the co-founder of Voodoonauts (an Afrofuturist summer workshop nominated for a community Ignyte Award). Shingai is a creative writing teacher, an eternal student, and a lover of all things soft and Black.

T.L. Huchu's work has appeared in *Lightspeed*, *Interzone*, *Analog Science Fiction & Fact*, *The Year's Best Science Fiction and Fantasy 2021*, *Ellery Queen Mystery Magazine*, *Mystery Weekly*, *The Year's Best Crime and Mystery Stories 2016*, and elsewhere. He is the winner of a Hurston/Wright Legacy Award (2023), Alex Award (2022), the Children's Africana Book Award (2021), a Nommo award for African SFF (2022, 2017), and has been shortlisted for the Caine Prize (2014) and the Grand prix de l'Imaginaire (2019). His Edinburgh Nights series is now on its fourth instalment. Find him @TendaiHuchu.

Wole Talabi is an engineer, writer, and editor from Nigeria. He is the author of the Nebula, Locus and BSFA award-nominated novel *Shigidi and the Brass Head of Obalufon*, which the *Washington Post* called one of the ten best science fiction and fantasy books of 2023. His short fiction has appeared in places like *Asimov's Science Fiction*, *Lightspeed*, *Africa Risen* and is collected in the books *Convergence Problems* and *Incomplete Solutions*. He has been a finalist for the Hugo, Nebula, BSFA, Igntye, and Locus awards, as well as the Caine Prize for African Writing. He has won the Nommo award for African speculative fiction and the Sidewise award for Alternate History. He has edited five anthologies, including *Africanfuturism: An Anthology* and *Mothersound: The Sauútiverse Anthology*. He likes scuba diving, elegant equations, and oddly shaped things. He currently lives and works in Australia.

Xan van Rooyen is an autistic, non-binary storyteller from South Africa, currently living in Finland where the heavy metal is soothing and the cold, dark forests inspiring. Xan has a Master's degree in music, and – when not teaching – enjoys conjuring strange worlds and creating quirky characters. You can find Xan's stories in the likes of *Three-Lobed Burning Eye*, *Daily Science Fiction*, and *Galaxy's Edge*, among others. They have also written several novels including YA fantasy *My Name is Magic*, and adult aetherpunk novel *Silver Helix*. Xan is also a founding member of the Sauúti collective. Feel free to say hi on socials @xan_writer.

About the Illustrators

Akintoba Kalejaye hails from Nigeria. He is a lawyer, comic writer, and graphic artist. Akintoba has brought to life over twenty comics under the umbrella of the award-winning publisher Comic Republic, including the critically acclaimed *Visionary* and *Metalla*, both inspired by Yoruba mythology and Nigerian way of life. His contributions to the comic world have garnered him numerous accolades, including winning Best Traditional Comic at the 2017 Comic Connect Award and earning a nomination for Best Writer at the 2023 Glyph Awards. When he's not crafting storylines or practicing law, Akintoba enjoys programming, photography, and video games. His source of inspiration remains his wife and their three young children.

Stephen Embleton is a South African writer resident in Oxford, after his 2022 academic fellowship at the African Studies Centre, University of Oxford. Stephen was awarded a literary grant by the Royal Literary Fund in 2024, recognising the literary merit of his body of work and literature-related activities.

About the Editors

Cheryl S. Ntumy is a Ghanaian writer of speculative fiction, young adult fiction and romance. Her work has appeared in *FIYAH Magazine of Black Speculative Fiction; Apex Magazine; The Best of World SF Vol. 3* and *Botswana Women Write*, among others. Her work has also been shortlisted for the Nommo Award for African Speculative Fiction, the Commonwealth Writers Short Story Prize and the Miles Morland Foundation Scholarship. She is a member of the Sauútiverse Collective, which created an Afrocentric shared universe for speculative fiction, and Petlo Literary Arts, an organization that develops and promotes creative writing in Botswana.

Eugen Bacon is an African Australian author of several novels and collections. She's a British Fantasy and Foreword Indies Award winner, a twice World Fantasy Award finalist, and a finalist in other awards, including the Shirley Jackson, Philip K. Dick Award, as well as the Nommo Awards for speculative fiction by Africans. Eugen was announced in the honor list of the Otherwise Fellowships for "doing exciting work in gender and speculative fiction". *Danged Black Thing* made the Otherwise Award Honor List as a "sharp collection of Afro-Surrealist work". Eugen's creative work has appeared worldwide, including in *Apex Magazine*, *Award Winning Australian Writing*, *Fantasy*, *Fantasy & Science Fiction*, and *Year's Best African Speculative Fiction*. Visit her at eugenbacon.com.

Stephen Embleton was born in KwaZulu-Natal, South Africa and is now a resident in Oxford, United Kingdom, since being an academic visitor to the African Studies Centre, University of Oxford in 2022. Stephen was awarded the Best Novella by an African in the 7th Nommo Awards presented in person at Glasgow WorldCon in August 2024 for his Sauúti-based novella, "Undulation". His first short story was published in 2015 in the *IMAGINE AFRICA 500* speculative fiction anthology, followed by the 2016 Edition of *Aké Review*, the debut edition of *Enkare Review* 2017 and more. He is a charter member of the African Speculative Fiction Society and its Nommo Awards initiative. His then unpublished fantasy novel, *Bones & Runes*, was a finalist in the 2021 James Currey Prize for African Literature, and published in the UK in 2022. Stephen is the editor of the 2023 edition of the posthumously published final novel of Flora Nwapa, *The Lake Goddess*. Stephen's academic essay, "Cosmologies and Languages Building Africanfuturism", appears in the Bloomsbury essay collection *Afro-Centered Futurisms in Our Speculative Fiction*.

Glossary

A–Z TERMINOLOGY (General)

bés (bez): standard day

Boãmmariri (Bow-ahm-mah-ree-ree): conference of planets held every five juzu (years)

boa'oba (boa-obah): baobab tree

d'hiamomo (dai-a-moh-moh): diamonds

Da'unspasha (dah-uhns-pahshah): The Federation Headquarters' Name

Eh'wauizo (Eh-wah-oo[as in look]-ii-zoh): The spirit realm / the afterlife, a dimension of the dead, souls and ancestors

hoguro (ho-goo[as in look]-roh): made-up drink in the Sauútiverse

janlele (jah-n-leh-leh): made up, water dog

juzu (joo-zoo): standard year

khwa'ra (k-wah-rah): to seed, conceive, receive

owo (oh-woe): currency

ra'kwa (rah-k-waa): offspring

ririni (rih-rih-nih): Energy crystals from the planet Órino-Rin – sources of energy and can also be used as currency in barter

ya'yn (yah-ii-nn): mother

CREATURES

chekele'le (check-e-ley-ley): hyena, derived from "cheka" – it means "laugh" in Swahili

Iboriiwili (i-boh-ree-wee-lee): intangible spirit being that possesses minds

impudu-pudu (imp-poo-doo-poo-doo): derived from the impundulu, a mythical lightning bird in African folklore

Intigitih (in-tee-gee-tee): tentacled whisper worm covered in mouths; a creature without a voice that possesses people and takes their voices. In ancient times those with strong minds used it to listen to silent spirits

kudu-kudu (coo-doo-coo-doo): kudu (type of gazelle, or galloper)

kunkun (koon-koon): a ferocious, carnivorous large cat native to Wiimb-ó (akin to a lion)

kwa-achi (kw-ah-ah-chee): were-leopard; human who can turn into a large yellow spotted cat; derived from "kwac", the Luo word for leopard

t'apiapia (t-a-pi-a-pi-a): tilapia (fish)

t'embo'oo (t-eh-m-bo-o-o): elephant, derived from "tembo" in Swahili

tetekute (teh-teh-kuh-teh): sentient leopard-like cat with an array of specialized vocalizations nearly hunted to extinction, highly sensitive to vibrations from its side stripes. Indigenous to Órino-Rin

tikolokolo (tee-koh-loh-koh-loh): made-up, spirit gremlin

yasa (yah-sah): caterpillars (food)

MUSICAL INSTRUMENTS

balafofo (ba-la-FOH-foh): balafon, African musical instrument

du'undun (doo-OON-doon): dunun, African musical instrument

k'hora'aa (kho-rah-aa): kora, African musical instrument

luhte'te (loot-e-tey): lute, African musical instrument

mbi'ira(m-BEE-rah): mbira, African musical instrument

ngonini (n-go-ni-ni): ngoni, African musical instrument

tambi'ibinn (tah-mbi-i-binn): wood-carved flute

PLANETS

Ekwukwe (Eh-kwoo-kweh): echo planet, from the Igbo word "ukwe" which means "song" or "anthem"

Mahwé (Mah-weh): dead planet, uninhabited, sometimes referred to as Mahwé-Pinaa (meaning Mother of Pinaa, the inhabited moon)

Órino-Rin (Oh-reen-oh-reen): gas giant with sonic storms, from the Yoruba word "orin", which means "song"

Pinaa (Pee-nah): inhabited moon, from the Setswana word "pina", which means "song"

Wiimb-ó (Wee-m-boh): Earth-analogue planet, from the Swahili word "wimbo", which means "song"

Zezépfeni (Zey-zey-fey-nee): elite planet of the "original race", from the Amharic word "zefeni", which means "song"

PLANTS

j'hani'ni (jah-ni-ni): acacia grass, derived from "jani" in Swahili – it means "grass"

kaka'pa (kah-kah-pah): sour fruit with fleshy seeds

kalabash (kah-lah-bash): calabash – see also klalabash

klalabash (kla-lah-bash): calabash – see also kalabash

mopane (mo-pah-neh): also butterfly tree, commonly found in woodlands near the Zambezi River, and southern parts of Africa

t'embo'oo (grass) (t-eh-m-bo-o-o): elephant (grass), derived from "tembo" in Swahili

TRADES

inatani (ina-tah-nee): scholar who teaches initiates and novices

maadiregi (ma-aa-dee-rey-ghee): tradesperson/professional e.g. engineer, technician, architect

mahadum (mah-ha-doom): institution of learning, derived from Igbo word for university

menigari (meh-ni-gah-rii): (singular/plural) a person who is spiritually attuned

raevaagi (rah-ey-vaa-ghee): bearer of history, a messenger, bard, storyteller, orator

Sâkoukou (Sah-kow-kuu): secret warrior group from the now dead and uninhabited planet Mahwé, whose function was assassination/military attacks

Susu Nunyaa (Soo-soo-noo-n-yaa): elite order tasked with interpreting lost language

Taq'qerara (Tak-keh-rah-rah): special-born and gifted with the magic to feel sound aura

Tsamanãrari: order of watermancers, from the Tsadiri'Tdidi region (Salt Pan Region)

uroh-ogi (oo ["oo" as in "look"]-roh-o-ghee): healer

zéhemgwile (zey-hey-m-g-wee-ley): guild of tailors

Beyond & Within

THE FLAME TREE Beyond & Within short story collections bring together tales of myth and imagination by modern and contemporary writers, carefully selected by anthologists, and sometimes featuring short stories and fiction from a single author. Overall, the series presents a wide range of diverse and inclusive voices, often writing folkloric-inflected short fiction, but always with an emphasis on the supernatural, science fiction, the mysterious and the speculative. The books themselves are gorgeous, with foiled covers, printed edges and published only in hardcover editions, offering a lifetime of reading pleasure.

FLAME TREE FICTION

A wide range of new and classic fiction, from myth to modern stories, with tales from the distant past to the far future, including short story anthologies, Collector's Editions, Collectable Classics, Gothic Fantasy collections and Epic Tales of mythology and folklore.

•